BESTSELLING AUTHOR

ACE COLLINS

IN *The* PRESIDENT'S SERVICE

EPISODES 1–3

BEST SELLING AUTHOR
ACE COLLINS
A DATE *with* DEATH
IN THE PRESIDENT'S SERVICE SERIES : EPISODE 1

BEST SELLING AUTHOR
ACE COLLINS
The DARK
IN THE PRESIDENT'S SERVICE : EPISODE 2

BEST SELLING AUTHOR
ACE COLLINS
HER
IN THE PRESIDENT'S SERVICE : EPISODE 3

Cover Design: Jeff Gifford
Model: Alison Johnson
Interior Design: Cheryl L. Childers
Editing: Kathi Ide, Kathy Macias, Tish Martin, Deb Haggerty
Published in Association with the Hartline Literary Agency

PUBLISHED BY: Elk Lake Publishing, Inc., 35 Dogwood Dr., Plymouth, MA 02360

Library Cataloging Data
Names: Collins, Ace (Ace Collins)
In the President's Service: Episodes 1-3 Ace Collins
438p. 23cm × 15cm (9 in. x 6 in.)
Revised copies of the first three books in the In the President's Service Series.
Identifiers: ISBN-13: 978-1-946638-50-2 (e-bk) |
978-1-946638-51-9 (POD paperback) |
978-1-946638-52-6 (Trade paperback)
Key Words: Helen Meeker, Teresa Bryant, World War II, The Manhattan Project, Nazis, Suspense, Murder
LCCN 2017948778 Fiction

BEST SELLING AUTHOR

ACE COLLINS

A DATE with DEATH

IN THE PRESIDENT'S SERVICE SERIES : EPISODE 1

To Alison

Chapter 1

Sunday, September 21, 1941
A field in France

Just past midnight, Private Nigel Andrews lay flat on his stomach, hiding in some tall weeds just beyond a French pasture.

The twenty-seven-year-old Liverpool native was a college graduate. Blond and green-eyed, he was stocky, just a touch over five-eight and an ounce short of 150 pounds. But in this situation, size didn't matter.

He was tough as shoe leather and hard as iron. In his unit's boxing tourney, he had whipped men six inches taller and more than fifty pounds heavier. So in spite of his schoolboy appearance, those who knew him never crossed him.

His strength and grit notwithstanding, Andrews had once wanted to become a pastor and was even engaged to a preacher's daughter he'd met at Hope College. But for the moment those plans had been supplanted by a driving desire to get off French soil alive. His mother and father had already lost one son; they likely couldn't survive losing two. They'd even fought his being drafted.

He hated the military and everything about it. So, no matter the odds, he vowed he would survive this unholy war. He also vowed to make sure that whatever it took, short of his death, ultimate victory would be realized.

"Where is that blasted plane?"

Andrews turned his attention from the horizon to an obviously frustrated Col. Reggie Fister. Speaking to no one in particular and likely just yapping to defuse his anger, Fister continued to lash out. "It was supposed to be here and ready for takeoff. Blimey! We do our impossible job perfectly, and the Air Force can't even manage to get the easy part right. Whose side are they on anyway?"

For the past week, the elite unit's secret mission in Nazi occupied France had gone much smoother than expected. After a night parachute drop, they'd met with the underground and gotten the lay of the land. Over the next six days, they observed German emplacements, studied and recorded troop strengths, and photographed two air bases being constructed for attacks on London. There had been a few close calls, but not once during their time behind enemy lines had they been spotted. Now, in the witching hour, just as their mission was supposed to be concluding, the British Air Force plane that should be waiting on this dark, grassy field to take them back home was nowhere in sight.

Just like his commanding officer, Andrews knew that in a mission based on complete precision, this should not have happened—especially to an elite British unit. After all, everything up until this moment had been done just the way the English liked it—by the book and exactly on time. Now everything was upside down. The game was no longer being played by a set of formal rules, and it looked as though they were going to have to ad lib.

His gut churning and a growing fear gripping his heart, Andrews lifted his chest and rested on his elbows to study the French countryside. Except for two sheep, it was completely void of life.

"Sir?" Andrews screwed up the courage to ask the question that was surely crowding deeper and deeper into everyone's mind.

"What?" Fister barked back.

"Do you suppose the Jerries shot it down?"

"Could be," the colonel replied. "And that would mess up the whole works, wouldn't it?" He paused a second before adding, "Let's give them some more time. But I sure don't like being hung out to dry like yesterday's wash. Churchill will not be on my Christmas card list after this. Neither will Monty."

"And if the plane doesn't get here?" Andrews asked. "What happens then?"

Fister's grim expression lightened up a bit. "It could be worse, son. I've always wanted to date a French lassie. I'll wager you have too."

Even now, when it appeared they didn't have a chance in Hades, Fister's sarcastic humor and positive attitude remained true.

The colonel was the kind of person Andrews both respected and despised. He loved war, seemed to live for it and relished the moments when his life was being challenged. He all but wrapped himself in the Union Jack and almost shouted out the lyrics of "God Save the Queen" whenever it was played. On top of that, he was a man's man, a no-nonsense kind of leader who never put his squad in unnecessary danger. If there was fighting to do, the tall, ruggedly built, dark-headed, blue-eyed Scotsman would be leading the way. In a different time, he would have been a knight on a white horse, charging into battle with a smile on his face and a glint in his eye. Minus the steed, those qualities had been evident all week during this mission. Fister had always been a step ahead, constantly getting his men out of harm's way just before a group of Nazis happened onto their position. It was almost as if he were psychic.

But now Fister was in a place where he had no control. He was helpless, and his forced grin couldn't hide that fact. As badly as Andrews needed to get out of this bloody war and go home, it did his heart good to watch his commanding officer squirm.

Pushing his helmet back, the angry colonel ran his hand through his wavy hair and spat. After checking the horizon, he turned his gaze back to Andrews and whispered, "Don't worry, Nigel. I will get you out of this mess. You'll be kissing your sweet Becky before the sun sets tomorrow."

Andrews certainly hoped that was true. All he wanted was for the fighting to end and for his life to go back to the way it was before. Who really cared about France, Austria, or Poland anyway? Why not find a way to satisfy Hitler so he'd leave the British Isles alone?

The colonel looked toward the other ten Brits who'd volunteered for this dangerous mission. "Stay low to the ground," he instructed. "The plane will be here soon. The Jerries are not going to spoil this holiday for us. The information we have is too important for us to be left stranded here. I wouldn't be surprised if Princess Elizabeth herself is on board to greet us each with a kiss."

The intelligence they'd gathered was indeed important. Andrews knew that well. But it had the potential to do exactly what he didn't want or need—make the war last even longer. What he wanted was for the fighting to end and for life to go back to the way it was before. Who really cared about France, Austria, or Poland? Why not just find a way to satisfy Hitler so he would leave the British Isles alone?

Realizing it was going to be a while, Andrews figured he might as well get comfortable. Taking off his helmet, he rolled over onto his back and gazed at the clear sky. At this moment on a peaceful fall night, it was hard to believe there was a war raging all across Europe. It was also nearly impossible to imagine this serene pasture in France was in the middle of it. Yet Europe was aflame, the Germans were destroying London piece by piece from the air, half of his schoolmates were dead, and he'd already fought on the African sands and tramped through the French countryside on this undercover mission. And he'd come to know death as well as he knew the streets of his hometown.

Watching the Grim Reaper work had hardened his heart and made him question his faith in God. He knew hell was real, for he had lived there the past twenty-four months, but he was not so sure about heaven. Was there really such a place, and was his brother Bobby looking down on him from there right now? Did it matter? Did anything matter beyond getting the information they'd gathered back home?

"There it is," Fister barked. "Look over to the west; she's coming in now."

As Andrews turned his head to the right, the colonel pulled a large flashlight from his backpack and clicked it on and off three times. He waited for thirty seconds and repeated the actions. The plane began to descend from the sky toward their position.

"Okay, laddies," Fister called out, "our bus has arrived. But don't get too excited yet. Stay on your bellies until she lands and turns around. Only when she comes to a complete stop and the door flies open do we move out."

Rolling onto his stomach, Andrews rammed his helmet back into place and observed the plane's approach. The bright moon meant there was no need to light the makeshift runway; the pilot could easily see it. And the field was plenty long enough for the American-built Douglas DC-3 to land, turn, and take off.

As it dropped close to the ground, the pilot cut the engines and glided in. Andrews smiled. The less noise, the better.

"Hold your spots," Fister called out as the airship almost noiselessly set down in the eight-inch-high grass. The plane taxied a few hundred yards. Then the pilot re-fired the twin engines and turned the craft around.

As the plane once more came to life, Fister flashed his light three times. A few seconds later the signal was returned, and the metal bird's side door flew open. "Time to go home, boys. Your country will be proud of the work you did here."

Andrews and his friends pushed off the damp ground, grabbed their gear, and jogged toward the plane. They had covered half of the 150 yards to their ride when gunfire exploded from the woods to their left.

A second later, four feet to Andrew's right, Basil Homes screamed and fell to the ground. Blood gushed from a huge wound just below the intelligence officer's breastbone. There was no doubt he was a goner. His life was no longer numbered in years but in seconds.

"Get to the plane," Fister screamed from behind. "Don't stop until you're on board, laddies. I'll hold them off."

With gunfire popping like corn, Andrews felt an urge to grab the dying man and hold him as the life oozed from his tall, thin body. Homes had a wife and kids. He was smart, funny, and charming. Of all people to die, it shouldn't be him. But that was the way war was; the ones who shouldn't die always did. Just like his brother. There had never been a finer lad in the whole wide world.

"Andrews," Fister screamed, "get moving!"

After taking a final look at his fallen comrade, Andrews turned his attention to the plane. As he and the other nine picked up their pace, the colonel dropped to the ground, grabbed his machine gun, and aimed at more than fifty Nazi infantrymen who had emerged from the woods and were racing toward his position. As he frantically fought against overwhelming odds, Fister screamed, "Get on that bloody plane, and get the information back to London. Then have a pint for me!"

With the sound of gunfire echoing all around him, and the DC-3's pilot revving the plane's twin engines, Andrews and the other nine members of the team continued running. Behind them Fister kept his gun blazing, offering at least a bit of cover and a few more moments to get to safety.

Andrews was the last of the group to leap through the aircraft's doors. No one bothered closing the oval-shaped entry as the pilot opened the throttle and urged the DC-3 across the field. While the plane struggled to make speed for the takeoff, Andrews crawled over to one of the small windows and glanced back toward the spot Homes had fallen and where the war-loving, brash Fister was fighting. At least two dozen Germans were lying on the ground, and the colonel was still shooting. But as the woods came alive with the continuous flashes of gunfire, the foolhardy Scot, who was trading his life for theirs, surely couldn't last much longer. In fact, by the time the plane left the ground a few seconds later, Fister's gun had gone silent.

A dozen men had come on this suicide mission, but only ten were returning home. For the military, that would make this undercover operation a huge success. But what kind of success was worth men dying?

"What a man!" Robby Penny yelled over the plane's motors. "Fister saved us all."

Andrews nodded. "He's the man, all right—the kind who treats war like the ultimate game. No doubt he'll be awarded the Viking Cross." He shook his head and grimaced. "Or at least his family should get it. He earned it by killing a bunch of Germans who were drafted into their army just to be tossed out like lambs for the slaughter. I hate this war. I can't wait for it to be over."

Chapter 2

Wednesday, March 4, 1942
The White House

Helen Meeker glanced down at her watch. At 8:30 p.m., the White House still hummed with activity. It had been that way since December 7. No matter the time, day or night, the building was always alive with ringing phones, muted voices, and the sound of doors opening and closing.

Somewhere in the background, a radio played a Glenn Miller song. Meeker could barely hear it over the hundreds of other sounds filtering down through the building, but what she could make out didn't seem to fit. The tune was too upbeat, too happy, when in Washington smiles were in as short a supply as milk or butter. And no amount of money could buy so much as a grin on the black market. Even the upbeat strains of a swing band couldn't change the overriding dark dynamic that defined today's reality.

The blue-eyed, auburn-haired Meeker had just uncovered information that shook her to the core. That was the reason she was here, sitting just outside the oval office, where she'd been waiting for forty minutes. Though she knew J. Edgar

Hoover wouldn't buy it, she felt she had information with major security implications. Problem was, she couldn't pinpoint what they were.

Not having the definitive answer to that question might destroy her case and torpedo her unique request. But her gut was rarely wrong. She had to try to convince Franklin Roosevelt of the need for her to join with an old friend on a trek that might save an innocent man's life. Even at a time when millions of innocent men and women were dying all over the planet, wasn't one man's life worth a bit of time? She thought so. But would the president?

As she crossed her legs, the pump on her right foot slipped off her heel. Meeker put it back on, then fiddled with the blue purse in her lap. Waiting was not something she did well. It was certainly not part of her normal nature. Then again, nothing was normal now. Normal had stopped with Pearl Harbor. Now every day had different demands and goals, and that meant an everchanging schedule. It wasn't just that way for her; it was like that for everyone at the White House and probably for people all over the globe. And no one's life had changed more than the man she was waiting to speak to now.

Every moment of every day there was a decision FDR had to make. There was no time for evenings off or trips to the country or even a long weekend with his family. He couldn't be away from phones. He always had to be ready, day and night, to make gut-wrenching calls that ended with young Americans dying. It was not a life anyone would embrace. Yet it was what Roosevelt had been given, and he had to deal with it.

When the door to the Oval Office finally opened, Meeker's attention was yanked away from thoughts of pain and suffering and the overwhelming nature of the president's job. Secretary of State Cordell Hull stepped out into the hall, followed by Secretary of War Henry Stimson. Hull hurried by without a word, but Stimson stopped in front of her. The dark circles under his bloodshot eyes highlighted the deep concern on his face as he dug his hands into his pants pockets. After almost half a minute of stark and disturbing silence, the elderly man forced a smile. "How are you today, Helen?"

She clutched her bag, uncrossed her legs, and stood, staring directly into the eyes of one of the world's most powerful decision-makers. "I'm fine, sir."

"Good," the thin man replied. Perhaps it was the strain of his duties or maybe just the hour, but he looked every bit of his seventy-four years. After pushing his right hand through his close-cropped gray hair, Stimson sighed. "Oh, to be young again. Just don't know if I've got the stamina for this job anymore."

"I didn't think you ever aged," Meeker replied with a wink. "At least that's what they say around here."

"Aging happens." Stimson shrugged to make his point. "But only to those who are lucky. A lot of the boys on the front lines aren't ever going to know the trials or blessings of old age. In fact, there are a lot of things they'll never know. Should be a way for the young to stay home and folks who've already lived a long life to go off to battle. At least that kind of war wouldn't last as long."

There was no way to respond to his sober observation, at least none that carried any weight or hope. Meeker nodded in sad agreement.

"By the way," Stimson continued, "the president told me to send you straight in." He pushed a long breath between his lips, then turned without saying good-bye and trudged down the hall. Meeker studied him for a moment before gripping the knob on the most important office door in the world.

Though she'd been in the Oval Office a hundred times and every facet of it was deeply imprinted in her mind, there was still something intimidating about crossing this threshold. It was like no other room in the world. This was the heartbeat of the nation and contained perhaps the last hope of the free world.

Taking a deep breath to steady her nerves, she twisted the knob, silently opened the white door, and entered.

The room's sole occupant, dressed in a black suit, white shirt, and blue tie, sat behind his desk, a stack of newspapers piled on a table to the left. Beside them, fanned out like oversized playing cards, were updates from the various battlefronts. To the right, on a small bookcase, sat photographs of the president's family, including his spoiled Scottish terrier. Meeker imagined Fala had more security clearance than any cabinet officer, and she smiled as she thought of the good times she'd spent in the company of the playful canine. After enjoying a few seconds of happy memories with Fala, she turned her attention back to the man who called this oval-shaped room his office.

The president—his long, thin cigarette holder pinched between his lips—seemed lost in thought as he stared at a painting on the far wall. Meeker peered behind his wire-rimmed glasses and into his eyes. She sensed Roosevelt's mind was not contemplating the art but was actually a few thousand miles away.

After she had taken a seat in one of two leather-backed wooden chairs in front of his desk, he turned to greet her. "Helen," he said in his clipped New York accent, "I trust you are well." Before she could reply, he said with a smile, "That blue suit looks lovely on you. Have I ever told you you're the spitting image of your mother when she was your age? What a woman she was!"

Meeker nodded. "I remember her spunk. Dad always said I got it in spades."

"That you did, my dear." The president leaned forward on his elbows. "I've often called on you to do a job for me. But I can't remember the last time you came into my office without an invitation. I don't have to be Sherlock Holmes to guess this must be important."

Was it really that important? She'd thought so earlier. But now that she was here, she wondered if what she had to share was worth stealing time from the world's most powerful leader. Maybe not. But it was too late to turn around now. She had to go with her gut and hope he could read between the lines, as she had.

"Mr. President—"

He waved his hand to cut her off. "If I've told you once, I've told you a thousand times—call me Franklin. My goodness, young lady, I've known you your whole life. In fact, you called me Uncle Franklin when you were a child."

Meeker nodded. "Yes, sir." She tried to form his first name with her lips but couldn't. It didn't seem right to be that familiar with the leader of the free world. Instead she skipped personalizing her comments as she pushed forward.

"Sir, about a month ago, I requested a car from the motor pool."

The president's laughter filled the room and echoed off the rounded walls. "You mean that bright yellow Packard you're so proud of finally gave up the ghost?"

She shook her head. "No, sir. My sister was visiting and she needed it for a few days. But I had to follow up a lead the OSS had given me."

"They're proud of you over there. Arthur is begging me to let him have you full time." Roosevelt shook his head. "But I can't do that. There are issues here that I only trust you with."

"Actually, sir, I believe one of those issues is the reason I'm here."

"Well, then, let's hear about it."

She took a deep breath. "The car I got from the motor pool was a 1937 Lincoln-Zephyr sedan."

Roosevelt leaned back in his chair and clasped his hands together. "A great car. I really like the V-12 engine. And that model has great lines."

"The vehicle was seized in an espionage case. It belonged to

Wilbur Shellmeyer."

"The Lutheran minister we arrested for spying for the Nazis."

"That's him. He's due to be executed on March sixteenth."

"Sad case." Roosevelt sighed. "I understand he has a wife and three children."

"He did," Meeker corrected. "One of the girls supposedly died about six months ago. The mother and the other two children live in Germantown."

The president tilted his head to one side and raised an eyebrow. "Supposedly died?"

"I'll get to that," she assured him. "On my second day of driving Shellmeyer's car, I opened the glove box and found a notebook containing detailed information about the car's every fill-up, oil change, and maintenance. At first, I didn't think much about that. But as the hours passed, my curiosity got the best of me, and I started wondering about a man who would be such a stickler for recording everything."

Roosevelt pointed a finger in Meeker's direction. "Curiosity has killed many a cat, my dear."

"I know," she shot back. "But it's why I'm good at what I do."

"Touché. Now, what did your curiosity lead to?"

"I had to know why a preacher and father would turn spy. So I dug into his case file. In a box of his belongings, I found his Bible, which had countless detailed notes in the margins. He even kept a record of his children's heights in the notes section. The man's journal, which he called a logbook, was just as comprehensive. I can tell you everything he ate at every meal for three years. I know how much rain fell on what days. I can even give you the key points of his sermons and who he visited at hospitals."

"Sounds like a perfect spy to me. Good at getting information, a person people trust, and an eye for details."

"That's exactly what bothers me." Meeker lowered her voice a bit, even though they were alone in the room. "The case against him was pat, but the materials the FBI found didn't have any detailed information. And the code in his notes was so easy to break a child could have done it."

"But didn't he confess?"

"Yes. And that bothers me too. There wasn't enough evidence to hold him, much less convict him, but as soon as our people showed up at his door in response to that anonymous tip, he gave them a stack of documents proving he'd worked for Hitler for five years. It was as if he knew they were coming and was waiting for them. He could have burned that stuff, but he didn't."

The President shrugged. "Maybe he panicked, or perhaps guilt got to him."

"I thought about that." Meeker crossed her right leg over her left, then pulled her skirt's hem down over her knee. "But those confessions didn't fit with the detailed notes I found in his Bible and his logbook. So, I went to his church and examined their records. Turns out he was performing a wedding on a day when he claimed he was photographing our shipyards in Norfolk. Another time, when he was supposedly stealing files at Fort Bliss, the church records say he was at a funeral. There are a dozen more examples that dispute what he told the FBI."

"Why wasn't this discovered before?"

"Because he confessed. And because there were photographs

and papers in his home that matched up with what he claimed. No one thought it was necessary to look deeper. And with everything that's going on right now, we didn't want to look a gift horse in the mouth. So we just saddled him up and took him for a ride."

The President rubbed his chin. "But he confessed. As I recall, he offered no defense. He didn't even try to make a deal to give us information on the people he was working with. And if I'm not mistaken, he's said nothing since going to prison."

"Which leads to one of three conclusions. Either he's completely loyal to the Nazis. Or he doesn't want to rat out a friend. Or he's afraid of something even more than death." She locked eyes with her boss. "I'm beginning to think it's the latter."

"One of your hunches?"

"Maybe. But I've discovered something else. His oldest daughter, Ellen, drowned while on a family vacation in Mississippi last October. But they didn't bring her body home for a funeral. The day after the drowning, she was buried in a small rural cemetery in Georgia."

"So?" The President shrugged. "A lot of folks bury their loved ones near where they die. Maybe their grief was so great they felt an urgent need to put matters to rest."

Meeker shook her head. "I don't think so. Every member of the Shellmeyer clan, going back three generations, is buried in the same cemetery in Germantown, New York. Ellen should have been buried there too. And if they couldn't take her to New York, why would they go to Georgia for the funeral? It doesn't make sense."

"Well, young lady, you've certainly set forth a lot of interesting conjecture. I trust you have something more than assumptions."

"I think I do." She got up from her chair and walked to the window overlooking the rose garden. After glancing into the darkness for a long moment, she turned back to her boss. "But to prove it I need to get into that girl's grave."

"Are you crazy? Her family would never agree to exhuming the body."

"I'm sure they wouldn't. But if it were a matter of national security, they'd never have to know."

Roosevelt pulled a cigarette from a box on the desk, pushed it into his holder, lit it, and took a draw. "So, what's your theory about the 'supposedly dead' daughter?"

Meeker moved to the corner of the desk nearest her boss and leaned against the antique piece of furniture. "My guess is that Ellen is being held somewhere by the powers behind this deal. They're buying time until they can pull off something really big. If Shellmeyer talks, she dies. And the pastor is perfectly willing to be executed to make sure his daughter isn't killed."

"That's a pretty wild story, Helen."

"But it's the only thing that makes sense. And my gut tells me this is something we need to pursue. However, I don't want to go through regular channels."

The President looked over the top of his glasses. "Why not?"

"I think there might be a German mole in the White House, though I don't have a guess as to who it is. So, I want to do this off the record. I need a cover to make it look like I'm working on something else."

"I'm sure you can make one up." He smiled. "And when you do, I'll issue an official order."

Helen pushed off the corner of the desk and returned to the chair. She reached into her purse, pulled out a letter typed on White House stationery, and placed it in front of her boss.

He skimmed the three paragraphs. "So, you want me to grant you permission to interview some experienced law-enforcement officials who might be officer material."

"Yes, sir. I also need something else."

"What's that?"

"Henry Reese."

"Why him?"

"I believe the notes in Shellmeyer's Bible and journal are written in code. Reese can break that stuff down better than anyone I know. Besides, he's a good shot, and I'm thinking there's going to be some shooting before this is over."

Roosevelt set his cigarette in an ashtray and looked back at the painting he'd been studying when she walked in. The room grew still. One minute became two, then three. The ticking of the grandfather clock by the entry grew louder.

After a good five minutes, the nation's leader finally spoke, his eyes still fixed on the far wall. "I wonder how many of our boys have died during our little chat. I wonder that a lot. When I eat breakfast, I consider how much American blood has been shed in the time it took for the cook to fix my eggs. How many more died as I went through my morning ritual of putting these braces on my legs, getting dressed, and being moved into my wheelchair? That kind of thinking must seem strange to you."

"No, sir."

"You've made a good case for Shellmeyer's innocence. But those boys who die in battle are innocent too. Their only crime is being too old or too young to be drafted. They didn't ask to die, didn't want to die. But I sent them to a place where they did."

Once more the room grew eerily silent. The clock ticked. And Meeker waited.

Finally, Roosevelt's eyes left the painting and met hers. "I can give you what you need. But I can't give Shellmeyer a reprieve unless you get me proof that he's innocent. We can't look soft on espionage agents at this point in the war." He glanced at the calendar on his desk. "You've got twelve days before his execution."

"Then I'd better get moving." Meeker was halfway to the door when he called her name. She turned and looked at him.

"There's something I need you to do as well."

"What's that?"

"I want you to spend some time with a man England has designated as a hero of sorts."

"Excuse me?"

"Let's just say I want you to go on a few dates for your country."

"You can't be serious." The thought of feigning romantic interest in a stranger, especially as a job requirement, turned her stomach. But the serious look on the President's face told her she had no say in the matter.

Resigned to the worst, she returned to the chair and sat down to hear the details of her fate.

Chapter 3

Wednesday, March 4, 1942
The White House

Meeker tilted her head and frowned. She couldn't believe the President would ask her to date someone for political reasons. This was not what she had signed up for, not at all.

Roosevelt smiled. "I see I have your attention." He settled back into his chair and pushed his fingers together. "What do you know about Colonel Reggie Fister?"

"The English Viking Award recipient?"

"Yes."

She shrugged. "Just what I've read in the newspapers. He held off scores of Germans while the men in his undercover operation got on a plane and escaped occupied France. The reports I've read indicate the information gathered during the mission led to a number of successful English bombing runs."

The President grinned. "You know the story well. Are you aware of a member of that unit named Nigel Andrews?"

She nodded. "I've seen photos of him with the king and Princess Elizabeth. He was chosen to raise money for bond initiatives and give a few speeches to rally the troops. As I understand it he was the member of the unit who was closest to Fister. So, he's kind of serving as a substitute for the dead hero."

"That seems to be the general consensus, yes. Turns out Andrews got promoted to corporal and was assigned to be one of Churchill's personal assistants."

"As a bodyguard?"

"Essentially. In a few weeks, Churchill will be coming here for some secret meetings. No one must know about it. He will be hidden away on an estate in upstate New York. Andrews will be with him while he's here. But to give the illusion that Churchill is still in London, the British corporal will arrive in Washington a few days early. He'll appear at a few bond rallies, do a bit of meet-and-greet, participate in various social events. Whenever he's in the public eye, I want you with him."

"With all due respect, sir, I don't have time to be a decoration on some soldier's sleeve. A man's life is on the line, and I have to get to the bottom of it before we execute him. Can't you hire some Hollywood starlet for the job? The press would eat that up."

"Andrews is a valuable symbol for the Brits, and we have to show England we recognize that fact." Roosevelt's tone was firm. "He needs a beautiful, professional, intelligent woman by his side during his visit. Besides, the gossip you'll create by being a part of my staff will take up far more of the press's time and attention than some starlet would." He took a puff on his cigarette. "This is not a request."

Meeker suppressed a moan. "I understand."

"Good. The first event is in six days, so you've got some time to get a start on your other project. After that, Mr. Reese can cover for you on the days you're with Andrews."

"Okay." She sighed. "Let me know when I'm needed. In the meantime, I'll do everything I can to get to the bottom of something that's far more important than serving as a dizzy debutant."

Roosevelt's eyes sparkled. "You never know where you might find something important. Your days with Young Nigel—as Winston has taken to calling him—might just open up something that will change your life."

"I don't have time for marriage," she grumbled.

"Who said anything about that?" He laughed. "But as I know you don't fear fear, the only thing you really have to fear is your fear of commitment."

She shook her head. "I'm not afraid of that either. I'm just not the type to bake cakes and darn socks, that's all."

Without giving the President a chance to reply, Meeker headed for the exit. Just before closing the door behind her, she said, "I'll keep you informed on both fronts."

"I'm sure you will." Roosevelt turned his attention to one of the reports on his desk. "I'm sure you will."

The clock in Meeker's head ticked even louder than the one in the Oval Office. She was on a mission and time was at a premium. A man was going to die if she didn't find out some answers—and fast.

Chapter 4

Thursday, March 5, 1942
FBI Headquarters

Dressed in a navy-blue suit and white blouse, Helen Meeker marched into the FBI offices in the Justice Department Building. Having once been on loan to the Bureau, it was a place she knew well. After checking in with the receptionist, she made her way back to the familiar confines of Henry Reese's office. A quick glance through his open door proved his absence.

"You looking for Agent Reese?"

Meeker turned and stared into the dark, scorching eyes of a tall woman with broad shoulders and a dead-serious expression. She was likely between fifty and sixty; her short, curly gray hair framed a square face unadorned by makeup. Her eyes were deep brown, almost black, and her jaw was firmly set. She seemed as warm as a pit bull protecting half a dozen new pups.

"I'm Helen Meeker from the White House."

"I know who you are," the woman snapped back. "Reese has spoken of you the way some folks talk about Joan of Arc. That doesn't mean much to me. Reese is just like every other man." She raised her eyebrows. "Impressed more with a good set of pins and a haunting smile than a solid brain. Well, not me. I've seen your type before. Just another woman trying to charm her way into a man's world—and you know what I mean by charm."

"If it's what I think you mean, then you need to go wash your mind with a bar of lye soap."

The pit bull frowned, crossed her arms, and tapped her right foot. Meeker was not put off by the assertive manner or harsh expression.

"I have an order here from the President, which has been approved by Mr. Hoover, to take Agent Reese with me to investigate something with national-security implications. Now, where is he?"

"At the First Continental Bank."

"When will he be back?"

"When the bank robbers free the hostages and are arrested," she hissed. "So, it looks like your little adventure will have to be put off for a while."

Seeing no reason to continue the conversation, Meeker spun around and retraced her steps. As she exited back onto the street, a thought crossed her mind. We need that woman on the front lines. She'd scare the Germans to death!

Chapter 5

As Meeker drove up to the bank, she saw that DC police cars had blocked off the streets around it. She parked in a lot just off Vine. After paying the attendant, she pushed through a crowd of curious spectators and up to the barricades.

The scene in front of her looked like it had been staged for a Jimmy Cagney film. There were no signs of life on the street for as far as she could see. Either the cops had evacuated everyone or folks were staying behind closed doors.

As she leaned farther over the wooden barrier, a uniformed cop, who appeared to be in his sixties, rushed over. “No one gets in, lady,” he barked. “We got a dangerous situation on our hands here.”

She flashed her smile and her credentials. “I’m Helen Meeker. I need to be taken to wherever FBI Agent Henry Reese is holed up.”

“I’m Sergeant O’Hara.” The man lifted his hand to slightly above his head. “Is Reese about so high, built like a football player, with a face girls swoon over? Or is he the short, stocky guy who looks a bit like a mule?”

"The former."

"Jackson," O'Hara yelled to a younger cop. "You watch things here. I need to take this pretty young woman to see the FBI men."

As the tall, slim Jackson took up his position, O'Hara led Meeker across the street, down an alley, and to the back of a red brick building. Another cop glanced over her identification before opening the service entrance into a flower shop. He then pointed to a rear staircase.

The cop and Meeker made their way up about twenty steps into a large room with four windows looking out on the bank building across the street. In front of those windows sat two men dressed in suits. One was her old friend and former partner.

"Hey, Henry," she called out. "What has Hoover gotten you into now?"

Reese glanced back from the window and smiled. "Nothing that should concern the President. Shouldn't you be putting sugar in Roosevelt's coffee or taking Fala for a walk?"

"I only draw those details on Tuesdays," she shot back.

The two of them walked to a corner of the room, which Helen hoped was far enough away from the windows that Reese's partner couldn't hear their discussion.

"So why are you here?" he asked.

"The President has issued a request for you to help me with a matter that he feels needs a couple of sharp eyes and good minds. You and I have to get to Georgia ASAP."

"Sounds like a trip I'd want to take," he replied. "But I can't go until we get this mess solved."

"Can't you call in a backup?"

"Nope. I'm the only guy the lead hood will talk to. So, until we end this thing, I'm stuck by the phone."

Meeker moved to the window and looked out onto the street. It might have been just an hour before noon on a busy shopping day, but there was nothing moving except one stray dog, who'd obviously found something he liked in a trashcan. He had knocked it over, and now only his back half was visible.

"What's the score?" she asked.

"Three armed men walked into the bank about an hour ago. They demanded all the cash on hand. One of the patrons managed to sneak out the back and called the cops. When two policemen showed up, the robbers locked the door and made their demands. So far no one has been injured. But the situation is a bit explosive."

"What do they want?"

"The usual," the agent next to Reese interjected. "Safe passage to the airport, where we're supposed to have a DC-3 fueled and ready for take-off. Basically, they want to get out without being handed a go-directly-to-jail card."

Reese nodded at his partner. "This is Rod Giger."

"Nice to meet you. I'm Helen—"

"Oh, I know all about you." Giger's eyes fixed on her. "I love the story of you tying Big Nose McGrew to the hood of your Packard and taking him for a ride."

Meeker smiled, but she was determined not to get sidetracked.

"So why can't you just go in and take those men out?"

"They have six hostages," the long-faced, droopy-jawed agent noted. "The bank president, two male tellers, and a woman with her two small kids."

"Children change the dynamics," Meeker noted.

"Don't you know it," Giger groaned. "No way we can run in with guns blazing or even use tear gas."

Meeker's eyes shot back to the bank building. She studied the two-story brick building. "How are you communicating with them?"

Reese pointed to a phone on the windowsill.

Noting a stack of newspapers sitting against a far wall, Meeker got an idea. "Call them. Give me a chance to talk to the man in charge."

"Why would I do that?" Reese asked.

"They might be more prone to listen to a woman."

Reese shook his head. "Your sex appeal isn't going to convince them to change their plans."

"It worked on you." She followed her quip by batting her eyelids and grinning.

Reese shrugged and picked up the receiver. "Fine. I don't mind watching you hit the same wall we have." After a few seconds, he said into the phone, "This is Reese. I have someone who wants to talk to you. It's a woman."

He covered the receiver and whispered, "The guy's name is Ben. He appears to be the leader. By his accent I'm guessing he's from the Midwest."

Meeker grabbed the phone and took a deep breath. "Ben, this is Helen Meeker. How would you like to visit with a reporter from *The New York Times*?"

Reese and Giger's confused expressions made her smile.

"And why would I want to do that?"

The gruff voice caused Helen to tremble, but she kept her voice steady. "The more the public knows your story, the better chance you have of winning sympathy and getting what you want from the FBI. And if you're in *The Times*, you'll be famous. Warner Brothers will probably want to make a movie about your life. Maybe they could get Gable to play you."

After an interminable wait, he grumbled, "I guess that'd be all right."

"Great. I'll walk out of the florist shop in about a minute. I'm wearing a blue suit. You be ready to let me into the bank when I get there." She hung up.

"What are you doing?" Reese demanded.

"I have a really important job to do, and I need your help. We've got a plane to catch tonight. If I wait for a man to solve this dilemma, it might take days."

"These guys are ready to kill anyone who gets in their way."

"Then I'll try to stay out of their way." Meeker smiled as she turned and hurried down the stairs.

"Helen," Reese called out as he followed, "I don't want you doing this."

"Don't worry. It'll be a piece of cake," she assured him as she hurried toward the front door of the flower shop.

She grabbed the knob, pulled the door open, and walked out in the street before Reese could talk her out of her insane plan.

Chapter 6

The sixty steps across Third Street were the longest of Helen Meeker's life. She felt eyes on her from every direction, and she knew a few of those folks had guns trained on her.

On the far side of the street, she crossed between a 1941 Buick sedan and a 1938 Studebaker coupe, stepped up on the curb, and made her way to the front entrance of the Continental Bank. She rapped on the glass. A few seconds later she heard the latch release, and the door eased open just enough for her to slip in. Taking a deep breath, she crossed the threshold.

"You the reporter?" asked a tall, heavy man in a dark suit.

Instead of answering she allowed her gaze to take in the scene. There were no surprises; it looked like every big bank in the country. The large lobby held one long, high counter, a desk with a swivel chair, two filing cabinets, and four chairs for customers. Six teller windows on a wall dissected the middle of the room, and off to the right was the bank president's office. Behind the tellers' cages, on the floor in the corner, the obviously frightened hostages sat huddled together. A hallway on the far side of the room likely led to the vault.

Crouching beside one of the front windows and peering through a tiny opening in the closed blinds was a man who appeared to be no older than twenty. He was dressed in ill-fitting gray sports coat and blue slacks. He looked scared.

Behind the teller cages, guarding the hostages, was a short, stubby, gray-haired man in a black suit. He held a .38 pistol in his left hand and a cigarette in his right. He seemed as cool as a late fall breeze.

Beside her, gun aimed at her gut, stood a middle-aged man with red hair, a pockmarked face, steel-gray eyes, and a firm, square jaw. He wore a navy-blue pinstriped suit that appeared to be made of silk. He looked more like a bank officer than a bandit.

"I asked if you were the reporter."

"No," she said. "I'm Helen Meeker."

"But you said you were from *The Times*," he growled.

"No," she corrected him. "I asked if you would like to speak to a reporter from *The Times*. I didn't say I was that reporter."

"You lied," he screamed as he shoved the pistol forward.

"No. You assumed." She slowly strolled across the lobby, her heels clicking on the marble floor.

"Are you with the FBI?" he demanded.

"Surely you know Hoover doesn't allow women as agents. I'm from the Office of the President of the United States, and I have the credentials to prove it."

All three gunmen stared at her, jaws dropped.

"Now, who do I talk to about working out a deal here?"

"Me," said the one with the .38. "I'm Ben."

"Where's the vault?"

"Down that hall."

"Is it open?"

"Of course. How do you think we got the cash?" He nodded at five canvas bags on the floor next to the front door.

She headed to the far side of the room, her pace steady and fast.

"Where are you going?" Ben demanded.

She stopped and turned back toward him. "We are going to the vault. I've got to make sure you didn't get a certain something out of there. Once I can guarantee it's still there, we can talk turkey and get you that plane you want." She glanced at the hostages, who peered at her with guarded hope. "But first, you need to let the woman and her little girls go."

"No one gets out of this bank until we're free."

Meeker folded her arms across her chest. "I am one of the O's most valued employees, and having me here means a whole lot more than having a mother and a couple of kids."

His forehead furrowed, as if he saw the merit in her assessment.

"Call Reese," she demanded. "Tell him you're letting three hostages go. After they're released, I will explain why you stumbled into something that's worth the President helping you get away with the money and your freedom."

Ben studied her face a few moments before looking back to his pal behind the teller cages. "Stan, take the woman and the kids to the front door."

As the older man signaled for the trio to get up, Ben moved to the phone and dialed. "We're letting the woman and her kids go. They'll be coming out in a few seconds. Don't try anything or we'll shoot them in the back and then take out the rest of the hostages, including the woman you just sent over."

The mother, wearing a green print dress and black flats, grabbed the hands of the two blonde girls, both about four years old, and hurried them to the front door. When Stan opened the entry, she yanked the youngsters out into the sunlight. A split second later the door was closed and latched again.

"Tell me when they're across the street," Ben barked to the young man by the window.

A minute later he announced, "They're there."

The leader looked back to Meeker. “Okay, now, what’s so important in the safe?”

“You and Stan follow me back there, and I’ll show you.”

Ben looked across the room to the older man and then back to her. “Why both of us?”

“Because it’ll take both of you to open the box.”

“What box?”

Helen released a drawn-out sigh. “Look, this situation has FDR spooked. He’s more worried about you right now than he is about Hitler.”

“He is?” Stan asked. “Why?”

Helen looked around, then lowered her voice. “If the material in that box fell into German or Japanese hands, it would likely cost us the war.”

“I don’t want to cost us the war,” Ben said, a worried look crossing his face. “I might be a bank robber, but I’m still an American through and through.”

“Didn’t figure you were anything but,” Meeker countered. “But because you picked this bank, those papers are your ticket to getting pretty much whatever you want. Now, where do you want to go?”

“Mexico,” Ben answered.

“Mexico, it is. I just need to make a call.”

“To who?”

“The President.”

Ben’s eyes widened. “How do I know you’re not tricking me, like you did before?”

Meeker shrugged. “I’ll let you talk to him yourself if you want.”

He nodded at the phone. Helen picked up the receiver and dialed a number few people knew. A few seconds later a familiar voice answered.

“White House.”

“This is Helen Meeker. Is the President in?”

As the three astounded hoods looked on, the receptionist connected the call.

"Franklin," she said, knowing he'd be tipped off that things weren't normal by her use of his first name. "I've made it to the First Continental Bank. If we give the three robbers safe passage to Mexico, they'll agree to release the hostages and not give the Exodus Plans to the Japanese or Germans. But to assure them that we'll agree to these conditions, they need to talk to you."

"I knew about the bank robbery," the President whispered. "Are you on the inside with the men?"

"Yes, sir."

"I ought to strangle you."

"Maybe. But we have more important things to deal with now."

"And you want me to assure them there's something of great value there?"

"I do."

"All right. Let me talk to the man in charge."

Meeker held the phone out to Ben.

He took the receiver. "Is that really Roosevelt?"

"You'll know in a second."

His eyes wide, Ben spoke into the phone, "Mr. President."

Meeker remained close enough to hear both sides of the conversation.

"Ben, I'm disappointed in you."

"Sorry, sir," he answered, a tremble in his voice. "But if you can get me out of this, I promise I'll mend my ways."

"I believe you, Ben. However, if you sell this information to the enemy, we will track you down and make you wish you had never been born. Do you understand?"

"Yes, sir."

"Take the cash. But don't hurt anyone."

"You have my word," Ben replied.

"Let me talk to Helen."
Ben pushed the receiver back to Meeker.
"Helen, are you sure you know what you're doing?"
"Yes, sir," she replied. She hoped it was true.

Chapter 7

With the two bank robbers watching her every move, Helen Meeker crossed the threshold of the vault, which was flanked by a twelve-inch-thick vault doorway. At the back of the twenty-foot-deep chamber lay bags of coins on the left and a wall of safety deposit boxes on the right. When she got to the one marked 1776, she traced the locked drawer with the fingertips of her right hand and nodded.

"I need to make sure the plans are still here. Are either of you good at picking locks?"

Ben nodded. "Stan's one of the best, and he has his tools in his vest. But I promise we haven't taken them."

"I have to have proof," she insisted. "My job is on the line here." Meeker moved back to the entry and stood beside the pair. "The plans are in drawer 1776. I guess you can figure why we chose that box."

"The Revolutionary War," Stan said.

"Yep," she replied. "And if you can get it open, you win the prize—a long vacation in Mexico."

Slipping his gun into his pocket, the older man moved to the back of the vault and studied the drawer. A few seconds later, he looked back at Ben. "It'll take two of us. When I get one lock tripped, you'll have to hold the tool until I get the other to release."

Ben glanced at Meeker. "I can still shoot you just as easily from back there."

"No doubt."

Rubbing his hand over his mouth, the big man ambled back to where his partner was working on the drawer.

"Okay, I tripped the first one," Stan said. "Hold this tool just the way it is, and don't let it move."

Ben kneeled down, set his gun on the floor, and grabbed the short piece of wire. As he did, Meeker picked up a canvas bag filled with coins.

"What are you doing?" Ben growled, grabbing his gun and pointing it in her direction.

"Dang," Stan grumbled. "The tool moved. Now I've got to do it all over again."

"What are you doing?" Ben repeated, his gun still pointed at Helen.

She lifted the big bag of coins up to her waist. "I just wanted to see how much they weighed. They're really heavy."

"Well, back up against that far wall," Ben ordered. "And quit playing around."

The bag of pennies still in her hand, she took five long backward steps until her back was against the wall near the door.

"Okay," Stan said, "I've got it tripped again. This time hold that wire until I get the other one unlocked."

Once more setting his gun on the floor, Ben turned his attention back to the drawer. As soon as he grabbed the wire, Meeker wrapped the fingers of her free hand around the edge of the vault door. It moved noiselessly a few inches forward. She stepped quietly through the doorway, then slammed the door shut.

After dropping the coin bag to the floor, Meeker spun the lock, which looked like an old sailing ship's wheel, and smiled.

She retrieved the bag of pennies, slipped off her pumps, and silently made her way down the hall. A peek around the corner revealed that the one remaining bank robber was still in his position, gun drawn and studying the street through the slit in the blinds. Hugging the wall, she slowly advanced toward his position.

When she was inches away from his shoulder, he must have sensed her presence, because he jerked around. But before he could aim his gun, Meeker brought the full weight of the canvas bag full of coins down on his head.

He gasped, then fell face forward onto the hard floor. After kicking the gun from his hand, she dropped the bag, picked up the .38 revolver, and hurried to the desk to call Reese.

It occurred to her that she didn't know the number of the phone he was using. She was about to head out the front door when she spotted a bank deposit slip with numbers scrawled on it. When she dialed those numbers, a familiar voice answered.

"Reese, it's me. I have everything under control here."

"Really?"

"One of the hoods is sleeping like a baby. Let's just say I gave him a bit more change than he was expecting." She smiled. "The other two are locked in the vault."

"How did you—?"

"Never mind that. You just get over here and do whatever you have to do. I need to call the President and tell him my plan worked."

Setting the receiver back into the cradle, she shook her head. Perhaps now old J. Edgar would realize that women really did belong in the FBI.

Looking over her shoulder at the confused hostages cowering behind the teller cages, she announced, "Party's over. You can relax now."

Chapter 8

After buckling his seat belt, Henry Reese looked out the airplane's window at the Capitol Building. Once more overriding the powers at the FBI, Helen Meeker had somehow accomplished the impossible and pulled strings to again make them a team for a mission. But that was the way she was. Just about the time he thought he had her figured out, she pulled another surprise to prove he had underestimated her again.

In her case, he loved to be proven wrong.

As the plane lurched forward, he smiled. He might actually enjoy this midnight flight to Georgia, especially since he and Helen were the only two in the plane beside the pilot and copilot.

As the Army Air Corps C-48 lifted off the ground, Reese turned his eyes away from the landscape outside the aircraft and to the woman sitting across the aisle. He never got tired of looking at her. She was uniquely beautiful. Her long, cascading hair perfectly framed her expressive, deep eyes and high cheekbones. Her full lips, arched brows, and angular nose gave her the appearance of a fashion model, but they also pointed to an intelligence few could fully fathom.

A couple of years before, Reese had looked beyond her beauty and discovered she was shrewd, intuitive, and deep. It was a lethal combination for anyone who might try to cross her. But if she was on your side, it could prove the difference between living and dying. And when he was with Helen, he really felt alive.

As she crossed her legs, displaying athletic calves mounted on thin ankles, Reese's mind flew back to the only time he'd ever kissed her. He could still remember every detail of her soft lips pressing against his. Just thinking about that moment caused his heart to race and brought a flush to his cheeks.

"Are you hot?" Helen asked.

Jerking his eyes to her face, Reese shook his head. He felt like a kid who'd been caught with his hands in the cookie jar.

"Well, you look warm." She had to raise her voice to be heard over the Pratt and Whitney's motors. "Even your ears are red."

He shifted in his seat as he sought for a way to change the conversation's direction. "I'm always flushed on flights.

Something about the altitude."

She laughed. "Yeah, we must be all of five hundred feet off the ground by now."

Loosening his tie, he stammered, "How did you get us this flight? I figured low-level employees like us would have to take a train."

She winked. "This was a snap compared to what I did this afternoon at the bank."

Reese relaxed, regaining a sense of control. "You had no business taking that kind of risk."

She shrugged. "If they hadn't bought my story, they would have had one more hostage. But they couldn't afford to shoot me. If they did, you all would have come in with guns blazing."

"You should have waited," he groused. "Hoover had his best minds working up a plan back at headquarters."

Helen laughed. "I couldn't hold off that long. I needed to get you on this plane."

"So, this is all about your impatience."

Helen's face lit up with that perfect Hollywood smile of hers. "More about needing to get a mother and her two kids out of that situation. Besides, I knew I could come up with a plan once I got a feel for the situation."

His eyebrows lifted. "You didn't have one before you went in?"

"How could I? I hadn't seen the landscape yet. You can't clean up a room until you visit it." She kept her eyes fixed on him for a moment. "I saw a picture of you at a banquet with Hedy Lamarr. Some say she's the most beautiful woman in the world."

"I was assigned to that duty," he snapped. "Besides, she's married. She and her husband have invented something that might help us in the war effort. Hoover asked me to take her out while he and her husband talked."

"That's a good cover."

"It's true," Reese retorted. "I bet you'll get stuck with that kind of duty sometime."

She frowned. "Let's not talk about that."

He grinned. "You already have! Who is it?"

She shrugged, clearly trying to act nonchalant. "I have to be seen with some British soldier at a few social events."

Reese laughed. "I bet you're dreading it."

"I am," she insisted, her mouth forming a distinct pout.

He'd hit a sore spot. He enjoyed having something to rib her about. Since he rarely had the upper hand, he pushed harder. "Tell me about him. Is he as good a kisser as I am?"

"How would I know?"

"Surely you remember that night in Illinois when we wrapped up The Yellow Packard case."

She tiled her head. “I vaguely remember something about that. Didn’t you give me a peck on the cheek?”

“That was no peck. Gable didn’t kiss Vivian Leigh with that much passion in *Gone with the Wind*.”

“Boy, are you sensitive. What I meant was that I’ve never even met Nigel Andrews, much less kissed him.”

“Oh.” He frowned, realizing she once again had the upper hand.

She reached into her briefcase and pulled out a file. “We can chat about old times later. Right now, I need you to look over this material and see if you notice the same holes in the case that I found. And if that doesn’t convince you, I have a Bible you need to read.”

“What could a Bible have to do with this case?

“I think there’s a code hidden in some of the notes in the margins. The Bible was owned by a Lutheran minister named Wilbur Shellmeyer.”

“I worked that case.”

“I know. But you might have missed something.”

More than a bit miffed at the insult, Reese grabbed the file and looked through the report. Within fifteen minutes he realized that Helen Meeker had once again seen something everyone else, including he himself, had missed.

Chapter 9

Friday, March 6, 1942 Shady Grove, Georgia

Helen Meeker had never been to Shady Grove, Georgia, a sleepy town located in thick woods along a river named for a former president from Tennessee. From what she'd read about this area, most of the residents didn't have phones, some didn't even have electricity, and a few had yet to install indoor plumbing. Agricultural and lumber work offered enough jobs to put food on the table but rarely enough income to do much else. Poverty was the accepted norm, and the best way to escape it was to join the military. Thus, with a war going on, there were very few young men left in the town or the countryside around it.

After the flight landed at Atlanta in the wee hours of the morning, she and Henry had grabbed a couple of hours sleep at a tiny motel. Following a quick breakfast, they had taken one of the FBI's two-door Fords on the hundred-mile trip to Shady Grove. By the time they parked the five-year-old sedan in front of the local sheriff's office, Meeker had fully shared with Reese her theories on the case. If he was convinced about what was—

or wasn't—in Ellen Shellmeyer's grave, he didn't show it. In fact, he stayed strangely quiet until the moment they arrived in the small town.

"You okay?" she asked as he switched off the motor.

"Fine." He paused for a moment. "Actually, I'm not. I'm stuck here in the States while all my friends are overseas. They're doing the grunt work, taking the risks, and I'm essentially laying low and playing it safe. Hoover won't let me go into the military, and it chaps my hide."

"We need people here too." Meeker rested her hand on his arm. "In truth, you might be doing work that will keep your friends from dying."

"Not so far," he grumbled. "School crossing guards save more lives than I do."

"I have a suggestion."

He looked at her with a hint of hope in his eyes. "What's that?"

"You want to really help the war effort?"

"You know I do."

"Then get Hoover to send your secretary to face off against the Germans. Sixteen-millimeter artillery shells would likely bounce off that woman's hide."

Reese chuckled. "I take it you met Agnes."

"I left before she challenged me to a wrestling match, so I didn't catch her name." She grinned. "Now, we have a job to do here, so let's get started."

Armed with two .38s and a presidential order, they climbed out of the sedan and made their way up wooden steps to the slightly elevated concrete sidewalk. As Meeker smoothed her dark blue skirt and adjusted her matching wide-brimmed hat, she looked around at the dozen or so stone buildings that made up the business district.

"Not much going on around here," Reese said. "I feel like we've stepped back in time to 1922. I haven't seen a dozen

Model Ts all parked on the same street in years. Our car is the newest one here."

Meeker watched three small children tag behind their mother into a feed store. "This is one of those towns the Depression still calls home. Sad. But, since my social calendar is about to get filled up with a man who salutes the Union Jack, let's get this over before I have to head back to Washington."

Reese chuckled. "I can't wait to see pictures of you and the Brit in Life magazine."

"I'll be sure to autograph a copy for you," she grumbled. "Come on, let's get to work."

Meeker led the way into the small structure that housed the area's only law-enforcement officer. The single room was as stark as the main street and almost as dusty. Yellowed wanted posters hung on one wall, a file cabinet sat against another, and two cane-bottomed chairs parked in front of an ancient mahogany desk. Sitting behind stacks of magazines, empty tobacco tins, and a half-eaten sandwich was the man in charge, reading the Grit newspaper.

In his fifties, the sheriff was perhaps six-two and weighing in at likely 280 pounds. He had graying dark hair and wore wireframed glasses. His double chins were clean shaven, and he wore a gray shirt and slacks.

Evidently deciding his guests were not going to leave, he finally set the newspaper to one side, lifted his green eyes to study the two strangers for a few seconds, and then, with considerable effort, pulled his large frame off the wooden swivel chair.

"Brice Johnson's my name," he said, his tenor voice drenched in a southern drawl. "Who might you folks be?"

"I'm Henry Reese, with the FBI." After flashing his credentials, Reese cocked his head toward his partner. "And this is Helen Meeker, special assistant to the President."

"The president of what?" Johnson almost spat as he spoke.

"The United States. Name's Roosevelt. You might have heard of him."

"Oh, I heard of him," the sheriff growled. "But I didn't vote for him. He's too uppity for me. I could never trust a man who smokes with a cigarette holder."

"I don't think that'll bother him much," Meeker observed with a wry grin.

The big man shook his head. His expression made him appear more bovine than human. "What brings you down my way? Nobody of any importance has been to this place since President Davis raced through here trying to evade the Yanks. By the way, given the chance, I would have voted for him."

Meeker pushed up onto the toes of her high heels. "We need a couple of men to do some digging for us."

Johnson shook his head, his cheeks wobbling like jelly. "What do you mean by digging?"

"Dirt," Meeker explained. "We need to dig up a grave at the Grove Cemetery."

The sheriff's eyebrows rose. "You paying?"

"We are," Reese assured him. "And we have a court order for the exhumation."

Johnson nodded. "There are a couple of colored boys, the Wilson brothers, who could do that for you." He narrowed his eyes. "Mind if I ask whose grave you're digging up? After all, this is my town. I have a right to know."

"You can ask," Meeker said, "but we aren't required to tell you. And I doubt the FBI or the president believe you have a right to know any more than you already do. Now, where can we find the Wilson boys? And who do we talk to about getting into the cemetery?"

The sheriff stood up straight. "I don't take that kind of talk from a woman."

Before Meeker could jump down the ill-mannered man's throat, Reese intervened. "I wouldn't recommend crossing her.

This woman brought in Big Nose McGrew single-handedly. You might have read about that in the *Grit*."

As the color drained from his face, the sheriff's eyes darted to her. He rubbed his throat as if trying to push out a frog. "You the one that strapped him over your hood like a deer?"

Meeker rocked back on her heels. "That was easy compared to the bank robbers I nabbed in Washington yesterday." She crossed her arms. "Now, who's in charge of the cemetery?"

Words came tumbling out of Johnson's mouth like rocks sliding down a Georgia hillside. "Mort Graves is the undertaker. And before you ask, that's his real name. He's in charge of the graveyard too."

Reese grinned. "Sounds like he was born for that job. We'll need him to be there when we do ours."

"Mind if I go too?" Johnson asked.

"You can be there," Meeker said, "but you can't talk about what we're doing to anyone. You got that?"

"I can keep a secret," the sheriff assured them.

"If you don't, there'll need to be a special election in this town, because your mail will be forwarded to a government facility in Leavenworth. Do you understand?"

The big man nodded.

Reese buttoned his gray suit coat, smoothed his black tie, and pulled his white shirtsleeves over his wrists, all without taking his eyes off the squirming but conciliatory lawman. "Got a place to eat in this town?"

"They fix sandwiches down at Jenkins Cafe. Got a jukebox you can play there too. Only a nickel per song. I love Dinah Shore."

"Sounds good," Reese replied. "While Miss Meeker and I have some breakfast, you round up Graves and the Wilson brothers, then meet us at the restaurant. We'll buy all of you something to eat."

Johnson shook his head. "Mort and I can eat with you, but they don't serve colored folks in the café. So, the Wilson boys will have to wait outside."

"They will join us today," Meeker said, her tone firm, "or none of us will be eating."

"But—"

"No buts. I don't care how things are done here on most days. Today the team that works this case will eat together. You got that?"

"Yes, ma'am," the sheriff replied.

Reese turned toward the door. "You make whatever calls you need to make, but be sure to alert the café that there'll be new rules in play today." He grinned. "And if they want to argue about that, tell them they can take it up with the gal who got Big Nose McGrew. You got it?"

The sheriff nodded.

"And Johnson?" Reese pointed to the six wanted posters tacked on the far wall. "Three of those men are dead, and the others are in prison, so you can pull them all down."

The big man scratched his head. "When did that happen?"

"We got the first two in 1937. The rest of the cases were closed a bit more recently—1938."

"Wow. I just put them up last year."

Meeker moved toward the door, but turned before exiting. "We'll see you at the café as soon as you round up what we need. And remember, don't tell anyone what this is all about."

Stepping out onto the sidewalk, she glanced at her partner. "He clearly doesn't have much respect for anyone who's not local."

Reese laughed. "I get that a lot. Comes with being in the FBI. State cops almost always look at us as either invaders or interlopers. And you know how they feel about women. But your taking down McGrew set the table for this gig to be played by our rules. I wish J. Edgar could have seen that."

Chapter 10

Helen Meeker enjoyed the fried ham, scrambled eggs, and toast at Jenkins Café. But never had such a simple breakfast created so much interest. Folks from all over town came in to watch the Wilson brothers eat at a table with white folks. It likely surprised more than a few when the building didn't collapse during the meal.

After eating their fill, Meeker, Reese, Mort Graves, Sheriff Johnson, and the Wilsons climbed into four vehicles and made the mile-and-a-half trip out to Grove Cemetery.

The century-old rural graveyard was typical of those found in almost every state in the Union. The stones were modest, and only a handful of the graves were adorned with flowers. There were a few scattered trees. On the north side of the grounds stood a small frame chapel, its white paint peeling and its tin roof showing a hint of rust. The six-inch-high grass growing in the path leading to the front door of the twenty-by-thirty-foot building revealed that it was rarely used.

Under cloudy skies, Meeker looked the undertaker in the eye. "Mr. Graves, I believe that last October you sold a grave to some folks from up north, a Lutheran minister and his wife. Their name was Shellmeyer."

Graves, a slightly built man in a dark suit and white shirt, nodded. "I did. Quiet folks. Kind of nervous, as I recall."

Meeker gazed at a stone well to the right of the chapel, wondering how best to explain their objective.

"So," the sheriff said, his high-pitched tone displaying his impatience, "is the preacher's grave the one we're going to dig up?"

She shook her head. "He's still alive … at least for a few more days." She pointed toward the chapel. "What's that building used for?"

"We hold services there during bad weather," Graves explained in a deep, rhythmic baritone.

She looked into the man's sunken, dark eyes. "What's inside?"

He shrugged. "About what you'd expect. A few pews, a piano, a podium."

"Does it have power?"

"We aren't as backwoods as you might think. Got a bathroom too."

The dark sky had been threatening rain all day. If the clouds let loose before they finished their work, at least they'd have a dry place to examine the body.

"Where is the plot you sold the Shellmeyers?"

Graves extended a short, bony finger. "About forty feet beyond that maple tree, toward the back of the property."

"Did you do the embalming work on their daughter?"

"No. Never saw the body. They came here with it already in the coffin."

That fit with the scenario she had imagined. "Was the Shellmeyer family alone when they arrived?"

"Let me think." Graves stroked his jaw. "Besides the two other daughters and the parents, there were two middle-aged men. They did most of the talking. They weren't from the South,

I'll tell you that. Sounded a bit like my cousins who live up by Chicago."

"Was there a graveside service?"

"Not much of one. The father just said a prayer, and then the two of us lowered the coffin into the grave. They all stayed while Amos and Zeb here tossed the dirt on it. Then one of the middle-aged men gave me money for the headstone they ordered. That was it."

Meeker studied the Wilson brothers. They were solidly built, wide-shouldered men in their forties. Clean shaven, they dressed in flannel shirts, bib overalls, and brown work boots, and had coarsely cropped hair. Amos was a touch over six feet, his brother a bit under. Knowing the reason they had been called to this place, they both held shovels.

Meeker addressed the brothers. "Were either of you within earshot of the Shellmeyers at the graveside?"

Amos cleared his throat. "We was both near enough to hear the prayer."

"Kind of a strange one it was," Zeb added.

"In what way?"

The young men looked at each other. "It was short," Zeb said. "And it sounded less like a prayer for the family than a warning. I never heard anything like it at a funeral, and I've been to a lot of 'em."

Reese took a step closer. "What made it sound like a warning?"

Zeb's eyes widened. "I'll never forget. The preacher said, 'Please, Lord, let her body rest in Zion's graces, and let no man ever disturb this vessel, for if they do, they will meet you sooner than later.'"

Meeker hurried past the maple tree to the plot the undertaker had pointed out. The white stone marker was simple and direct. It listed only the name, Ellen Shellmeyer. There was no date of birth or death.

Meeker grimaced. The pastor's wish for eternal rest was about to be rescinded. It was time to see if her theory was right.

Chapter 11

It took almost an hour for the Wilson brothers to dig deep enough into the Georgia soil to strike pay dirt. By that time a light rain had started falling, and the brothers' boots were caked with red clay.

As Helen Meeker looked on from about ten feet behind the marker, the Wilsons succeeded in getting ropes around the coffin's rails. Then, with Sheriff Johnson's help, Graves and Reese managed to wrestle it out of the ground and to a resting point beside the open grave. As the men paused to catch their breath, Meeker approached the coffin, circling it twice to make sure she had viewed it from every possible angle. It was a standard-sized, fairly ornate gray casket with a rounded top and silver rails. As she had picked out her father's coffin not many years ago, she was familiar enough with them to realize this model was anything but cheap. It hardly seemed the choice a minister with two other children would have made. Because it had been in the ground for such a short time, the sides, where the rain had started to wash away the clinging clay, still showed a shine.

"Mr. Graves," Meeker asked, "what can you tell me about this casket?"

The small man wiped his brow. "For starters, it's much nicer than anything I carry. Nobody around here would lay out the kind of money it takes to buy one of these. You could purchase a new Ford or Chevy cheaper than this."

"Do you know who made it?"

"The Batesville Casket Company of Indiana. You can see their name on the end. They've been around a long time. They're one of the top names in the industry."

She nodded. "How difficult is it to open?"

"Just takes a special key. I've got one with me. Since this one hasn't been in the ground too long, it shouldn't take any time at all."

Meeker stooped and studied the two places the key would fit, then glanced at the sky. The clouds were getting darker, and the rain was picking up.

"Let's get this thing inside the chapel," she suggested. "I don't want the body in this casket getting wet before we examine it. I'll help the Wilsons on this side. You three get on the other side."

After all six had taken their positions, Graves directed, "Lift on three. One, two, three!" Motivated by rain that was now falling hard, they managed the trip to the chapel in a minute or less.

The makeshift pallbearers braced the heavy box against the step railing while the undertaker checked the ring of keys he pulled out of his pocket. When he finally found the key to the building's only door, they brought the coffin inside the musty building.

"Let's take it up by the podium," Meeker suggested.

After they arrived at that spot, they turned the box so it was parallel to the pews and placed it on the wooden floor. While

Reese walked back toward the entrance to snap on the lights and close the door, everyone but Helen took a seat on the front pew.

Only the Wilsons were not breathing heavily.

"You want me to unlock it now?" Graves asked.

"In a moment." Meeker ran her hand along the lip of the box, pausing at a point just above one of the two locks.

"Why is it so important to look at this body?" Johnson asked.

"We need to make sure it's her," she explained.

"Why wouldn't it be?"

Meeker lifted her gaze and directed her answer to all the men. "If Ellen Shellmeyer died in a swimming accident on the Gulf Coast, why bury her here? This wasn't her hometown, and the Shellmeyers had no obvious connection with Shady Grove."

"So what?" Johnson grumbled. "What difference does it make where some kid's buried?"

Meeker tilted her head. "If your father had been accused of being a Nazi spy, it might make a lot of difference."

The sheriff's eyes widened. "Do you think they might have buried important papers with the girl? Could we be sitting on something right here in Shady Grove that might help bring down the Nazis and Japs? Or maybe it was gold or cash."

"I don't know about anything being inside," Meeker replied, frowning as she noted the red clay caked on her navy pumps. "But I do think there's something important that might be revealed here that could help us in the war." She moved her eyes from her soiled shoes to Mort Graves. "How many people are buried in this cemetery?"

"Maybe three hundred. Counting the really old graves, might be double that."

"How many of those are from places other than Shady Grove or the area around here?"

The undertaker shook his head. "None that I can think of." He paused. "No, I take that back. There was a salesman who died back in 1933. We couldn't find any family, so we buried him here. If I remember correctly, he had a heart attack or stroke. He's resting up the way about a hundred feet."

She looked back at the coffin. "Interesting."

"Well, let's get this box open and take a look inside." Johnson rubbed his hands together and grinned. "This is better than Christmas."

Meeker ignored the enthusiastic sheriff's impatience and turned to her partner. "Henry, have you got that photo of Ellen?"

He reached into the inside pocket of his coat and pulled out a four-by-four snapshot. He handed it to Meeker. She studied it for a moment, then looked toward Graves. "Unlock it."

"Now we're cooking," Johnson almost shouted. "Get moving, Mort."

The undertaker fished into his pocket, pulled out a large key ring, and moved toward the casket. He bent over and examined the lock toward the foot of the box, chose a key, dropped to his knees, inserted it, and gave it a twist to the right. The lid released and raised a fraction of an inch. He moved to the head of the coffin and repeated the process with the same results.

"You want me to lift the lids?" Graves asked.

"Before you do," Meeker said, "what kind of shape do you think the body will be in?"

"If it was embalmed, and the mortician did a good job, it'll be easy to tell if it's the girl in that photo."

"And if it wasn't embalmed?"

"Still should be able to do it, though there'll be some decomposition." He looked at the box. "The lack of air in the sealed coffin slows the process down. And this casket wouldn't allow much humidity in, if any. But seeing as how there's no smell oozing out after breaking the seal, I'd have to believe she was embalmed."

"All right, then. We might as well see what we've got."

Graves reached for the front of the lid, but Meeker grabbed his wrist. "Wait a second."

Johnson stood from his spot on the pew. "We've wasted the better part of the afternoon doing this. Let's get moving and see what kind of secrets we find in there."

With rain peppering the tin roof, Meeker studied the oversized sheriff and the eager undertaker before turning her attention back to the coffin.

Graves rose to his feet. "A dead body can't hurt you, lady. There's nothing to be scared of."

"I'm not scared," Meeker replied as she crouched by the casket. "I just don't like the feeling I'm getting."

"Hogwash." Johnson groaned. "Women don't have the stomach for real law-enforcement work. Never have and never will."

Johnson's opinion grated Meeker, but that was the least of her problems at the moment. Her hunches were usually good ones, and something told her she didn't need to rush into finding out what was inside this box.

She walked to the back of the coffin, then moved back about five feet away to get a full view. The sheriff uttered a curse and all but leaped up to the casket. Before Meeker could protest, he grabbed the lip of the lid and jerked it up.

As he and Graves stared inside, Meeker's ears picked up on a sound she knew all too well. "Get out of here!" she screamed.

Her gut told her she didn't have time to make it to the door, so she hit the floor, rolled over onto her back, slid under a pew, and scooted across the dust-covered wood toward the front wall. Above her the Wilson brothers took three long strides and jumped through a large glass window. Reese, who was closest to the door, had the quickest route out. By the time Meeker had pulled herself under the third pew and was reaching for the fourth, the agent was opening the door.

Meeker peeked out through the aisle and saw Graves, still at the coffin, staring into the open box. The sheriff stood beside him, frozen in the same position.

Before she could shout another warning, an explosion rocked the chapel. Meeker ducked for cover under the pew.

The deafening roar, though lasting only a few seconds, shook the rafters. It blew out five windows and splintered the first two pews, knocking the next one onto its side. The podium was blown into a thousand pieces, and the metal coffin was turned into hundreds of shrapnel-fueled rockets, flying at light speed across the width and breath of the structure. Large sections of the tin roof fell to the floor, allowing the pouring rain inside the building.

For almost ten seconds the sound rocked Shady Grove, and then there was silence. That silence spoke even louder than the blast.

Chapter 12

Her ears ringing, Helen Meeker stared at the gash on her right arm. A sheet of tin rested on the pew above her, blocking her view of the sky and shielding her from the pouring rain.

Rather than shove the shredded metal panel away, she grabbed the pew and pulled herself to the back of what was left of the small structure. Pushing to her knees, she took a deep breath, then got to her feet.

Just as she managed to stand, Henry Reese stepped through the open door. Except for being soaked, he seemed fine. Apparently, he'd gotten out soon enough to escape injury.

He knocked a sheet of tin out of the way and moved to her side. "You okay?"

"Yeah. Except for a nasty ringing in my ears." She glanced toward the front of the chapel, where parts of the coffin rested between two men, lying on the ground. She didn't have to check the sheriff's pulse to know the consequences of his slow reactions. His body had been sliced to pieces and tossed against the right wall.

On the other side of the room, Graves was covered with blood but he was still breathing. Pushing through the wreckage,

Meeker worked her way to the man's side. Bending down, she grabbed his hand.

"Mr. Graves," she whispered as she leaned near his horribly lacerated face.

"There was no body," he moaned.

"It was a booby trap." She glanced over her shoulder. "Henry, get some help. This man needs a doctor."

As Reese rushed out the door, Meeker returned her attention to the undertaker. She pressed her hand against a large wound just below his neck in an effort to slow some of the flow and give the man a few more moments of life.

"Don't bother," he whispered, his thin, almost blue lips forcing a smile. "I know when a person is beyond help. Besides, death doesn't scare me. I'm more than ready to sing with Jesus. I just hope he'll forgive the fact I can't carry a tune."

"My partner went to get some help," Meeker assured him. "You hang on."

"Nothing to hang on to," he said. "But I do want to know something."

"What's that?"

"Why would anyone turn a casket into a bomb?"

Meeker shook her head. "I don't know, at least not yet. But I think it has something to do with why a man waiting for an execution is willing to die for something he didn't do."

"But what happened to the girl?" The undertaker's breath came in gasps.

Meeker was formulating a way to answer that question when the man's eyes rolled back and his mouth gaped open. Graves was dead.

As Meeker stood, Reese reentered the chapel. "The Wilsons are on their way to get help."

She shook her head. Unable to help the dead man, Meeker studied what was left of the casket.

"Did you see what caused the explosion?"

"No. But I know it was a grenade. When Johnson yanked the lid open, it pulled the pin."

"How did you know if you didn't see it?"

"I heard the ticking." After glancing at the two dead men, she added, "Shellmeyer's cryptic prayer wasn't answered in the way he'd hoped, but his fears were realized. Can't say we weren't warned."

"Was there anything else in the coffin?" Reese asked.

"Graves said there wasn't a body. He lived long enough to tell me that."

"Is that what you expected?"

"I didn't think Ellen was dead, but I wasn't anticipating a bomb." She turned her eyes toward her partner, her emotions a jumble of fear and confusion. "This is even bigger than I thought. Shellmeyer knows something with major consequences and the key has to be finding his daughter and getting her to safety."

"Miss Meeker?" a voice called out from the chapel door.

She looked up and saw Zeb Wilson, appearing none the worse for his experience. "The doctor's coming."

"No reason now. The other two are dead. But thanks for your help." She paused. "Is your brother all right?"

"We're both fine. Got out in the nick of time. The good Lord was watching over us. He surely was."

Meeker moved carefully through the debris to the door. "Zeb, can you tell me once more what the preacher said when he prayed over the grave?"

He nodded. "I'll never forget it." Zeb looked back toward the gravesite. "He said, 'Please, Lord, let her body rest in Zion's graces, and let no man ever disturb this vessel, for if they do, they will meet you sooner than later.' He was sure right about that last part."

"There was nothing else?"

"No, ma'am, that was it. Expect that he added an 'amen.' And then the folks left, and we covered the casket. Sure wish it had stayed covered."

"Thanks, Zeb." She patted his arm. "You might as well go now. Nothing anyone can do here."

"Guess we'll be digging two more graves," he murmured. Then he turned and walked down the steps.

Meeker turned to Reese. "Shellmeyer's notes in that Bible or the logbook have to mean something. Let's get back to Washington and start digging."

As the two walked down the steps and through the rain to the car, Meeker thought about her last visit to the President's office. He had warned her that curiosity killed the cat. She still wasn't sure about the cat, but there was no doubt it had led to the death of a small-town Georgia sheriff and undertaker.

Chapter 13

Saturday, March 7, 1942
Washington, DC

Just past six in the morning, the plane carrying Helen Meeker and her partner touched down in the capitol. She'd had two hours sleep since Thursday, had barely escaped being blown to bits, and had taken six stitches in her arm, but the answers she got on her trip to Georgia only created more questions. Worse yet, the clock was running, and Shellmeyer would meet his maker in just over a week. That gave her very little time to operate.

Yet even with her mind whirling, she had to sleep. Two minutes after arriving at her apartment, she dropped into bed without even removing her clothes. She immediately fell into a heavy slumber that offered both escape and peace.

At four, her ringing phone yanked her from a dream that included a romantic date with Henry Reese at a posh New York nightclub. He'd just asked her to dance when she emerged from the fog, crawled across her bed, and reached for the receiver.

Even as she answered she could swear she still heard the strains of the nightclub's orchestra.

"This better be good," she mumbled into the phone.

"I hope you found what you needed in the sunny South."

After rubbing her eyes, she looked at the clock and sighed. Couldn't the President have waited until tomorrow or even tonight?

"Well, sir," she began, hiding as best she could her displeasure with his timing, "I found out enough to feel certain I'm right about Shellmeyer. But I don't have the proof you need. Still, I'm going to get it. Reese has the logbook and the Bible right now. I'm hoping I'll have something concrete for you by Monday."

"Glad to hear that. Now, you need to get yourself fixed up really nice. You have a formal evening at the British Embassy tonight."

"What? I thought my arranged dating life didn't kick off until toward the middle of next week."

"Change in plans. The Brits have scheduled a banquet tonight for about a hundred guests, and you'll be representing the White House. It's formal, and you'll be sitting with Nigel Andrews. I'm sure there will be lots of press climbing all over one another to get a picture of you two. I see this as an opportunity for an arms-across-the-ocean kind of thing. People love that."

"When did this come up?"

"Winston called me from London an hour ago. He said there was going to be some kind of huge surprise announcement during the banquet. When that happens, you need to be on the arm of our hero. And if the British corporal wants you to kiss him on the cheek, do it."

"That's just great," she groaned.

"Be there at seven. And look your best. Thanks." He didn't give her time to respond before hanging up.

After pulling herself out of bed, Meeker wandered over to the dresser mirror and gazed at her reflection. Her face looked more like the Wicked Witch of the West than one that belonged to a member of the social elite. Her hair was still filled with dust from the chapel explosion, her makeup was smeared, and she had huge circles under puffy eyes. Turning toward her bathroom, she wondered if three hours would be enough time to transform herself into Cinderella. She doubted it. Still, her country called, and even if this was something trivial, it went with the job.

Chapter 14

Having heard the evening was supposed to be cool, Helen Meeker chose a long-sleeved, jade-green dress with a high neck and low back. She added long white gloves to hide her stitches, a gold necklace, green pumps, and a fur wrap. After driving her Packard through the massive gate and onto the embassy grounds, she parked, presented her identification, and made her way up to the front entry of the stately red brick building at 3100 Massachusetts Avenue.

The embassy seemed to be a cross between a city library and an English country mansion. The columns gave the building somewhat of a Roman look. The rest of the structure clearly showed its British roots.

Walking through the front door, down the hallway, and into the banquet hall, she caught the eye of a dozen men of all ages. As she paused at the entry, four formally dressed males nearly tripped over one another racing to her side. A heavyset fellow, about fifty, with silver hair and a red cummerbund, won simply because he avoided a parade of waiters carrying drinks to a group of twenty or so guests visiting by a massive fireplace.

Meeker waited for the other three to make it to a position in front of her before smiling at the winner and posing a question none of the men likely wanted to hear. "Could you direct me to Corporal Nigel Andrews?"

The member of the quartet closest to her shook his head and frowned. "Oh, that's the way you are. Pip, pip, so be it. Can't win them all, you know." He looked toward the other three and announced, "I'll take this."

After they left, he introduced himself. "I'm John Babcock, of the Brighton Babcocks." An elderly gentleman, he sported a distinguished handlebar mustache and wore a long-tailed jacket.

"I'm Helen Meeker, of the official White House dating pool."

After bowing he took Meeker's hand and led her to the far side of the room. There, by a side table, stood a handsome young man who looked quite dashing in his dress uniform.

"Nigel," Meeker's temporary escort announced, "this woman wishes to meet you." Babcock leaned closer to him. "Your fortune and my loss." After a final forlorn look at her, he headed back to the entry.

"You must be Miss Meeker," the soldier said in a Liverpool accent. "I've heard a great deal about you, but no one mentioned how beautiful you are."

She smiled. "Did they make you practice that line for very long?"

The Brit grinned. "Let's just say they wrote it for me and taught me how to deliver it properly. But it wasn't a lie; you are a devastatingly lovely woman."

"Thank you. And I can honestly say that it's nice to spend the evening with a man who can legitimately be called a hero."

"Oh, I'm not so sure about that," he said, his smile fading. "I was just one of the blokes who was lucky enough to get back."

"That's every soldier's goal," she assured him. She was about to ask about the decorations adorning his jacket when she felt a tap on her shoulder.

"Might we have some pictures?"

As Meeker turned, she came face-to-face with half a dozen members of the press corps, ready to record this moment in history. And record it they did. It was a good thing film wasn't being rationed. For the next five minutes, flashbulbs popped and a series of meaningless questions were asked and answered.

When the first wave of the press finally moved off, Meeker suggested, "Let's step out on the patio for a few moments. That might give us a bit of peace and a chance to get to know each other."

After crossing the room as quickly as decorum allowed, the pair escaped through a set of French doors into the cool evening air. Shutting the doors behind them blocked out much of the noise coming from inside the hall.

"This is far better than being in a stuffy room," he noted, "listening to that string quartet."

"Much," she agreed. "So, do you know what this quickly tossed-together affair is all about?"

"I don't. I was touring the DC sights this morning when I got the word. But it must be something big. The embassy staff has pulled out all the fine china. Still, I wish I was somewhere else." Apparently sensing he'd said something wrong, he added, "I don't mean I don't appreciate being with a beautiful woman like you."

Meeker held up her hand and grinned. "You're fine. I understand. This tore me away from something too. But, since you're not putting the moves on me, like most men in uniform seem to be doing, I'm guessing you have a girl back home."

He got a faraway look in his eye. "I do. Becky's cute, kind of short, and doesn't know much about sophisticated gatherings like this one. But she's all I need or want."

"Good for you." Meeker patted his arm. "She sounds pretty special."

"As special as the first robin in spring. Would you like to hear more about her?"

"I'd love to. As long as she's not a part of the Brighton Babcock clan."

"What?"

"Nothing." She swallowed a smile, feeling a bit sorry for her weak attempt at humor.

As only a British man could do, Andrews took Meeker's elbow and guided her to a railing overlooking the grounds. After glancing up at the sliver of a moon, he began his tale of romance. "I met Becky in grammar school. I still remember that day. Her hair was fixed in strawberry curls, and she wore a fluffy blue dress. The first thing she said to me was, 'You're a might strange sort.'"

Meeker laughed. "I take it she wasn't impressed."

"No. She wouldn't give me the time of day until we were in our teens. But on a fall night in October, at a school party, we danced for the first time, and my heart has been dancing ever since." He chuckled. "That's sounds silly, doesn't it?"

She shook her head. "It sounds nice. No, better than nice. It sounds wonderful."

"You know what's so special about Becky?" Meeker waited for him to tell her.

"It's the way she …" He shook his head, his brows drawing together slightly. "I'm sorry. It actually hurts to talk about her."

"Why?"

"Because of this stupid war. It killed my brother. It killed my best friends. It demolished the home I lived in as a child. It destroyed some of the greatest buildings ever constructed in Europe. And it hasn't helped my relationship with Becky."

Meeker wondered how the war had affected their relationship—other than keeping them apart, of course. But it seemed too personal a question to ask.

"We should just give Hitler Europe and make peace. I don't think France would care about Great Britain if the Nazis were leaving them alone. And I doubt anyone would have gotten too upset if Russia had invaded Germany. Who would have come to their defense? But rather than seek peace, we fight. We slaughter innocents and bomb civilians, and there are men who love every moment of it."

Meeker frowned. "You can't be serious."

"The men calling the shots treat people like equipment. Life means nothing to blokes like Reggie Fister."

"Fister?" She gasped. "He was your friend, your leader. And your country's biggest hero."

"He was a lover of war." Andrews's voice took on a bitter tone. "He lived for battle and women. He bragged about his conquests in both areas. Oh, he was charming all right, and he had a wealth of courage and spunk. You would have liked him—every woman did. But he was the kind of guy who draped himself in the flag and looked for ways to prove his manliness."

"Is that bad?" Meeker asked. "I mean, aren't those the kind of men we need right now?"

He looked her in the eye. "If there were no men like Reggie, there wouldn't be any wars. No, we need people who realize that being with loved ones is far more important than killing men who have their own loved ones waiting for them at home. Someone should tell Churchill that."

"You're working for him," Meeker reminded him. "Perhaps you can tell him."

"He won't listen. No one wants peace."

"I do. And so do many others. However, saving Europe from Hitler is of monumental importance. We cannot allow him to make a mockery of freedom."

"I understand why you think what you do. Maybe if you had been there, as I have … if you had known the French arrogance and the—"

The double doors opened. "Nigel," a staff member called out.

"Yes?"

"They're about to make the announcement. You two need to come back inside."

Meeker tucked her hand into the crook of Nigel's elbow and allowed the bitter Brit to escort her back into the banquet room.

"We're supposed to sit at that table," he whispered, leading her to a place near the podium. He pulled out her chair. She had just taken her seat when the British ambassador to the United States stepped up to the microphone.

"Ladies and gentlemen, distinguished guests, and members of our military, on behalf of the king and the British Government, as well as the entire Allied forces, I am here tonight to share a tale of one of the bravest men ever to wear the British colors. You all know his story. One of those here tonight, Corporal Nigel Andrews, served with him in Africa as well as on that secret mission in France. You have no doubt all read of the way Colonel Reggie Fister held off hundreds of German troops so that his men could escape back to England and share the intelligence they uncovered on their mission."

Meeker glanced at Andrews and noted his face was twisted in an expression of both pain and anger. This tribute to a fallen hero, a man he evidently neither cared for nor admired, was likely too much for the resentful man to stomach.

"Tonight," the ambassador continued, "I have additional news to share with you about Colonel Fister. But why should I deliver this report when there is a man far better suited for that duty?"

The ambassador paused, waved his hand toward the side of the room, and smiled. “Ladies and gentlemen, may I present to you Colonel Reggie Fister.”

All eyes went to a door as it opened, and a distinguished looking man in uniform stepped into the room. As those in attendance jumped to their feet, clapped, and shouted out greetings, Meeker’s eyes fell back to her escort. Andrews had not risen, and he was not clapping. Rather, he looked stunned beyond belief.

Chapter 15

An hour after the meal, and more than two hours after he'd been introduced, Colonel Reggie Fister finally escaped the onslaught of press and fawning dignitaries and made it to the table where Helen Meeker sat with Nigel Andrews.

Andrews had said almost nothing the whole time. The unbelievable news that his dead friend was still alive seemed to have put him in a near-catatonic state.

"Nigel," the black-haired, green-eyed hero called out as he approached. "My, it is good to see you."

Andrews looked like a frightened rabbit as he awkwardly rose from his chair and saluted.

"None of that," Fister barked. "Open up those arms and give me a hug." Showing none of the normally stiff English reserve, Fister grabbed Andrews in a bear hug and almost squeezed the life out of him. He then stepped back and announced with a wide grin, "You're looking good, lad."

"Thank you, sir," Andrews mumbled. But the wild, nervous look in his eyes remained.

If Fister noticed his friend's apprehension, he didn't show it. Instead he turned to Meeker, allowing his eyes to slide from the top of her head to her pumps and back up. "My goodness, this one is beyond what I dreamed of when the underground was nursing me back to health."

She smiled, not sure whether she should feel complimented or repulsed, and extended her hand. "I'm Helen Meeker."

"Helen, eh? I believe the name is Greek for torch or flame. And beauty like yours would likely set any man's heart aglow. If I survived everything I went through in France only for this moment, it would be more than enough." He caressed her gloved hand.

Fister was a combination of English charm and American brashness with a hint of Scottish rogue. He was like no one Meeker had ever met. If he didn't come off as such a gentleman, his leering gaze would have made her uncomfortable. But he had been away for a while, and likely he would want to be in the company of any single woman. So, for the moment she could forgive him. And forgiveness was easy when a man was as attractive as Reggie Fister.

"Miss Meeker," Fister sighed more than said, "is there is a place we can go and get to know each other better?"

She shook her head. "I'm not familiar with the embassy. This is only my second trip here." She glanced at the ashen-faced Andrews. "Nigel, do you know of a spot?"

The corporal swallowed hard and nodded toward a door just across the entry hall from the banquet room. "There's a small study that's likely not being used right now."

"Perfect," Fister announced as he continued to stare into Meeker's eyes. "Nigel, why don't you lead the way?" As the corporal stepped out, Fister took Meeker's arm and tucked it into his. "This makes being turned over to the Americans by the underground all the better."

"You mean you haven't been back to England yet?" Meeker asked as he led her around tables toward the study.

"No. When I was rescued, they felt it best to debrief me here in the States. I will get to head home when the delegation that Nigel is a part of goes back." He smiled, his eyes shining like lighthouse beacons. "And suddenly I have no problem with that delay. In fact, I hope it goes on for months."

Meeker could almost feel her cheeks flush.

Andrews opened the door and pushed on the lights in the study. As he did so, Meeker's eyes were pulled from Fister's dynamic smile to the room. It was no more than twenty by twenty, with bookcases lining all except the far wall—which, based on its French doors, likely bordered a garden area. There was no desk, but the room contained a half dozen high-backed green leather chairs. Judging from the lingering smell of cigar smoke, it was likely a place where the staff gathered for relaxed, after-hours conversations.

The colonel led her to a chair on the far side of the room and took a seat directly across from her. Without a word, he watched her movements as she crossed her left leg over her right knee and folded her hands in her lap.

After almost a minute of awkward silence, Andrews moved to a chair on her right and finally spoke. "Colonel, I don't understand how you escaped. When I looked out the plane's window, the woods were filled with Germans, and you were out in the open."

"Ah." Fister grinned. "And thus begins a story that is part miracle and part the nature of German arrogance." The Scotsman leaned forward in his chair and folded his hands over his right knee. "When I quit firing, they assumed I was dead. One man came up and rolled me over, and I played the part. After checking on poor Homes, their commander ordered one of his men to find a local farmer to take care of the dead limeys. I stayed there, not moving, with Germans all around me, for at least a half hour. Finally, some sleepy-headed old man showed up and the Nazis moved off. When the farmer left, probably to get a shovel, I got up and headed toward the house of Frank Colbert. You remember him, Nigel. He was one of the underground men who helped us with our mission. I almost bled to death before I got there."

Fister leaned back in his chair, stretched out his long legs, and crossed one ankle over the other. "Colbert patched me up the best he could and hid me away. I stayed there until after Christmas, regaining my strength. When more Germans were transferred into the area, Colbert and his group moved me to a hiding place just outside of Paris. Later, I was smuggled to Spain and finally given over to a group of merchant seamen. They got me on a ship bound for America. When I arrived in New York, I came straight to Washington and checked in with the embassy."

"Amazing," Meeker said. "Did the Nazis ever get close to capturing you during your months behind lines?"

"A couple of times. I had to kill two Gestapo agents with my bare hands," Fister bragged. "I thought I was a goner when some lads spotted me. But they were soft; they didn't offer much of a fight."

"When did you get to Washington?" Andrews asked.

"About three weeks ago. I had my injuries checked out at Walter Reed Hospital and have been in debriefings ever since I was released. Hopefully what I saw will help us knock out some Jerry installations. When I get back to England, I'll receive my promotion, working for the high command. So, I'll be dealing with Monty and Ike on a regular basis."

"That's quite an honor," Meeker said. "You'll soon know more about the war and Allied plans than even Roosevelt and Churchill."

Fister grinned. "I doubt that. But I will be in a position to give a regular soldier's viewpoint before we charge off into battles. Maybe that will help us save a few chaps like Nigel here. If so, I will have done my part."

The colonel leaned farther forward, his eyes all but staring through Meeker. "I do hope in the next few weeks you'll make time to show me some of the sights in this beautiful city. I've heard so much about Washington over the years and would love to have someone like you be my guide."

Meeker nodded, her palms clammy. "Perhaps. But only if it doesn't interfere with my work for the President."

An astonished look framed the Brit's sparkling eyes. "You mean Mr. Roosevelt?"

"Yes. I'm his special assistant and we're in the middle of an important assignment right now." She glanced at her wristwatch and noticed the time. "As a matter of fact, I need to check in with my partner now. So, if you'll excuse me, I must be heading out." She stood, and the two men followed suit.

At the door, Fister extended his hand. "I trust we will meet again and you can show me your city."

"If time allows."

"How can I reach you?"

"Just call the White House." She turned to Andrews. "Nigel, thank you for your time, and I do hope you get back to Becky very soon. I too pray we will find a way to end this war, sacrificing as few lives as possible." She flashed a smile at each of them. "Good night, gentlemen." She headed to the door. After opening it, she turned and found Fister close behind her. "Welcome back from the dead, Colonel."

Without waiting for a response, she hurried down the hall to the front door. As she drove her yellow Packard toward home, though she was completely alone, she still felt Reggie Fister's hand touching hers. It was too soon to determine if that was a good thing or the right temptation at the wrong time.

Chapter 16

Monday, March 9, 1942 Germantown, New York

Helen Meeker studied the traffic on Ivy Street from the passenger side of the 1935 Dodge panel truck. The cold day felt more like winter than spring, so she appreciated the warmth of the standard-issue blue-gray Red Cross uniform, with its wool gabardine jacket, skirt, coat, and cap—though it was hardly the usual attire for a president's assistant.

"How do I look?" she asked her partner.

Reese pointed at the emblem on her jacket sleeve. "Just like a real member of the Red Cross."

"As do you."

He sighed. "I still wish I could wear my marine uniform."

"I'm sorry J. Edgar blocked you from that. But these clothes will work better today. We don't want anyone who might be watching the Shellmeyer home to know who we really are."

"I suppose you're right," he muttered as he parked the distinctly marked vehicle used by the Red Cross for blood drives. "But this is not one of my favorite covers."

Meeker didn't dignify his complaint with a response. "You take this side of the street; I'll take the far side. Knock on a few doors and say you're looking for donations. If they seem agreeable, ask if you can come in out of the cold to explain the importance of our program. Then it won't seem strange when I gain entry to the Shellmeyer house. Assuming I do."

"Got it."

They stepped out of the truck.

"Honk when you need me to end my cold day of humiliation." Meeker rolled her eyes at him.

Reese strolled up the sidewalk to a home, knocked on the door, and went into his spiel. Assured he was going to play his role like a pro, Meeker crossed to the other side of the street. For an hour and a half, she worked her way toward the Shellmeyers' modest two-story white clapboard house. During that time, she met nine lonely housewives, four children, and an old maid, and gathered eighteen dollars in donations.

Smoothing her coat, she took a deep breath and strolled up the walk toward her real objective. After climbing three steps, she crossed the covered porch to the front door. She twisted the bell.

A few moments later, a too-thin woman, with pale skin and sunken deep-blue eyes, opened the door. In spite of her gaunt appearance, Meeker recognized Virginia Shellmeyer from the pictures she'd seen in the files. The woman looked sadder than anyone she'd ever seen.

"May I help you?" she asked in a lifeless voice.

Meeker began her rehearsed lines. "I'm with the Red Cross, and we're seeking donations to better serve our soldiers, both here and overseas."

"I'm sorry," the woman mumbled. "We have no extra money. The only reason we have a roof over our heads is that my brother loaned us one of his rental houses."

As Mrs. Shellmeyer stepped back and began to close the door, Meeker hurriedly added, "I understand that, and I sympathize with you. But I've been on the streets most of the morning, and I'm really cold. Would you perhaps have a cup of coffee you could share with me? I'll be happy to pay for it."

"All right," came the weary response. "That's the least I can do."

As the door swung open, Meeker scooted inside. After closing and latching the entry, her host said, "Let me take you back to the kitchen. I have some coffee on the stove."

"Mrs. Shellmeyer," Meeker cut in, "I don't really need the coffee. And I'm not with the Red Cross."

What little color there was in Mrs. Shellmeyer's face drained away.

"I'm working with the FBI and the Office of the President. And though I might be one of the few, I don't believe your husband is guilty."

She glanced out the window. "You shouldn't be here," she whispered. "If they see you, they'll …" Her voice trailed off as she stared at the street.

"What will they do?"

"Nothing. You need to go."

Meeker moved into her hostess's line of vision and stared into the woman's frightened eyes. "Mrs. Shellmeyer, I am absolutely certain your husband is not a spy."

"You shouldn't say such things," she pleaded. "Now, please leave before they find out you're here."

"Who are they?"

"I don't know," she whined, wringing her hands. "I've never met them face-to-face. But they told me they're watching our every move."

"How did they tell you?"

"Through phone calls and letters. And I know it's true. I can feel their eyes on me. They can hear what we're saying right now. They might even know what we're thinking." She shuddered.

Meeker looked toward the hall and into the dining room. Though convinced that no one was in earshot, she whispered,

"What does Zion mean?"

Mrs. Shellmeyer's face registered surprise at the question. "It's heaven."

"I know that. But what did your husband's prayer at the graveside mean?"

"I have no idea." The woman sobbed. "He was grief-struck. He probably didn't know what he was saying."

Meeker placed her hand on the woman's arm. "What happened to your daughter?"

She wiped a tear from her cheek with the back of her hand. "We were on vacation. Ellen disappeared from her bed, and Will went out to find her. He was gone almost all day. When he came back, he told me she'd been swimming in the ocean and a shark attacked her."

"Did you see her body?"

She shook her head. "Will said I shouldn't because it was so mangled. He didn't want me to remember her that way."

"Did you have any idea that he was spying?"

"No. And I still say he couldn't be a Nazi spy. He loved America. That's why we were on that vacation. He had some kind of important news he wanted to share with a man who was with some government group. They'd gone to college together." A sudden look of fright crossed her face. "I shouldn't have said that. Will made me promise never to tell anyone."

"It's all right. I'm here to help." Meeker patted the woman's trembling shoulder. "Can you tell me where this meeting was supposed to take place?"

"I don't know. I guess somewhere in Gulfport, Mississippi, since that's where we went. But Ellen died before the meeting could take place."

Meeker glanced out the front window. Seeing no activity on the street, she continued. "Who were the two men at the cemetery with you?"

"They were from the funeral home in Gulfport. They led us to that place in Georgia."

"Did you talk to them?"

"No," she all but whispered. "They rode in a different car."

"Did you get their names?"

Mrs. Shellmeyer shook her head. "Sorry."

"What did they look like?"

"They were probably in their thirties, well dressed, pretty big. I remember thinking they looked like they could have played football or maybe boxed." She paused. "One of them had an ear that looked kind of beaten up, like a fighter's. And he had a scar under his right … no, wait, his left eye."

"Hair color?"

"Dirty blond."

"Any details on the other one?"

She shifted her gaze to the far wall. "He had kind of a square jaw, and a mole above his dark eyes. When he reached out to grab Ellen's coffin, I saw some kind of tattoo on his left wrist."

"A tattoo of what?"

"It was barely visible beneath the sleeve of his shirt. It might have been an arrowhead. I'm not sure."

"Thank you. You've been a big help."

"With what?" Shellmeyer's tone turned bitter. "Making my husband look even more guilty?" She glanced out the window. "Or maybe the government thinks I'm a spy too."

"I don't believe either one of you could be guilty of that. And I'm hoping to be able to prove that."

Mrs. Shellmeyer shot her a glare. “Will is going to die in a week.”

“I know. But have faith.”

“Faith in what?”

Meeker wished she had an answer.

Chapter 17

Helen Meeker hit a half dozen more homes before she headed back to the truck and blew the horn. Within a minute, Reese was back behind the wheel and had the Dodge pointed south. Two miles down the road, he'd nursed the panel truck up to fifty. Apparently, he couldn't wait to get back to New York, give the old vehicle and uniforms back to the Red Cross, and once again don the more familiar role and appearance of an FBI agent.

"Mrs. Shellmeyer believes her daughter is dead," Meeker announced.

"Did you tell her any different?" Reese asked, keeping his eyes on the road.

"No. I couldn't get her hopes up when we aren't sure where the kid is … or if she really is alive."

"What does she think about her husband being a spy?"

"She doesn't buy that. And she doesn't seem to know why he confessed. But there was something she said that might point us in the right direction." Meeker stared out the window at the passing New York countryside.

"You going to fill me in or not?"

She turned back to face him. "Have you come across anything in Shellmeyer's logbook that indicates he planned on meeting someone in Gulfport?"

He shook his head. "There's absolutely nothing about that whole week in the book. This guy went into great detail on almost every facet of his life before Gulfport, but he barely noted anything about the trip or the days leading up to his arrest."

Meeker sighed. "His wife told me he was meeting someone down there, an old college friend, and he was going to give him some kind of information the US government would be interested in."

"He did mention some friends in the book. I could go back through those names and see if any of them went to college with him and have a connection to Gulfport."

"It's about all we have to go on." She paused for a moment and admired Reese's square jaw and rugged good looks, but stopped short when her perusal morphed into a comparison of Reese and Fister. She'd no more than thought of the Scotsman when the man she was admiring said his name.

"So, what were you able to find out about Reggie Fister?"

"Oh, not much," she said, feigning disinterest.

"Surely you picked up some details. Give it to me like an agent would."

"All right. He's … interesting. Very smooth and charming. He's got those English manners that most men on this side of the pond don't have." She shrugged. "I guess he's the kind of guy a lot of girls could fall for."

Reese smiled. "So you fell for him. It's that stupid accent, isn't it?"

"No," she shot back. "You asked me about him, and I gave you a report. That's all!"

He laughed. "He has you under his spell." His tone took on an edge of sarcasm. "Men in uniform always get attention."

"There you go again, feeling sorry for yourself," Meeker jabbed. "You're doing just as much for your country right now as any of those boys in the military. Besides, you look pretty dapper in that uniform you're wearing."

"Yeah, sure," he grumbled.

As the old truck approached a sharp curve, Reese eased off the gas and slipped his foot over to the brake. But the truck did not slow down.

"Take it easy," Meeker suggested. "Just because you're mad, you don't need to be playing around."

"I'm not." Jamming the clutch to the floor, Reese shifted into second. The gears screamed. The truck lurched and groaned. It slowed a bit, but not enough to safely maneuver the upcoming bend in the highway.

"What's going on?" Meeker shouted.

"No brakes!" Reese gripped the wheel with both hands and pulled hard to the right.

Just ahead, a two-ton milk truck came around the curve. With only one lane at his disposal, Reese gave the emergency brake a hard pull. Nothing happened.

"Hang on," Reese hollered. "We may need some of that Red Cross blood soon," he muttered through gritted teeth.

As Meeker braced herself against the dashboard, the panel truck's right tires dropped off the pavement and onto the grassy shoulder. A hundred feet after leaving the asphalt, the front tire found a large pothole.

The hole pulled both the front wheels sharply to the right, pushing the truck off the road and toward the woods. Meeker covered her face with her arms and pushed her feet into the floorboard. Reese, still fighting the steering wheel, tried one final time to change the truck's course. He failed.

The old Dodge skimmed a century-old oak with the driver's side fender, then careened into an impressive maple on the right side of the car. The maple pushed the truck down a steep draw. The passenger-side tires left the ground, and the truck rolled over onto its side.

Meeker was thrown on top of Reese as the vehicle skidded another fifty yards. He threw his right arm around her in a protective gesture that did little to shield her from the glass that shot onto them as a tree limb broke the truck's windshield.

"You all right?" he asked when the wild ride finally came to an end.

"I'm fine." Meeker pushed off her partner and glanced through what was left of the front glass. She was bruised and shaken, but nothing felt broken.

"Cover your face," Reese ordered as he aimed his shoes at what was left of the windshield. "If I kick out the remaining glass, we can get out through there."

It took three strong kicks for him to accomplish his mission. After he did, Meeker pulled herself around the steering wheel and fell out onto the bank of a slow-moving creek. She had just managed to stand when Reese stepped out of the cab.

"What happened?" she asked.

"I'd say you got us a bum truck," he snapped back.

After she'd regained her equilibrium, Meeker walked around the front of the vehicle. With the truck lying on its side, she could easily study the undercarriage.

"Virginia Shellmeyer was right," she announced as Reese joined her.

"About what?"

"She said someone was watching her and could hear everything we were saying."

Reese frowned. "And you believe her?"

Meeker moved to the back of the vehicle and pointed to a spot near the rear passenger tire. "Tell me what you see."

Reese sucked in a breath. "The line's been cut."

"So has the emergency-brake cable."

"Who would do that to a Red Cross truck?"

Meeker thought back to her meeting with Mrs. Shellmeyer. She had seen no one, and the free manner in which the woman spoke surely meant they were alone. So how had their identity been revealed?

"There must be bugs in the house," she said.

Reese rubbed his jaw. "Do you think this was a warning? Or was it meant to kill us?"

The words had no sooner left his lips than a shot rang out, the bullet striking the tire just above Meeker's head. Three more volleys followed. She fell to the ground and crawled around the truck. Reese rolled through the grass and joined her a second later.

"Does that answer your question?" Meeker whispered.

Chapter 18

Helen Meeker peeked around the edge of the upturned panel truck and toward a stand of woods on a hill from where the shots had come. She could see no one. Another round bounced off the vehicle's rear bumper, causing her to duck back.

"What do you think?" Reese asked.

"I figure there's only one of them. If there were more, we would've been peppered with firepower. Where's your gun?"

"In the cab of the truck."

"Mine too. In my handbag."

Four more shots rang out, all hitting the truck's underbelly.

"Why is he wasting bullets?" Meeker asked. "He can't see us."

Reese crawled up toward the front of the vehicle and crouched behind the hood. "He's going for the gas tank."

"Can he blow us up?"

He shrugged. "That works pretty well in Hollywood movies, but the odds are a bit longer in real life. Still, he could get lucky."

"I was too close to an explosion once already this week. I don't need more stitches in my arm."

Ducking down, Reese slid into the truck's cab. The attacker ripped off five more rounds. Reese rolled back out onto the ground, Meeker's purse and his gun in his hands and crawled to where she was sitting, her back pinned against the vehicle's roof.

"He's on the move," she told Reese as he sat beside her.

"How do you know?"

"The angle of the shots is changing. He appears to be heading south. We're going to be sitting ducks within a minute or so if we don't get up that hill and into those woods."

Reese grimaced. "Do you smell what I smell?"

Meeker took a sniff. "Gas."

"The tank is leaking. He must have hit his target at least once. Do you have any matches in your purse?"

"Yes."

"Give them to me. I'm going to start a fire. I'm betting that when he sees the smoke and flames, he'll move back to get farther away from the truck. That should give us a few seconds to make our getaway."

After digging out the matchbook and handing it to Reese, Meeker glanced toward the trees. "Looks to be about thirty yards to the woods. Bet I can beat you there."

"You're on." He crawled to the rear of the truck and fell to his stomach about three feet from a puddle of gas. After placing his gun on the ground, he pulled out a match and struck it against a nearby stone. When it flamed, he tossed it toward the puddle. It went out before it landed. As he pulled out a second match, two shots hit the dirt just in front of his head.

"I could use some help," he barked.

Meeker aimed her Colt into the woods and squeezed off four quick rounds. Reese lit the second match and held it against the cover until the cardboard caught on fire. Within seconds the rest of the book's matches sparked. Rising to his knees, he tossed the flaming box toward the puddle. It landed dead center. In one fluid movement, he rolled over, grabbed his gun, fired two quick rounds and headed toward the woods.

After pulling her trigger one more time to give Reese a bit of cover, Meeker raced toward the trees. Two shots rang out from behind her, peppering the hillside to her left. A second later, she heard the roar of the gas exploding. From the corner of her eye, she watched the back of the truck lift off the ground and twist to the side.

"Keep moving," Reese called out.

She didn't need his order. She wasn't about to stop for anything or anyone.

Finally, she dove into the wooded area and behind a tree, her partner a split second behind.

"Told you I'd beat you," she taunted as she opened her purse and reloaded her weapon.

"You cheated," he grumbled. "You started before I did."

"A victory is a victory. So, what do you suggest now?"

"The highway should be about a hundred yards through these woods. We should be able to flag down a ride."

After putting her gun in her purse, she rose to her feet and moved deeper into the woods. Reese was with her step for step. It took them five minutes to push through the timber and make it back to the two-lane highway.

Looking down the road, Meeker noted a rusty Model AA truck headed their way. As Reese slid his firearm inside his jacket, she stepped out onto the highway and waved to the driver. The truck came to a stop.

"Can we help you folks?" a teenage girl asked from the passenger-side window. The fresh-faced redhead gave Reese a coy smile.

Meeker nodded. "We had some car trouble back a spell and need a lift to the nearest town."

On the far side of the decade-old, ton-and-a-half vehicle, the driver's door creaked open. A middle-aged man wearing bib overalls got out and moved around the front of the truck to greet them.

"My name's David Sellers. I own a farm about ten miles back. Me, the wife, and my daughter are taking a few hogs to town." He eyed the emblems on the ragged-looking pair's sleeves. "You two with the Red Cross?"

"You have a good eye," Reese said.

Sellers gave them a big grin. "Well, then, you folks are welcome to jump in with us. The cab's full, so you'll have to ride in back with the hogs."

"Beggars can't be choosers," Reese quipped.

"Just climb in over the back gate. Those hogs are pretty big, but they won't hurt you."

As they got to the rear of the old truck, Reese grabbed Meeker's waist and lifted her until her feet touched the bottom the back gate. As she climbed over the three wooden rails to the top, she lost her grip and fell onto one of the hogs. The black-and-white beast squealed and lurched forward, then turned around and nosed the intruder's lips. Grabbing the side of the truck, Meeker pulled herself upright, wiped her mouth with her sleeve and glared at the pig. Reese snickered. She shot him a scorching glare too.

After climbing over the gate and dropping gracefully into the back of the truck's bed, Reese grinned. "I think he likes you. And I bet he has the same delicate charm and manners as Reggie." He laughed. "Can't say you didn't bring home the bacon."

As Sellers put the truck into gear and it eased back on the road, Meeker snarled at her partner. He laughed and pointed to her skirt. "I hope that's just mud."

She looked at her soiled skirt. "Doesn't matter now. The uniform did its job." She glanced between the slats at a car that was following about a hundred yards behind them. "Do you suppose that's the guy who tried to plug us?"

He glanced back. "No way to tell. Just to be safe, let's keep hunkered down where he can't see us."

Holding on to the railing for balance, Meeker studied the blue sedan behind them. "Henry, how many states do you think have towns named Zion?"

He shrugged. "Scores, probably."

"Have the folks at your office find all of them, starting with those in the South. My gut tells me Ellen Shellmeyer might be in one of them."

He nodded. "I can send out an alert to our people in each state where there's a Zion. But I'll need a photo of the girl."

Meeker pushed her grunting new admirer with the heel of her pump. "I'm sure her school in Newport has one. We could probably get hold of a copy of last year's school annual."

Reese groaned. "And while I'm hopping all over the country, what will you be doing with your time?"

She fluttered her lashes. "Why, I'll be working for the President, of course."

"Doing what?"

She shrugged. "I'm having dinner with Reggie Fister tomorrow night."

Reese frowned. "I have a suggestion."

"What's that?"

"Take the pig along."

Chapter 19

Tuesday, March 10, 1942
Washington, DC

Helen Meeker chose a simple purple blouse, gray jacket, and matching skirt for her dinner engagement with Reggie Fister. After dressing, she drove her Packard to the Royal Hotel. He was waiting on the sidewalk just outside the ornate, well-lit entry, dressed in a charcoal tweed suit, white shirt, and dark tie. He looked dashing, to say the least.

During the ten-minute drive to Rigatti's Café, one of the city's popular hot spots, Reggie filled the car with a string of compliments about everything from the shape of Meeker's ankles to the color of her eyes. If the trip had taken any longer, he might have mentioned an area that would have required her to slap him.

Once inside the restaurant, they sat at a corner table near the piano. He ate spaghetti, while she opted for a salad. Their dinner conversation centered on what Fister had observed during his last two days in Washington. After the meal, the waiter removed their empty plates and brought two steaming mugs of coffee.

"I'm glad you're enjoying our city," Meeker said as she sipped her hot brew. "Did your guides tell you that the British Army once burned it to the ground?"

Fister frowned. "That was not one of our better moves."

She smiled. "If you'd been serving in the military then, would you have followed those orders?"

"I'm a military man." He shrugged. "That's what we do. Our obligations are first and foremost to our duties. I don't believe I have ever disobeyed an order."

"I see." Meeker arched an eyebrow.

"However," he added quickly, "if you had lived then and we had met, I would likely have disregarded that one. I could not have left such a beautiful woman homeless, no matter what my superiors wanted me to do."

She smiled. "Of all your lines tonight, that one might well be the worst."

Fister gave her a sly grin, then took her hand in his. "To be honest, I didn't actually spend much time touring the city the past two days."

"Really?"

"I spent most of that time finding out more about you."

She was a little taken aback. What did he mean? And what kind of information did he uncover? She didn't care for folks snooping into her personal life.

He patted her hand and flashed his perfect teeth. "Don't get too concerned. It's not the way it sounds. The fact is, I realized the moment we met that I'd never known anyone like you."

"A lot of people say that. And they don't always mean it as a good thing." Despite her usually reticent nature, she felt almost pleased this handsome soldier knew so much about her. Part of her longed to tell him more.

He caressed her fingers. "The way you carry yourself is almost regal. Your beauty is addicting. Your intelligence and wit are beyond any I have ever known in the lassies back home. I could study you for the next year and never grow bored." He leaned closer. "I think of you as a flower that is ever in bloom."

Her cheeks felt hot. "Like flowers, I tend to wilt from time to time. You should have seen me yesterday."

"I'm not only impressed by your beauty. Your work amazes me too. Scotland Yard could use someone like you."

"Not if their rules are like those at the FBI. It's totally a boys' club."

Ignoring her quip, Fister gazed into her eyes. "I was especially fascinated by the case I read about where you found that little girl and reunited her with her parents. You uncovered clues that everyone else missed. That was quite impressive."

Meeker nodded. "That investigation also led to my reuniting with my sister. Alison has brought a great deal of joy to my life. When this terrible war is over, I hope I can get to know her even better."

"Is she still in Chicago?"

"No. She's at a small college in Arkansas. She's a bright girl, and I want her to reach her potential. This country can't remain a man's world forever. Maybe she can be one of those who changes that."

"Are you paying for her education?"

She shrugged. "I have more than enough to do that."

"Oh, that's right. Your family had some money."

She felt her heart skip a beat, and she drew her brows together. "Just how much research did you do on me?"

He grinned. "I know how much you weighed at birth."

"I'm flattered. At least, I think I am."

The smile left his lips. "I'm sorry if I've made you uncomfortable." He pulled back his hand and set his elbows on the cloth-covered table. "You must understand. I am military through and through, and I have a background in intelligence.

When I find an objective, I learn everything I can to better prepare me to achieve my goals."

"And am I part of a campaign? One of your goals?"

A bit of the sparkle returned to his eyes. "That doesn't sound like what I meant, but it might well be true. I have only a few weeks here before I go back to England, which means a very short time to convince you that your life cannot be complete without having me in it."

She shook her head, her emotions a jumble of curiosity and apprehension. "Reggie, we just met. I don't know how things work in England, but they don't move that quickly here—at least not with me."

He touched her arm. "Helen, there is a war on. Thousands die every day. We no longer measure our lives in years. We have to think in moments." He leaned across the table and allowed his lips to gently brush hers. "The moments I have I want to spend with you. You might well be the last woman I hold and the only woman I ever truly come to love."

As he sat back in his chair, his kiss stayed with her, and a fog, deeper than any that had ever invaded London, pushed into her mind. This man was good-looking, charming, and heroic. The kind of man who could sweep any woman off her feet. That made him not only desirable but dangerous.

His voice pulled her attention back from the cacophony of longing and warning sirens going off in her brain. "I'm glad you weren't hurt yesterday."

"Excuse me?"

He smiled. "When you were in New York."

Her breath caught in her throat. "How did you know I was in New York yesterday?"

"I called the White House to try to reach you. The woman who was taking your calls told me."

"Oh." Feeling uncomfortable, she glanced at her watch. "I hate to break up this incredible evening, but it's time for me to go."

"So soon? I was hoping we could go dancing."

"Not tonight." She rose from her seat. "I have an early day tomorrow."

He followed her to the door. No more words were exchanged until they got into her car and she drove back onto the street.

"I'm not sure how much time I have left in this country," he said in a somber tone. "I have some duties coming up that will require my full attention. But I would love to monopolize your time for the next few weeks."

"That's sweet. But I have an important job too. What I'm working on now might mean the difference between life and death for several people."

"Couldn't someone else handle it?"

"Not as well as I can."

"Are you sure about that?"

"Yes, I am."

From the corner of her eye, she saw him grin. "Maybe I could talk to the President and convince him how important it would be, to both me and Britain, to have you by my side while I'm in the States."

"Don't you dare," she snapped without taking her eyes off the road. "My work is important, so don't try to get in the way of it."

He paused. "May I ask what is so important about your current case?"

"No, Reggie, you can't. I'm not at liberty to talk about it, not even with my sister."

"I see." Meeker detected genuine sadness in his tone. "You don't trust me."

"That's not it," she assured him.

"Perhaps, with my experience and training, I might be able to help."

"If something comes up where I need you, I'll call you."

As they waited at a red light, she looked over to Fister. His face was drawn and tight, and his eyes were locked on the road ahead. "Reggie, I can't change what I do or who I am."

He nodded. "I understand. But please tell me you are safe. You're not doing anything that might put you in harm's way, are you?"

The light changed, and she pulled the Packard forward. After going through two shifts, she finally answered. "If you've done your research, you know I don't take the easy, safe route."

"And is your sister safe too?"

"What do you mean?"

"Can you be sure that what you're doing is not putting her in danger?"

She had never considered that. But the odds were long against anything she was involved in affecting Alison. Her sister was a long way from DC.

"All my sister has to worry about is making sure the guys in Arkadelphia don't fall all over each other while lining up for dates with her."

He laughed. "Then she must be as beautiful as you are."

Meeker pulled up in front of his hotel, put the car in neutral, and set the brake. She got out and walked her date to the door. "Thanks for the nice evening … and for your concern."

His arms wrapped around her waist and he drew her close. With their lips just inches apart, he whispered, "I could give you a life where you wouldn't have any risks … unless you consider loving me a risk." He covered her mouth with his and kissed her hard and long. The kiss took her breath away and left her knees wobbly. When he finally pulled back, she felt lightheaded.

After letting her slowly slide from his arms, he whispered, "Call me when you're free."

She watched him enter the hotel's revolving door before turning on her heels and hurrying back to her car. She sat in the driver's seat for a few moments, allowing her heart to slow, then released the brake and put the car into first gear.

A hundred feet or so down the street, she felt something cold on the back of her neck. "Keep going until I say to stop," a deep voice whispered. "And don't even think about calling out for help."

Chapter 20

Helen Meeker drove four blocks before her uninvited passenger in the sedan's rear seat removed the gun barrel from the back of her neck. "Where are we going?"

"Park by the Lincoln Memorial. And just because I no longer have my gun against your neck, that doesn't mean you're safe. There are a lot of ways to kill someone, and my training has taught me most of them."

The man's voice sounded familiar. She'd heard it recently but couldn't place where. She glanced in the rearview mirror, but the hat pulled low over his eyes kept her from seeing his face.

A quiet five minutes passed before she pulled into a parking place in the nearly vacant lot beside the memorial. She set turned off the car and waited for the intruder to give her further instructions.

"Get out of the car, and leave your purse here. I'm sure you have a gun in there, and I don't want to have to use mine. Do you understand?"

"Yes." She lifted the door handle and stepped out into the cool, damp air. As she waited for further instructions, she found herself wishing she'd opted to dance the night away with Reggie Fister. Perhaps, if he hadn't pushed the romance angle so hard, she would have. But that scared her even more than having a stranger hijack her car.

"Walk up to the top step," he ordered as he closed the Packard's back door. "And don't turn around. I'll be right behind you."

It took Meeker just over two minutes to climb the fifty-seven steps leading up to the top level of the memorial. When she reached the landing, she turned to face the man calling the shots.

Now face-to-face, she recognized him immediately. "Nigel?"

"That's right." The corporal was dressed in civilian clothing, and she didn't see a gun anywhere.

"What's this all about?"

"I'm not here to hurt you," he said, no longer trying to disguise his voice. "I just needed to get you alone so I could tell you something. Can we sit here on the steps?"

"All right." Smoothing her skirt, she took a seat on the top stair. He took a position about a foot to her right. "You didn't have to kidnap me just to talk."

"Sorry about the tough-guy act. But I don't have Reggie's confidence or charm." Andrews placed his hands on his knees and stared off into the distance. "How old is this memorial?"

"Two decades."

"Your country is very young."

"Compared to Europe, yes."

He silently laid his head on his arms.

"What's going on with you? I know you're disillusioned about the war and I understand how you feel about those who are sending men off to die. But what you did tonight doesn't fit your profile. You're a gentleman, with ideals and manners."

"I'm also a man who desperately wants peace." He lifted his face from his arms. "I was going to be a pastor. Did you know that? I wanted to teach men how to love one another. But my country turned me into a killing machine. I hate what I've become. And I hate the roll of playing the hero." He sighed. "I even hate that Reggie is alive, because it means he'll get the opportunity to kill even more men."

"That's a lot of hatred for someone who once considered going into the pastorate."

"I also hate that you're seeing him. You'll fall under his spell, just like everyone. It seems no woman can resist him."

Meeker smiled. "Is that what this is all about? Nigel, I don't know what he's told you, but I'm not the type of girl to get serious in a hurry."

"Even my Becky couldn't resist his charms," Andrews lamented. "The moment she met him, her feelings for me cooled."

"It was likely just a schoolgirl crush," Meeker assured him. "All women get those. It's nothing to worry about. They don't last."

"It doesn't matter. What's really wrong is that Reggie came back. I was there. He was surrounded by Germans. None of us should have survived."

"Miracles happen," Meeker assured him. "Sometimes God steps in and bends all logic."

"That's the only explanation that almost makes sense."

Meeker studied the man's face. He was obviously confused and deeply troubled.

"Have you ever had someone take a shot at you?"

"Yes." As a matter of fact, it had happened much more recently than she wanted to reveal.

"What happens when folks are laying down fire all around you?"

"Well …" She gave the question serious thought. "Dirt kicks up. Stuff around me gets hit. I can even hear bullets fly past my head."

"None of that happened the night we got away in France. Except for Homes, none of us was hit, even though scores of Germans were shooting at us. I saw the guns flaming in the woods, and I heard the shots echoing all around me. But, when I got to thinking about it last night, I realized that none of the rounds hit the ground around me. And there wasn't a single bullet hole in the airplane. There should have been hundreds."

His observation made sense. There probably should have been at least some damage and probably more casualties.

He locked eyes with her. "If Reggie's heroics had drawn the fire away from us, he should have been hit him numerous times. Yet he only took three bullets. No one is that bad a shot."

"What are you suggesting?"

"I don't know. But Reggie shouldn't be alive, and neither should the rest of us. And that plane should never have gotten off the ground. Those Germans had to be there all the time, just waiting for us. So why couldn't they stop us?"

He posed an excellent question. Meeker wondered why no one had asked it before.

Andrews stood and shoved his hands into his pockets. "Let's go back to your car. There's something there I need you to look at."

Meeker followed him to the Packard. He opened the back door and pulled out a folder, then slid into the front seat. She followed his lead and took her position behind the wheel.

"Could you turn on the dome light?" he asked.

Meeker flipped the switch.

"These are Reggie's medical files. I lifted them from the embassy. I want you to glance over them."

Meeker took the papers and skimmed through the reports of the colonel's evaluation at Walter Reed. She observed the diagrams of his three bullet wounds, studied a photo taken of the entry and exit locations of those rounds, read over the notes about his weight, height, and general health, then closed the file and handed it back to Andrews. "What did you want me to see?"

"The wounds. They were all flesh wounds."

"That's why he survived. If they'd been serious, he would have died."

"Wounds like his would have been made by small-caliber weapons. This was war, not a bird shoot."

Meeker traced her lips with her right index finger, intrigued by where this was leading.

"I'm being sent back to England tomorrow," Andrews said. "No one told me why. But Reggie will be taking my place as Churchill's personal guard." He looked her in the eye. "Don't trust him, Helen."

Before she could offer a response, Andrews pulled up on the car's handle and stepped outside. Then he leaned back in. "Do you believe in ghosts?"

"No."

"Neither do I. And I don't believe in miracles either." He shut the door and walked off.

When Andrews was beyond her sight, Meeker restarted her car and drove back across town to her apartment, trying to make sense of what she'd just seen and heard.

As she unlocked her front door, she heard her phone ringing. She rushed to the bedroom and grabbed the receiver. "This is Helen Meeker."

"You're finally home," Fister said. "I've called several times."

"I had some … work to do. What's up?"

"I don't know if I told you this, but I had a wonderful time tonight."

"I think you hinted at that when we said good night."

"I suppose I did." He laughed. "But that's not the only reason I called. I have something serious to tell you, and it must stay between us, at least for the moment."

"What's that?"

"I was given some reports this evening from British Intelligence, and they indicate that Nigel Andrews might be working for the Nazis."

"Really?"

"I always pegged him as a great lad. But the entire time we were in France, I sensed that one of my men was not on the up-and-up."

"What gave you that impression?"

"I found notes that had been dropped along a road that gave the location of a secret base in Wales."

"Is that it?"

"No. I got word last week that Colbert, a man who worked with us, was discovered and killed by the Nazis. Someone in our group must have blown his cover."

"That seems like pretty weak logic to me."

"There's more. The plane that took my boys home made it off the ground without having a single bullet strike. I have to wonder if the attack was staged. They killed one of us just to make it look good. But they needed to make sure Nigel got back to England so he could keep feeding them information. And his hero stature, along with his new assignments, give him access to plenty of information the Germans could use against us."

His conclusions didn't really add up, not after what Nigel had told her. But she didn't reveal her thoughts to him.

"If that's true, I wasn't a hero after all. I didn't need to hold off the Germans. They would have let me get on the plane too."

"Well, that does explain a lot about the miracle."

"Miracle?"

"Never mind." She sighed. "You sleep well, Reggie."

"You too, Helen. And please, stay away from Nigel. Whatever he tells you, don't believe it."

After placing the receiver back into the cradle, Meeker crossed the room and snapped the lock on her door. Who was yanking her string? Was it the recognized hero, or the man who had served as his stand-in? She wouldn't rest well until she knew.

Chapter 21

Wednesday, March 11, 1942
United States Federal Penitentiary
Lewisburg, Pennsylvania

While Reese stayed in Washington to put his efforts into finding out whether Ellen Shellmeyer was alive, and if so, where she was being held, Helen Meeker drove her yellow Packard to the prison where Wilbur Shellmeyer awaited death. After being processed, she was ushered into Warden Scott Dennis's office and given a seat across from the prison official's desk.

"Shellmeyer is not a typical guest for us," the middle-aged man explained. Smoothing his salt-and-pepper hair, he looked out into the prison yard. Though of average height and build, Dennis carried himself with an authority that would likely have intimidated most prisoners. His voice was deep and his dark eyes intense. "We usually cater to the organized-crime-lord types. I'm not used to someone as gentle and unassuming as Shellmeyer. He seems to me like a sad man who has given up on life."

Meeker smoothed her black jacket where it met her fitted gray wool skirt. "I think I might know the reason for that."

Dennis turned back to face his guest. "Care to share it?"

"Not at this time. But perhaps after I talk to him."

He nodded. "He's waiting for you in a room right off my office. Since he's shackled, you should be safe alone with him."

Meeker rose. "Thank you."

"Follow me." He led her out a side door, down a long hallway, and to a door where one prison guard stood vigil. Seeing the warden, the tall, powerfully built man stepped aside. With a turn of a knob, the door opened into a sterile, fifteen-foot room containing only a table and four chairs. A thin, tired-looking man in a gray shirt sat at the far end of the table. His blond hair was cropped short, and dark circles drooped beneath his light-blue eyes.

"Wilbur," the warden said, "this is Miss Helen Meeker. She's from the Office of the President. She wants to ask you a few questions, and I have agreed to allow her to be alone with you. I trust you will show her the respect she deserves."

As the warden left the room and closed the door, Shellmeyer's eyes remained on Meeker. She took a seat to his right, set her purse on the floor beside her, and forced a smile. He didn't respond.

"Should I call you Wilbur? Or do you prefer Reverend Shellmeyer?"

"It doesn't matter." His tone signaled an overriding sense of defeat.

"Okay, Wilbur. I know you didn't spy on the United States. I believe you're innocent. And I think you're willing to die for something you didn't do to protect someone you love."

His eyes grew wide. "I gave them the notes and photos. I told them what I did."

She reached into her purse and pulled out a notepad. After flipping through several pages, she looked back to him. "On the dates you were supposedly spying, you were officiating at weddings or funerals, conducting conferences, or preaching."

"You must be mistaken," he whispered.

"So, which is wrong? Your church records or the reports you gave to the FBI?"

"I don't know. But I did what I said I did, and I'm going to pay for it with my life next week."

"You can certainly do that if you want to. But you aren't dying because you were a spy. You're dying because you're protecting someone. So, who's really working for the Nazis? Is it your wife?"

"No," he shot back, exhibiting passion for the first time. "Virginia knew nothing."

"I believe you. I've met her, and she's not cut out for that kind of work. Which leads me to consider another option."

"Why can't you just believe I did it and let it go?" he begged.

"If you hadn't confessed, there isn't a court in this country that would convict you. But no one looked closely enough at the evidence to realize you were taking the fall for someone else."

"No," he moaned. "I did it."

"I've been to your daughter's grave, Wilbur."

His face registered shock.

"Now, tell me this. What did you mean when you said, 'Please, Lord, let her body rest in Zion's graces, and let no man ever disturb this vessel, for if they do, they will meet you sooner than later'?"

"It was just a mourning father's disjointed prayer," he mumbled. "I wasn't thinking clearly."

"That fact is obvious. Men who are thinking clearly don't forget to put a body in a coffin."

The chains clanked as he lifted his manacled hand and wiped his mouth. His expression displayed a combination of fear and resignation. "What do you mean?" he finally whispered.

"You know exactly what I mean, Wilbur. I don't know why you said what you did or whether you thought anyone would understand it. But the last part of your prayer was a warning about what was really in that box. I didn't figure that out until we dug it up and opened it."

"I'm so sorry." He buried his face in his hands. When he looked up tears were streaming down his face. "I wonder if he knew that."

"If who knew what?"

"Nothing," Shellmeyer whispered, shaking his head.

Meeker looked into the man's eyes. "The charade has gone on too long, Wilbur. Two innocent men have died. You'll soon be the third."

"I'm sorry," he repeated.

"Where is Zion?"

His eyes wandered around the room. "That's where Ellen is. She's safe in Zion. Zion is heaven."

Meeker studied him for a moment, considering his words. Suddenly she understood. Given his profession, it made perfect sense. "You're playing the role of Christ, aren't you? You're saving an innocent soul by allowing yourself to be executed."

"No," he replied, but his tone sounded more like a lie than a man committed to telling the truth.

"Okay." She leaned forward, playing a hunch that was the ultimate long shot. "What does the name Nigel Andrews mean to you?"

His frightened expression proved she had stumbled onto the truth—or at least part of it.

"Tell me what it is, Wilbur."

"He called yesterday. I got the message from the warden. But I didn't talk to him."

"Why not?"

He shook his head and remained mute.

"You aren't going to tell me anything more, are you?"

He sighed. "I can't."

Meeker dropped the notebook back into her bag and moved to the door. Before reaching for the knob, she turned back. "Only Jesus can be Jesus, Wilbur. And as I remember the story, he didn't die for a lie; he died for the truth." She pointed her finger at Shellmeyer. "I know you're walking to your death because of a promise that someone made to you. But think about this, Wilbur. They can't let Ellen go. She knows who they are. If they haven't already killed her, they will the second they know you've died and can't reveal their secret."

He cringed. Clearly, she'd struck a chord.

"On top of that, you're betraying your country. That's a steep price to pay for living a lie." She allowed her words to soak in. "If you give your life for this cause, it will serve absolutely no purpose. And if you take to the grave whatever it is you know, I'm betting a lot more people will die."

Sorrow filled his eyes. But no words came out of his mouth.

Meeker opened the door and walked out. Warden Dennis greeted her in the hall. "What did he tell you?"

"Not much with his words, but a great deal with his eyes." As the two walked back down the hall, she added, "I'm hoping he'll ask you to call me. You have my number."

"I do."

She stopped just outside his door. "He said you took a call from a man named Nigel Andrews."

"Yesterday, yes."

"What did he sound like?"

"A Brit."

What was the tie between Andrews and Shellmeyer? She had to find out. And that meant tracking down the English corporal before he left for England.

Chapter 22

A cold wind kicked up as if to remind Washington that winter was not yet over. Helen Meeker, her body exhausted but her mind still whirling, opened her apartment door at half past eight. She had no more than pulled off her shoes than the phone rang. She picked it up and was greeted by her partner's familiar baritone.

"Did you have any success with Shellmeyer?" Reese asked.

"He's still willing to die to make sure his daughter lives. And he told me very little that we don't already know."

"Well, I think I have something."

"Don't keep me waiting."

"Corporal Nigel Andrews is missing. He was scheduled to go back to England today, and he wasn't in his room at the embassy when they came to pick him up."

"So, the information Reggie gave us was spot-on."

"Could be, though no one at MI6 or SIS is talking. When I called my contacts there, they refused to comment on whether Andrews is suspected of passing information along to the Nazis.

The warrant that's been issued on him is AWOL. Right now, his absence seems to be a military matter."

Meeker glanced across the room to her front door, making sure she had remembered to lock it. "Andrews called the prison yesterday and asked to talk to Shellmeyer. Shellmeyer didn't speak with him."

"Maybe he was trying to make sure the preacher held his tongue."

"That's one possibility. Have you had any success in digging up suspicious activity in any of the Zions in the country?"

"I have two more reports I'm waiting on, but they're long shots. Looks like we're going to draw a blank there."

"Not what I wanted to hear." Meeker sighed. "We have to find that girl in order to convince Shellmeyer to give us what he's hiding."

"It might be easier to find the proverbial needle in a haystack."

"Well, needles are usually found there by sitting on them." She took a deep breath. "What about the preacher's notes and the Bible? Did you get anything out of those?"

"I deserve a bit more praise on that one," Reese bragged. "The man he was supposed to see in Mississippi is likely Russell Strickland. They roomed together in college. Strickland became a lawyer and worked awhile in the attorney general's office. About a decade ago he moved to Gulfport and set up practice there."

"So, we can run him down?"

"It's not that easy. Strickland is in England now, working with the OSS. He was too old for active service, so the US is using his skills with our intelligence department. I've sent cables to our people in London, and they're trying to locate him. As soon as I find him, I'll set up a phone call."

"We don't have much time," she reminded him.

"Believe me, I know." Fatigue clouded his voice. "One more thing. I assigned one of our agents, Collins, to go through the records of every church where Shellmeyer has pastored. I gave him the background on the case, and he'll call you if he finds anything."

"Good. Now, why don't you go home and get some sleep?

We have a lot of digging to do before March sixteenth."

"Think I'll take you up on that. Good night. Sleep tight."

"You too."

Meeker set the receiver into the cradle and eased down on the edge of her bed. She had slipped off her right shoe and was rubbing her foot when she heard a knock at the door. Putting the black pump back on, she walked across the small living area to her front door. Grabbing the knob in one hand and the lock in the other, she paused. "Who is it?"

A cheery voice on the other side of the entry announced, "It's your future husband."

She smiled and shook her head at the sound of Reggie's voice. When she opened the door, she found herself gazing into the eyes of the charming Scotsman. In his right hand was a dozen red roses, and in the other, a box of chocolates.

"What do you have on your mind?" she asked coyly.

"I probably shouldn't say. I don't want to get slapped before dinner."

"Dinner?"

"You owe me a dance or two, remember?"

"You have no idea how tired I am," she protested.

"Have you had supper?"

"No."

"Then that's your problem." Fister grinned. "Grab your coat. I'll buy you a steak. And after it has time to settle, we'll kick up our heels."

"You're crazy." She laughed.

"Crazy over you." The hero soldier smiled. "So, will you accept my invitation?"

"How could I refuse?"

Chapter 23

It was well past two when Fister returned Helen Meeker to her apartment. They lingered at the front door for a few minutes, trading small talk about the evening until he leaned over, swept her up in his arms, and kissed her … deep and long.

Pulling back at last, he whispered, "No reason for the fun to end here. After all, we don't know where we'll be next week."

Nigel Andrews might have lied about a lot of things, but he was spot-on when it came to Reggie. He was the most dynamic, irresistible man she'd ever met. Whenever she was around him, she became clay waiting for the potter.

She studied his eyes. It would be so easy to give in. Every chord in her body begged her to do so, and she might have except for one reason—Alison. Her sister looked up to her as a role model. If she gave in to temptation this easily, what kind of signal would that send to the kid?

"Not tonight, Reggie," she whispered.

"You don't mean that." He drew her close and kissed her again. Holding her in his arms, he pulled her face into his chest. She could hear his heartbeat.

He was right. She didn't mean it. She wanted what he was offering. Either of them might die serving their country over the next few months. Didn't that trump the old moral code? Besides, Alison was in Arkansas. She would never know.

After pushing out of his arms, Meeker opened her purse with nervous fingers and pulled out her key. Feeling like a high school girl at her first prom, she stuck it into the lock. The door clicked open.

She looked into her semi-dark apartment and considered how different this night had been than any other she'd known. The scrumptious dinner, the stimulating conversation, the dancing, the walk in the park. And that kiss! Reggie Fister was a hero, and he claimed to love her. Didn't he deserve this moment?

She felt his hands on her shoulders, nudging her forward. Yes, she was ready. It was time. He was the right one, and this was the right night.

The phone rang. She flipped on the light. Suddenly the situation looked different. As he tried to move her forward, she turned and said, "I need to get that call. I'm sure it's important."

"But—"

She cut him off. "I had a great time. Maybe too good a time. But this is getting in the way of something important … something I have to do."

The phone rang again.

"Nothing could be more important than you and me," he argued. "I'm convinced the war started just to bring us together." The phone rang a third time.

"Good night, Reggie," she whispered, pushing him back.

As soon as he cleared the entry, she closed and latched the door. Taking a deep breath, she raced to the bedroom and caught the phone on the sixth ring.

"Helen Meeker."

"Agent Collins here. I know it's late, but Reese told me to call you if I found anything, no matter what time it was."

"I don't know whether to thank you or hate you." She sighed as she sat down on her bed.

"Excuse me?"

"Never mind. What do you have?"

"A couple of interesting things. Before Shellmeyer pastored in Newport, he was in a small New York community called Germantown. He served that church for five years. I got hold of the church records, and it took me a long time to read them. The current pastor explained that Shellmeyer had a habit of recording everything. I can even tell you what they served at each of the Fourth of July picnics."

"That fits everything I know about him. So, what did you uncover?"

"About five years ago, a young man from England came over for a summer to assist the preacher."

"Was his name Nigel Andrews?"

"You beat me to it," Collins said with obvious awe.

So Shellmeyer did know Andrews.

"I've got something else. A year before Andrews came calling, Shellmeyer had another visitor from the UK. This one was a foreign exchange student, and he spent his senior year attending the local high school. He even stayed at the pastor's home."

"What's his tie-in to this case?"

"Perhaps nothing. But it's a really strange coincidence that this student later served with Andrews on that mission in France. His name is Reggie Fister."

"You're kidding!"

"No, ma'am. And after all that's been in the media, I was surprised to find out something I didn't already know about the British hero."

"What's that?"

"He was an orphan."

Meeker's finger went to the lips Fister had so recently kissed. She let it linger there for a moment. There was so much about the man she didn't know, so much she needed to learn. "Anything else?"

"Not from church records. But there's another area I want to dig into. If I find anything I'll get back with you right away."

"Thanks," she said and placed the receiver back into its cradle.

Chapter 24

Thursday, March 12, 1942
The White House

After spending all day running down false leads on anyone matching the description of Ellen Shellmeyer, Helen Meeker glanced at the clock on the office wall. It was just past six in the evening.

"You still here, Miss Meeker?"

She looked up at Joan White, one of the secretaries who worked the switchboard. The short, pleasant woman in her fifties had a sweet smile that matched her kind brown eyes.

"I'm about to give up for the day. How about you?"

"On my way home now. But I wanted to give you these messages." She handed Meeker several small slips of paper. "You've missed a few calls, all but one of them from Reggie Fister. He's been phoning every hour on the hour. Not sure why Ellie didn't put the calls through to you."

"I asked her not to. I needed to try to find some kind of lead on a case I'm working on."

"No luck?"

"No. Maybe tomorrow."

Joan smiled. "The other message is from the President. He'd like you to drop by his office before you leave."

Meeker nodded. "I'll do that right now."

She checked her hair and makeup in a mirror before walking from the office wing to the main part of the presidential residence. Even though she was passing some of the most treasured elements of history, things that had awed her in the past, she barely noticed them. Her mind was too busy playing a tug-of-war between her feelings for the British hero and her inability to make even a dent in the case she had claimed as her own. She was so caught up in her thoughts she almost didn't realize when she had arrived at her destination.

She was surprised to find the door to the Oval Office open. But rather than charge in, she gently tapped on the door. As she did, Roosevelt looked up from behind his desk. His smile couldn't hide the weariness in his eyes.

"You wanted to see me?" Meeker asked.

"Come sit down." After she had taken a seat in front of the desk, he leaned back in his chair. "You haven't filled me in on either of your two projects."

She offered a weak smile. "I have nothing new on Shellmeyer. I'm still certain he's not guilty, but I can't prove it. What I've gathered on the case is interesting, but not worth wasting your time with at this moment."

"I hope we don't execute an innocent man."

"I still have a few days. Maybe something will pop up."

He raised an eyebrow. "And your assignment with the Brit?"

Meeker blushed. "It involves two British soldiers now. The first one, Andrews, is AWOL and might be a spy. But the man who returned from the dead has been entertaining."

The President grinned. "The British ambassador tells me Colonel Fister has taken quite a shine to you."

"There's little doubt about that."

"What are your feelings?"

"I'm not sure. I like him a lot, but I'm not ready to toss my heart into a relationship that seems to have no way to play out in the long run." She shook her head. "My dad used to say that love is a marathon, not a sprint. But it's hard to embrace that wisdom during times like these, when every moment seems so precious and life is so fragile."

"I understand," he said in an almost fatherly tone. "By the way, Winston is coming in this weekend. Only those directly involved are aware of it."

She nodded. "Is the meeting still planned for the Grove Estate outside of Ithaca?"

"Yes," he said, accentuating his answer with a wave of his hand. "The owners are longtime friends of my family, the farm is private and secure, and the house can easily accommodate all those who'll be there. And to keep from drawing attention to the meetings, the security details will be minimal. Your name is on the pass list if you get a chance to come."

"I'll likely be working on the Shellmeyer case."

"I thought as much. But before you leave, I'd like you to give me a bit of information on what I can expect from Colonel Fister. He'll be at Churchill's side, and I'll likely get a chance to visit with him over dinner and during breaks."

Meeker shrugged, her eyes moving to a window as she took a deep breath. "He's rugged, charming, and very Scottish. Kind of a rogue too. He lacks some of the English reserve and is a bit more impulsive and outspoken than most Brits. He's very sure of himself and will not be intimidated by your presence."

The President nodded. "Sounds like Hollywood's version of a hero."

"Pretty close. But with a better accent."

Roosevelt chuckled. "Helen, I hope you can make it up to see us. I'd love for you to meet Churchill. He's a unique character."

"I'll do my best. If I haven't come up with anything to convince Shellmeyer to take back his confession by Monday, there'll be no reason to sit around and watch the clock tick down his final minutes."

"I hope it doesn't come to that."

A ringing phone signaled it was time for Meeker to take her leave. She moved toward the door as the President picked up the receiver.

A half hour later, she parked her Packard in the space in front of her apartment and strolled up the walk to her door. There on the steps lay several dozen roses. As she bent down to take in the fragrance of the beautiful red flowers, she noticed a note tacked to her door. The message was short and direct: "Must see you tomorrow. R. F."

Chapter 25

Friday, March 13, 1942

Much as she had the previous day, Helen Meeker avoided Reggie Fister's calls while she worked. Not so much because she didn't want to see him, but working with Reese on trying to track down Ellen Shellmeyer required her undivided attention. Unfortunately, the more they dug, the more she came to believe there were no needles in this haystack.

At six, after they had called it quits and were walking across the parking lot to their cars, Reese offered a piece of wisdom. "Sometimes innocent people die, and we can't do anything about it, no matter how hard we try. We may not be able to get the information we need to save Shellmeyer. But he's resigned to his fate. Maybe we should be too."

She stopped beside her Packard and shook her head. "He does not want to die. He just feels he has no choice."

"Whatever the reason, he is determined to do it."

Tears pricked her eyelids, and she blinked them back. "Do you think Ellen is still alive?"

He shook his head.

"I do. I can feel it. She's out there somewhere. I'm just afraid we're going to find her too late, and her father will have died for nothing."

"We all die for something," Reese noted. "Look, I feel for the man and his family. But Shellmeyer's death doesn't mean nearly as much to me as something else."

"What's that?"

His eyes, serious and focused, locked on hers. "I can't help but wonder how many people will die because of the information Shellmeyer is taking to his grave."

"I say, what's this all about?" Somehow Reggie Fister had snuck up on them.

"Nothing," Reese muttered, his expression clouding over. Turning on his heels, he brushed by the Scotsman and marched down the walk toward his car.

"What's wrong with him?" Fister asked.

Meeker shook her head, but she knew the answer. Reese was jealous of the chemistry he saw between her and Reggie.

"Would you like to go out?" the Brit asked. "This is my last night in town. For once, I'd like to make Friday the thirteenth seem lucky."

She nodded her agreement. But her eyes were still on Reese.

Chapter 26

After sharing dinner at a swank hotel restaurant, Helen Meeker and Reggie Fister listened to the Glenn Miller orchestra at a club downtown. When they were ready to call the public facet of the evening done, they hopped into her yellow Packard.

"I'll drop you off at the hotel," she said as she swung out of the club's parking lot.

"Why don't we head to your place instead? I can catch a cab back to the hotel later."

Against her better judgment, she pointed the car in the direction of her home. Ten minutes later, she unlocked the door and they stepped inside.

"Nice place," he said as he glanced at her modest living room. "Not large, but very tasteful. The sofa looks comfortable."

He opened the door to the bedroom, flipped the switch and glanced at the bed. Turning, he smiled and tilted his head slightly. "I like this place. I can picture you everywhere I look. Wish I'd been here before now."

"I'll bet you do," she quipped.

His cocky expression revealed that he felt sure how this night was going to end. And until a few hours ago, she might have granted his wish. But as they ate, listened to the band and danced at the club, Fister was not the only thing on her mind. The colonel now had to share space with a certain FBI agent. Deep in her heart, the two men were playing tug-of-war for her affections. The battle left her both confused and unsettled.

"Do we start out here?" Fister asked, pointing to her couch. "Or should we skip that step and move in there?" He shifted his hand in the direction of the bedroom.

"You're pretty sure of yourself." Meeker folded her arms across her chest.

He shrugged. "This could be our last night together. Who knows if we will ever meet again? We only have this moment, and we will regret it for as long as we live if we don't take advantage of it."

"Who will regret it more, I wonder."

He shook his head. "There is no one in this world like you, and I think I am pretty special too. I believe we would both miss something remarkable by not spending the rest of the night together."

Meeker knew what he meant. But the temptation she'd felt the last time was gone now. Why? What was missing? Was it her sudden realization that Reese was jealous? Or was it the fact that Shellmeyer was counting down the hours toward his meaningless death?

"Why the hesitation?" Fister closed the distance between them and slipped his arms around her.

"There's a lot going on right now," she said as she leaned away from his approaching lips.

"Forget Shellmeyer for a few hours," he whispered as he drew even closer.

His lips brushed hers, and for a moment she went limp in his arms. But she couldn't forget Wilbur Shellmeyer. He needed to be saved. He had to tell her what he knew, and she was determined to reunite that family. That was far more important than a few hours of passion. Until this case was resolved, she would not allow love, lust, or whatever this was to steal her focus.

Meeker pushed her hands into Fister's chest and freed herself from his grip. She spun on her heels, her swift action causing her hair to fly over her shoulders, and walked to the front door. She yanked it open, allowing the cool night air into the room. "You need to go."

His face registered shock. "Did I do something wrong?"

She smiled. "Without meaning to, you woke me up to what I need to be doing right now. This is not about you or me; it's about saving an innocent man's life. That's what I do. I couldn't live with myself if I didn't keep trying until the bitter end. And one night with you, no matter how tempting, is just not in the cards."

"Come on, lassie," he begged. "I might never have another kiss or get another chance to love someone. This is war, remember?"

"If all you need are lips and a body, there are a lot of women out there who would be more than happy to give in to the charms of a hero. Find the one that appeals to you the most. She'll likely take you wherever you want to go."

Fister set his jaw. "I fear you will always regret this."

"Perhaps," she admitted. "You're handsome, charming, and you earned the title of hero. But you're just a man. And while what you've done is impressive, it doesn't overrule the one thing that I just realized."

"What's that?"

"For you I'm just a conquest." She smiled. "You actually believe that you have more value than I do. You proved that when you asked me to forget my job and put you first."

His blank expression told her he had no idea what she was saying.

Meeker shook her head. "Because I'm a woman, you might see me as second rate. But in my mind, I'm your equal. And if you ever want to realize your dreams about me, you'll have to treat me as if I'm every bit as important as you seem to believe you are."

"And if I don't, we'll never see each other again?"

"Maybe. Maybe not. But one thing I can guarantee is that you won't see any more of me tonight." She nodded toward the exit. "Thank you for a lovely evening."

Fister moved toward the door. He didn't bother looking back as it closed behind him.

Chapter 27

Saturday, March 14, 1942

Because the decision she'd made to push Fister out of her apartment and probably out of her life had been such a difficult one, Helen Meeker had a tough time getting to sleep. Just as she finally managed to drop off, the phone rang. Pulling herself back to reality, she grabbed the receiver.

"I hope this isn't a wrong number."

"It's not," her partner assured her. "I've got a lead on what might be a sighting of Ellen Shellmeyer."

Suddenly wide awake, Meeker bolted upright. "Where?"

"Zion, Pennsylvania. I've got a plane that can get us there, but we need to leave in the next hour. I'll pick you up. Can you be ready in thirty minutes?"

"Already halfway there," she assured him, leaping out of bed. "Can you bring some donuts?"

"You bet."

Chapter 28

Zion was a small community in the middle of the state Ben Franklin had once called home. The town was typical of rural Pennsylvania—clean, quaint, and quiet. Everyone's dream of what life in America should be.

Helen Meeker drove the car that had been waiting for her and Reese at the airport. The five-year-old Studebaker's strong motor and good tires offset its suspect styling. At just past three, the two partners pulled up to a road leading to a farmhouse about two miles outside of Zion.

"See the name on the mailbox?" Reese pointed.

James W. Grace. Meeker recalled the part of Shellmeyer's prayer when he said, "Let her body rest in Zion's graces." Could that have been code for this place? "What do we know about the folks who live here?"

"Not much. They moved to Zion last year. They've kept a low profile. About a month after they arrived, the mailman spotted a blonde teenage girl on the porch, and he caught glimpses of her through the windows from time to time. He said she never goes to town with either of the adults who live here."

Meeker turned her attention to the house at the end of the half-mile-long dirt lane. The small white frame, surrounded by trees, had a front porch about ten feet wide. The lack of adequate cover meant there was no way to approach the structure without being seen.

"So, what's your plan?"

Reese smiled. "You're canvassing for the local Lutheran church. You'll drive up to the house, knock on the door and see if they'll let you in to answer some questions."

"And you?"

"I'll be hiding in the backseat. After you get their attention, I'll roll out of the car and check out what's inside the home through the windows. If I see the girl and she looks like Ellen, I'll catch them off guard and we'll grab her." He eased out of the passenger seat, stepped outside, and opened the back door.

"You really think it'll be that easy?"

He slid into the backseat and dropped down to the floorboard. "I guarantee it'll be far easier than seducing a British soldier."

"Hey," she grumbled as she put the car into first gear and pressed the gas pedal. "You're taking an awful lot for granted."

"I hope I'm wrong," he snapped back.

Meeker almost assured him that he was, but stopped short. For the time being it might be better to let him think the worst.

As she drove up the long lane, she scoped out the home and yard. A large yellow cat lounged on the porch rail, but thankfully, no dog appeared as she pulled into the yard. Though all the home's shades were pulled tight, she noted a side window where someone seemed to be peeking through the gap. A bright red, mid-thirties Nash sedan was parked on the left side of the house. She pulled up beside it, figuring that would give Reese the cover he needed to escape unnoticed from their car.

After flipping off the ignition, Meeker grabbed her purse and opened the door. "Shades are drawn, so it should be easy for you to work your way up there without being spotted. But I'm not sure you'll be able to see much inside." Reese didn't answer.

Walking around the Nash and over the thick brown grass, Meeker marched up the four steps, paused on the porch and rapped on the door. A few moments later, it opened. Filling the entry was a man, perhaps forty, about five-foot-ten and two hundred pounds. He wore slacks, dark shoes, and a white shirt. His unshaven face remained stoic as he waited for her to speak.

"Good day. My name is Helen. I'm doing a canvas for the area Lutheran churches and would like to ask you and your family a few questions about your church attendance." She looked in the man's dark eyes and studied his expressionless face.

"We don't go to church," he said.

"Perhaps that's because your church isn't giving you what you need. In these days of world war, faith is more important than ever. Don't you agree?"

He shrugged.

"Is your wife at home?"

"Step aside, Bob." A heavyset woman with a tiny chin and deep blue eyes pushed past the man. "We used to go to church, but quit a few years back."

"Well, could I come in and tell you about ours?"

The woman stepped to the side and waved her in. Meeker took a seat on a worn, wine-colored couch. To her left sat a potbellied stove; on her right, an oversized green chair, which the man sank into. The coffee table in front of her held several issues of National Geographic.

Meeker recalled the name on the mailbox outside the house: James W. Grace. But his wife had just called him Bob. Strange.

Glancing through the door into the kitchen, Meeker noticed a blonde girl, perhaps seventeen or eighteen, sitting at the table folding towels. Bingo!

"Perhaps your daughter would like our youth group," Meeker suggested.

"She's shy," the woman explained. "And a bit touched in the head. She doesn't get out much."

"I see." Meeker turned her gaze back to the woman. "Tell me, why did you quit going to church?"

"We moved," came the woman's straightforward reply.

Meeker looked back at the man, who was staring out the window. She noted a bulge in his left pocket. As he pulled the sleeves of his shirt off his wrists, she saw a tattoo that looked like a ship's anchor. Had they struck pay dirt?

Through the kitchen, Meeker saw the back door open and Reese creep inside. "Mr. and Mrs. Grace, could I get your phone number? I'm sure I have a pen and paper in my purse."

As she reached into her bag, she placed her fingers around her Colt. When Reese reached the doorway, she yanked it out and aimed it at the man of the house. "Don't go for your gun."

"What are you doing?" the woman shrieked.

Meeker pointed to the kitchen. "My partner and I are here on behalf of the FBI. We have some questions about that blonde girl."

The couple glanced at Reese. "I figured you'd catch up with us at some point," the man said. "We did take the girl. But we had good reason."

"And what reason was that?"

"My brother abused her," the woman explained. "He beat her up so often and so hard that her head's not right. And her back is full of scars. The poor thing doesn't trust anybody, and she's scared of her own shadow. If we hadn't taken her and run, I truly believe she'd be dead now."

"What's her name?" Reese demanded, glancing back at the teenager, who sat at the table, continuing to fold towels.

"Suzy Mertens," the woman replied.

"Is that true?" Reese asked the girl.

She looked up and nodded, then went back to her task.

"That's what she does for hours and hours," Mrs. Grace explained. "Folds and unfolds, all day long." She shook her head. "Maybe you folks can find someone who can help her. I've tried, and I just can't."

Meeker glanced from the teen to the woman. "You called your husband Bob, but the name on the mailbox is James."

"We made up new names when we moved here from Carolina," the man said.

"What did you do in Carolina?" Reese asked.

"We were both school teachers."

Mrs. Grace reached for a scrapbook on an end table. Opening it to a one page, she handed it to Meeker. Taped to facing pages were two teaching certificates.

Meeker turned to Mr. Grace. "What do you have in your pocket?"

He glanced down and retrieved a tobacco tin. "I roll my own."

Meeker slipped the gun back into her purse.

"I'll have to check out your story," Reese said as he put his gun away. "But for the time being, if you promise not to move from this location, we can leave the girl with you. Once we confirm she's been abused in the past, I'll find a place where she can be treated and get some help."

"Can you really do that?"

"We'll try," Meeker said. She stood and moved toward the door.

"Thank you," the woman called as her two visitors walked to the car.

Just over forty-eight hours remained before Shellmeyer would be put to death, and they had wasted an entire day on something that had no bearing on the case. On top of that, they had charged into a home where two people were doing nothing more than trying to save a child from pain and anguish. Meeker wondered if they'd ever get a break.

Chapter 29

Sunday, March 15, 1942
Washington, DC

Time was running out, and Helen Meeker didn't feel like she had even a prayer of saving Wilbur Shellmeyer. Then again, she hadn't actually been praying.

She felt so overcome with a sense of impotence that she couldn't sleep. After getting up and eating half a piece of toast, she called Henry Reese and asked if there were any more leads.

"We're out of Zions. I don't know what we can do that we haven't already tried."

"We're missing something," she said, her tone anything but convincing.

"But what is it, and how do we find it?"

"I don't know. But I've decided to attend the Methodist church down the street this morning. I need to put things in perspective, and I can't do it on my own. Doubt if I can in church either, but it's about the only thing I haven't tried. Could you pick up me up there around noon? I'm just going to walk and leave my car here."

"Sure. I'll see you in a couple of hours."

After dressing in a dark suit and light blue blouse, she made the five-block stroll to the gray stone building. As had been the case since war was declared, the sanctuary was almost filled. She found a spot on the edge of the pew next to the entrance and took a seat. After four hymns and two prayers, the sermon began and Meeker turned her thoughts back to Wilbur Shellmeyer.

While she had tried her best, she had done little for the man and his wife. By tomorrow evening that would be starkly clear. She wondered if his death would haunt her for the rest of her life. Over the next half hour, she wondered about a lot of other things, but her jumbled thoughts only plunged her into a deep pool filled with self-pity.

She was so busy beating herself up and rehashing all she knew about the case that she wasn't even aware the service had ended until the man seated next to her stepped in front of her to leave. Even that didn't prompt her to get up. She continued to sit there until everyone had left the sanctuary.

"Are you all right?"

She looked up into the kind eyes of a man in his declining years. He was slightly built, dressed in a black suit, and balding.

"My name is George Miles. I pastored this church until I retired a few years ago. Still go here, even though I'm a civilian now. You look a bit troubled. Do you need prayer?"

"No." She sighed. "More like a miracle."

"They still happen sometimes."

"What can you tell me about Zion?" she asked.

His face took on a confused expression. "We sing about Zion in hymns. It's mentioned in the Bible, and there are sermons preached on the subject. What exactly are you looking for?"

Meeker locked her eyes on his. "What does the word mean to you, as a preacher?"

He smiled. "For most Christians today, Zion means heaven. But the early believers likely used it to refer to the Holy City. I'm more of a scholar, so when I think of Zion, I go back to ancient Jewish history, where it conjures up images of the City of David. Does that help?"

"It probably should," she muttered as she rose from the pew. "But I have no idea how to put this puzzle together."

"It'll come to you in time."

"Sadly, time is the one thing I don't have." Lowering her eyes, Meeker walked out of the church.

Chapter 30

Reese's FBI-issued Ford was idling at the curb when Helen Meeker exited the church and walked down its ten stone steps. He leaned across the coupe's front seat and pushed the passenger door open as she approached. "How was the service?"

"I have no idea," she admitted as she picked up the Sunday newspaper sitting on the passenger seat and took its place. "My mind was on the case. I'm still trying to figure out the code at the grave."

"Maybe it wasn't code," Reese suggested. "Maybe Shellmeyer was just spouting a few random words before he gave the grave diggers and the funeral director that cryptic warning not to open the coffin."

"You may be right."

"I heard something interesting this morning. Andrews is still missing, and the Brits have asked the FBI to help find him. We've issued an All Points for him from coast to coast. The Canadian Royal Mounted Police are even involved."

"He can't hide forever." Meeker smiled as she noticed the headlines on the newspaper in her lap. The lead stories were about Churchill meeting with his team in London and FDR getting away from town for a holiday in Warm Springs, Georgia. The charade was working beautifully.

"There's a file on Fister in the backseat," Reese said. "When I stopped at the office, I ran into Collins, and he'd just finished writing it up. I told him I'd give it to you."

She reached over the seat, retrieved the folder, and pulled out the three pages of typewritten material. "Did you look through this?"

"I wanted to. But Fister is none of my business. Neither is what you do, or have done, with him."

Meeker smiled. "Well, let's just say that if it were a race, you'd be winning."

His eyes sparkled, and a smile stretched across the entire width of his face. "You mean that?"

She nodded. "He wanted more than I could give him."

"Did you want to?"

"I did … for an instant."

"What stopped you?"

"I think it was the fact that giving in to him meant not giving my all to the case. Shellmeyer is probably going to die, and there's nothing we can do about it. But if I gave up trying to save him just to indulge in something that could be saved for another place and time, what does that say about me?"

"It speaks volumes that you didn't give in to the crafty and charismatic Scotsman."

"I doubt it. But I'm glad you think so. Now, how about you take me out to eat? Maybe to a diner with some kind of greasy food."

"I know just the place." He laughed.

As Reese drove away from the curb, Meeker glanced at the file. Fister might have been an orphan, but he had a pretty good youth. After spending a year in the United States, he used the exchange program to study in Austria. After that, he returned to London and joined the service. By the time the war broke out, he was an officer and seemed destined to become just what he was now—the embodiment of the ultimate English hero.

Chapter 31

After lunch, Meeker and Reese went over every detail of the case. They spent hours trying to find something they'd missed, but came up completely dry.

Defeated and depressed, Meeker had her partner take her home, where she fixed a light supper and turned on the radio. The war news did nothing to improve her mood. A German U-boat had sunk a British naval ship in the North Sea, killing more than a hundred sailors. Another Nazi sub sank a US tanker a few miles off the North Carolina coast. MacArthur had been flown out of the Philippines. The general's leaving seemed the ultimate act of surrender.

She shut off her radio, picked up her phone and asked for the long-distance operator. After being shifted from one operator to another, she finally heard the phone ring at her sister's dormitory.

It took the dorm mother two minutes to find Alison.

"Hey, sis," Alison almost shouted.

"How are you doing, kid?"

"Great! I love it here at Ouachita. Best semester ever!"

"Does that mean you've found a boyfriend?"

Alison laughed. "You told me not to settle down yet. But yeah, I've had a few dates."

"Good. I want you to have fun. How are your grades?"

"No problems there at all. How are you doing?"

Meeker leaned back in her bed and sighed. "I'm struggling with a difficult case. I just can't get a good grasp on it. I feel like the answer is right in front of me, but I can't see it."

"I'm sure you'll figure it out. You always do."

"Maybe not this time."

"Hey, you found me, remember? Everyone believed I was dead, but not you. You knew I was alive."

"I just felt like you were."

"And how do you feel now?"

Meeker paused, considering the question. "I feel like the person I'm looking for is alive."

Alison laughed. "That's the spirit! You know, one of my professors says that life is a pilgrimage, and we just have to keep going until we find out where we're supposed to be."

Meeker chuckled. "That's a bit too vague for a logical mind like mine. Besides, I've got less than a day to get to where I have to be. If I don't complete my pilgrimage by then, it won't matter."

"Well, maybe you're not following the right map," Alison suggested. "The world's top destinations for pilgrimages are Mecca and Jerusalem. Maybe you should try going to one of those places instead of wherever you're stuck now."

"Alison, you might just be brilliant!"

"Really?"

"I love you, but I've got to go. I think you just gave me the clue I needed."

"Glad I could help, even if I don't know what I did."

"I'll talk to you later. Good night."

"I love you, Helen."

"I love you too, kid."

As soon as the line went dead, Meeker hit the button to get a dial tone. She then called Reese. He answered after only two rings.

"Henry, I think I might know what city Ellen Shellmeyer is in."

"Super!"

"Can you leave with me tonight?"

"Sorry. I've been assigned to run down a lead on Nigel Andrews. He was just seen in Baltimore. I'm about to leave. But where do you think she is?"

Helen smiled. "Zion."

"As in heaven?"

"As in the City of David."

"Jerusalem?"

"That's right."

"You're going to the place where Jesus died?"

"A little closer. I'm headed for Jerusalem, New York."

"Sounds like a hunch."

"It's a long shot. But it's the only shot I've got."

"Well, be careful. And call in backups. Don't try to do this alone."

"Once I'm sure I've figure it out right, I'll get the locals to help me. But right now, I need to pack a bag, put on some clean clothes and go. I'm heading off on an all-night pilgrimage."

Chapter 32

Monday, March 16, 1942
Jerusalem, New York

Intense blowing rain plagued Helen Meeker during her entire road trip. At times, the wipers couldn't keep up, and the gale-force winds almost pushed her off the road more times than she could count. As a result, the trip took much longer than she had planned.

At just past ten in the morning, she pulled into the hamlet of Jerusalem. The sign claimed a population just over two thousand.

She drove each of the city's streets, studying the various homes and businesses. She knocked on dozens of doors and showed folks the picture of Ellen Shellmeyer. No one could help.

One hour became two, two became three, and nothing jumped out as being the place where the girl might be being held. At one in the afternoon, Meeker finally pulled into a local diner to grab a bite to eat and try to regain her focus.

She had no more than sat down when a middle-aged, dark-haired waitress wearing a dress one size too small sidled up to her booth. “What do you want?” She snapped her gum while she waited.

“Could I get a ham sandwich?”

“Sure. On white?”

“That’d be fine.”

“You want it fully loaded? Lettuce, tomato, onion?”

Meeker shook her head. “No, thanks. Just mayo. And a Coke.”

“I’ll have them out in about five minutes.”

As the woman started to turn, Meeker stopped her. “Do you have a phone book I can look at?”

“Sure. I’ll grab it and bring it right back to you.”

In less than sixty seconds, the waitress returned to the table with the small book. Mentally reciting the pastor’s unusual graveside prayer, Please, Lord, let her body rest in Zion’s graces, Meeker flipped to the Yellow Pages. Sadly, there were no local businesses with “rest” in their name. So, she went to the white pages and looked up individuals’ names. She was up to the e’s when the waitress delivered her order.

“Thanks.” After taking a few bites of the sandwich, Meeker looked up at the clock. She had less than five hours to find the Shellmeyer girl and stop her father’s execution.

If the clue to where she was couldn’t be traced to the word rest, then where was the answer? Meeker considered each word of the pastor’s prayer. She even tried mixing up the words to find the right combination. “Please body. Lord body. Lord rest.”

She was still going through her word-scramble exercise when the waitress came back to the booth. The woman shook her head and smiled. “I was a kid when that place was in its prime.”

“What place?”

"The old estate house," the waitress explained between chomps on her gum.

"What estate house?"

"The one you were mumbling about—The Lord's Rest. It was a horse farm, named after the greatest racehorse the original owner ever bred. But it went under back in the 1920s. It's been abandoned for years. It's kind of a spooky three-story mansion. Folks around here call it the haunted house."

"Where is it?"

"You go a mile down the road to Oak Street. Turn right there and continue till you pass a couple of vacant businesses. Make a left on a dirt road and go about a quarter of a mile. It's muddy today, so you might get stuck. Anyway, you can't see it from the road because of the trees that have grown up."

"Thanks," Meeker said, glancing out the window into the pouring rain. As she did, the diner's lights flashed off and then back on.

"That's been happening a lot today," the waitress explained.

"If this storm keeps up, we'll lose power for sure."

"What do I owe you?" Meeker asked.

"Sixty-five cents."

As she rose, Meeker tossed down a five-dollar bill. "Keep the change."

"Wow," the waitress whispered. "Thanks."

As Meeker pulled on her coat, the waitress said, "Oh, there's something else you might need to know. Someone bought that old place last year. They said they were going to fix it up, but they haven't done much yet. It does have power, though. And there are some folks who stay there from time to time. I've never met any of them."

"I can't tell you how much I appreciate this." Meeker pushed by the woman and rushed out into the rain.

Chapter 33

Helen Meeker had just pulled out of the diner's parking lot when the lights went out all over town. As dark as the skies were and as hard as the rain was falling, it seemed more like night than early afternoon. With the Packard's wipers speeding up and slowing down depending on the motor's demands, Meeker had a difficult time seeing the road. She missed the first turn and had to make a trip around the block to correct her mistake.

A half mile later, she passed the two vacant businesses and spotted where she needed to be. She pulled into the lane and parked her car under a large elm tree just to the right of a dirt trail. Reaching over the front seat, she grabbed a set of rubber boots, a raincoat and an umbrella from the backseat. After taking her gun out of her purse and dropping it into her jacket pocket, she put on the slicker and boots, slid out of the car, and popped open the umbrella. Fighting both wind and rain, she pushed forward through the mud. Halfway down the lane, a wind gust turned her umbrella inside out. Meeker tossed it aside and moved on.

The ancient Victorian home looked like something out of the 1800s. At one time, it must have been a real showplace, but now its wraparound porches were sagging, shutters were either gone or hanging sideways, and there was very little paint left on the wood siding.

Meeker couldn't just walk up on the porch, knock on the door, and ask if Ellen Shellmeyer was in the house. She needed a plan.

As she hid behind a large oak and considered her options, she recalled a promise she'd already broken. She had forgotten to call the local cops for backup. There was no time to correct that oversight now. The clock was ticking, and she had only a short window of opportunity to save a man's life.

The pouring rain was joined by massive bolts of lightning, followed by loud blasts of thunder. But Meeker saw the storm as a godsend because it made for a great cover.

Opting to circle around the house to peer into a few windows and get the lay of the land, Meeker moved toward the old mansion. The first three rooms were void of furniture. The next was a large living room where two men, dressed in slacks and white shirts, sat in old, well-used high-backed chairs. This room also contained a desk, a few other chairs of similar style, and an antique Victorian couch. While there were several lamps and two overhead light fixtures, the room was lit only by two candles. The men, seemingly unconcerned about the weather, were smoking cigars and drinking a dark-colored liquid. She guessed it to be whiskey or scotch.

As she studied the scene, she focused closely on the men. They both fit Virginia Shellmeyer's descriptions of the ones who'd posed as funeral directors at the graveside. Satisfied she had the right location, Meeker circled the rest of the home to see if there were any more men she had to worry about. Besides the duo, she saw no one else on the ground level. If Ellen was there, she must be on either the second or third floor.

The kitchen seemed to be the most logical point of entry. Sneaking up onto the back steps, she tried the door. It was locked. Pushing her wet hair off her face, she moved back to the muddy ground and tried four windows. They were all locked too.

A flash of lightning struck a nearby tree, and the rolling thunder that followed almost split her eardrums. That gave her an idea. Pulling her gun from her inside jacket pocket, she moved to a window as far from the men as possible. She waited beside it until a flash of lightning lit up the sky. When the thunder roared two seconds later, she shattered the window with the butt of her gun.

After brushing away the remaining glass, she grabbed the window fame and pulled herself inside. After dropping to the floor, she moved into the shadows to see if the storm's fury had managed to cover her actions. She waited thirty seconds, gun drawn, before she breathed.

The kitchen was to her left. She noted the door and considered her options. When she'd peered in from the outside, she'd spotted a stairway in a hall outside the kitchen. While it was close to the room where the men were relaxing, if she was quiet she could likely make it up the winding stairs without them detecting her presence.

After setting her gun on the table, she yanked off her boots and pushed them under a chair. Then she removed the raincoat and laid it on the wooden plank floor. Picking up her Colt, she silently crossed the room in her stocking feet.

Leaning into the door she gently pushed it open, then stepped into a large kitchen that would have been modern in 1890. The cabinets were minimal and painted white. Beyond a couple of old-fashioned food cabinets against a far wall, there was a fairly up-to-date refrigerator. A six-by-four-foot table sat in the middle of the room, with two stools pushed under it. In the center of the table was an oil lamp filled with kerosene. It was lit, and the steady flame provided some light.

Meeker snuck across the kitchen to an open door leading to the hall. She hugged the wall until she got to the steps, then glanced into the living room. Neither man was looking her way. She climbed the winding, eight-foot-wide wooden staircase. Only one of the twenty planks creaked, and with the rain pouring down, she figured that noise was likely not noticed.

The second floor had eight rooms, four on each side, separated by a ten-foot-wide hall. The four rooms on the left were empty. They didn't even have furniture. The first room at the back of the hall was the same. The next was furnished, and some men's clothing lay on a couch. The third was a bathroom, dirty but functional. The final room on this floor was evidently where the other man slept. At the end of the hall was another set of stairs. These were much narrower.

After climbing the fifteen steps, she emerged into another dark hallway. On the left were two doors—to the right were three. The first two on the right were void of anything. The third door was locked. Silently falling to her knees, Meeker peered through the keyhole. She spotted a bed, two chairs, and a chest of drawers. Standing to the right, looking out the window, was a young woman dressed in a ragged dress. She was barefoot.

Setting her gun on the floor, Meeker reached into her wet hair and pulled out a bobby pin. It was time to put her Girl Scout training to good use, though this was a skill one of the other scouts had taught her and she hadn't earned a merit badge for it.

In less than a minute, she'd picked the lock. After tossing the pin aside, she grabbed her Colt and opened the door. The girl whirled, her face drawn and her expression fearful.

Meeker slipped her gun back into her jacket pocket and pressed her finger to her lips. Walking quickly to the blonde's side, she placed her hands on the captive's shoulders and whispered, "I'm here to get you out of this place. Do you understand?"

She nodded, her blue eyes displaying a blend of trust and apprehension.

"Are you Ellen Shellmeyer?" The girl nodded again.

"We have to sneak out quietly. Can you do that?"

"Yes," she whispered.

"Follow me."

With Meeker leading the way, the pair exited the room. After making sure the coast was clear, they slowly made their way down the hall toward the stairway. They had covered half the distance when a man stepped out of one of the empty rooms on the far side of the hall. He had a face only a mother could love and a smile that would have scared a goblin. He was big, sported an ugly scar beneath one eye, and had an ear that looked as though it had once been a dog's chew toy. But at this moment, the gun he held was his most impressive feature.

"Who are you?" he barked.

"I'm from the Office of the President of the United States, and I'm taking this girl with me."

He sneered. "I was considering killing you before. But if what you say is true, you just signed your own death warrant, lady."

His smile vanished as he aimed his gun at her. A second later a shot rang out, and smoke filled the hall. A confused look framed the man's face as he stared at the hole in Meeker's jacket, which had come from the inside out.

Yanking the still-smoking Colt into the open, Meeker watched the man fall to his knees and then forward onto his face.

She grabbed the girl's hand. "We've got to move."

After rushing down the stairs, they emerged into the second-floor hall. The other man wasn't there. Meeker charged down the winding staircase with Ellen on her heals. Making a U-turn, she rushed toward the kitchen. As she charged into the room, the man greeted her, gun drawn and ready for action.

"Drop it, lady, or I shoot you and then the girl."

Meeker lowered her weapon. As she dropped it to the floor, she moved a step to her right so the length of the table was between them.

"That's a good girl," the man said. "I take it you killed my friend."

"Probably," Meeker admitted. "He's lying face down in the third-floor hall. Look, you don't want to fool with me. I'm on FDR's staff. Kill me and the entire force of the United States government will be on your tail."

He grinned. "If I don't get rid of you, that'll still be the case." He aimed the gun at her head and studied her face, as if waiting for her to beg for her life.

A massive bolt of lightning struck the house and a blast of earth-shaking fury rattled the ancient home's windows. In that split second, Meeker grabbed the edge of the table and shoved it forward, striking her adversary just below the waist. She continued to push until he was pinned between the table and the cabinet. As he bent forward in pain, Meeker picked up the oil lamp and smashed it over the hand holding the gun. The flame jumped from the wick to the oil covering the man's arm. He screamed in pain and dropped his weapon.

Meeker shoved the shocked girl toward the door. "Get out of here. I'll be right behind you." Glancing back toward the man, she watched the flame spreading across his pants and up his shoulder.

Meeker grabbed her gun. As she did, he pushed the table away and lunged toward her. She slid her stocking-covered feet to one side. The man slipped and fell into the kerosene that had dripped onto the floor. A second later the fire reached him. He rolled around on his belly, screaming.

Meeker spun toward the door and raced out into the rain. The girl was waiting for her in the yard.

"Let's go," Meeker shouted as she pointed down the lane.

Glancing back toward the home, she noted through a window that the kitchen was a wall of flame. Even with the heavy rain, this fire would not go out until the structure had burned completely to the ground. Soon the Lord's Rest would be haunted no more.

Chapter 34

After dragging Ellen Shellmeyer down the lane and pushing the girl into the Packard, Helen Meeker drove to the local police station. Leaving the teenager in the car, she barged through the door a little past three a.m. A sheriff and deputy were sitting behind their desks.

"I'm Helen Meeker," she announced. She pulled her credentials out of her purse and tossed them toward the man in charge. "I've just rescued a young woman from kidnappers who were holding her in the old place known as the Lord's Rest."

The sheriff stared at her credentials in disbelief. "You work for FDR?"

"Yes, I do. There are two dead men in that old house, and it's on fire."

"Wow," the deputy exclaimed.

"I need to use your phone to call the federal prison in Lewisburg, Pennsylvania."

The sheriff handed Meeker her credentials. "I'd love to help you, but the storm has knocked out the power and phone service all over the central and western parts of the state. Even our radios aren't working."

"How long does it take to drive to Lewisburg?"

"It's almost a hundred and fifty miles. Even in good weather with a powerful car, it takes almost four hours."

"Then I'll do my best to set a new speed record."

"What's the hurry?"

"Got to save a man's life. Maybe I'll get lucky and run into a place in northern Pennsylvania where the phones are working."

Meeker ran back out into the rain, hopped into her Packard and backed out onto the street. As the car picked up speed, she glanced at the young woman in the passenger seat. "Hang on. This is going to be a wild ride. And if you know any prayers, now's the time to say them."

Chapter 35

Helen Meeker pushed the Packard to the limit, sliding around curves, racing through small towns, and pushing the gas pedal to the floor on long, straight stretches. A dozen times she almost lost control in the heavy rain, and on each of those occasions her frightened passenger looked at her as if she were mad. And perhaps she was. Yet she had to do whatever she could to save an innocent man's life. If she failed to make it, at least she would know she tried.

The storm had knocked out power and phone service not only in New York, but most of Pennsylvania.

At just past six, when Meeker practically flew into Lewisburg, the rain was finally starting to let up. If the execution had been carried out on time, it was already too late to save Wilbur Shellmeyer. But more often than not, these exercises in justice were delayed. Perhaps she still had a chance.

She glanced at the confused and scared girl in her passenger seat. How she wished she had the time to sit down and explain the situation to her. Instead, after stealing her from her kidnappers and killing two men right in front of her, she had taken her on a ride that made the Indianapolis 500 look like a

Sunday drive in the park. But at least she was here. Soon the kid would be reunited with her family.

Pulling up to the prison gate, Meeker ordered Ellen to stay in her seat until she called for her. Then she raced over to the nearest guard. "I need to see the warden right away. I've got evidence that will overturn the conviction of a man on death row."

"Sorry, lady. You have to be on the list to get in."

Meeker opened her purse and yanked out her credentials.

The guard looked them over. "You're Helen Meeker?"

"Yes. And if you'll check your records, you'll discover I was here last Wednesday. Now, do whatever it is you have to do, but I must see Mr. Dennis immediately."

The uniformed man stepped back into his booth and picked up the phone. While he was speaking, Meeker opened the door to the small room and pushed her way in. Grabbing the receiver from the stunned guard, she pulled it to her mouth. Her words flew out like blasts from a machine gun. "Warden Dennis, this is Helen Meeker. You have to stop the execution. I have Ellen Shellmeyer. Her father will talk as soon as he sees she's safe."

"Miss Meeker," Dennis said, his voice tense. "I wish you'd gotten her here ten minutes earlier. Mr. Shellmeyer has already been executed."

Meeker's throat constricted in pain. It couldn't be true!

"I'll instruct the guard to let you in. His wife is here. I'm sure she will get some relief in seeing her daughter again."

Meeker handed the receiver back to the man and slowly exited the tiny room. As she made her way back to the Packard, she didn't feel the rain or note the cool wind. She'd failed. She'd found the answer to the puzzle, but too late.

After opening the car door, she slid into the driver's seat as the huge gates swung open. She drove to the same parking space she'd used last week. After switching off the motor, she looked over to the disheveled young woman beside her. "Your mother is waiting for you inside."

A guard escorted the pair from the car to the warden's office, where Dennis was waiting for them. So was Virginia Shellmeyer, dressed in black and looking even thinner and paler than she had last week. Her eyes red and her face drawn, the woman opened her arms. The girl raced into them.

The reunion should have been infused with happiness. But Meeker's heart was bathed in pain and anguish. The father should have been able to feel his daughter's arms and see her face. But he was dead. And all because Meeker had taken too long to decipher a code.

"Miss Meeker?"

She turned her eyes from the bittersweet reunion to the warden, who stood close beside her. "Yes?"

"I thought you might want to know what Mr. Shellmeyer's final words were. They were … strange, to say the least."

"How so?"

"After saying good-bye to his wife and pleading for God's mercy for 'living a lie,' he called out, 'God save the President and Mr. Churchill.'"

What did that mean? Was he trying to prove his loyalty to the Allies and recant his confession? She shook her head. "It's not that strange. I mean, I've read far more bizarre final statements."

"Those were not quite the last words he said. There was a postscript directed just to you."

Her heart lurched. "What was it?"

The warden whispered, "'Tell FDR's woman to unmask the imposter before he kills them.'"

Meeker considered the message. The imposter had to be Andrews. Shellmeyer knew him. And he was currently missing, with a nationwide search going on for him. But who did Shellmeyer think Andrews was going to kill?

"Oh." The warden raised a finger. "And just before the lines went down, an FBI agent named Henry Reese left a message for you. He seemed to think you'd be here before the execution."

Well, he was almost right. "What did he say?"

"He told me to tell you, 'The bird has been sighted in Elmira and is on the move.' Does that make any sense to you?"

As a map of New York took shape in her brain, she started to panic. "I need to use your phone."

"Sorry. Service is still out all over Pennsylvania and New York. I hear it might be a day or more before anyone in this area can make any calls."

"But the guard used a phone to call you."

"That was on our in-house system."

"I need a New York map."

"There's one in my desk." The warden crossed the room to his desk and pulled out a map. After studying it, Meeker checked the office's wall clock.

"Okay," she said, more to herself than the warden. "It's six thirty. Even at top speed, it'll take more than three hours to cover the distance. But it's the only way."

"The only way to do what?"

"No time to explain. Have the guard open the gates. I'm in a hurry!"

Chapter 36

Helen Meeker drove out of the prison gates and pointed the Packard north. While the rain had slowed from monsoon intensity to gentle showers, the slick pavement and the darkness made driving just as dangerous as it had been on her trip to the federal correctional facility. While she'd arrived too late to save the life of an innocent preacher, perhaps she could beat the odds now and save the lives of the Allies' most powerful leaders.

As she pushed the gas pedal to the floor, she paid no attention to either the road conditions or the speed limits. While most highway signs listed a maximum speed of forty-five, Meeker doubled that. Except for slipping off the shoulder once in northern Pennsylvania, she had no problem keeping her car on the pavement.

She was five miles north of Elmira, over three-quarters of her trip completed, when a New York state patrolman gave chase. She grudgingly pulled over. Before he'd managed to walk up to her window, she was ready with her credentials. He looked them over, checked her license and sent her on her way with a request to exercise caution. She ignored it.

At just past ten thirty, she pulled into the lane leading to the Grove Estate. Despite the steady rain, a Secret Service man raised his arm, stepped into her path and demanded she stop. As he walked to the driver's side of the Packard, she rolled down her window. "I'm Helen Meeker. I'm on your pass list. I have important information to give to the President."

The man shined a flashlight in Meeker's face, causing her to squint, then flashed it down to her car.

"Hello, Miss Meeker," he said with a smile. "Sorry I didn't recognize your car, but I've never seen it all covered with mud."

"Since the phone lines are down, I've been driving like crazy to get here."

"Go on in. I'll radio ahead so the front-door guard will let you in the house."

"Thanks." Meeker headed down the long, paved road. After parking in front of the house, she grabbed her purse and rushed to the front door. A man she knew well opened it for her.

"Where's the President?"

"He and Churchill are in the back study," John said, "and he left word not to be disturbed. It's all very hush-hush. Barnes and I are the only agents in the house. And there's only one other person in the room with them. A Brit."

Meeker started down the hall. "On the right or left?"

"The left," he shouted. "But it's locked."

Stopping in front of the entry, Meeker rapped on the walnut door.

"Who is it?" Clay Barnes's gruff voice demanded.

"Helen Meeker. I need to see the President. It's urgent."

A moment later the latch was flipped, and a tall, stern Secret Service agent opened the door. Meeker pushed by him. The President and Prime Minister sat on a couch on the far side of the study. Reggie Fister leaned against the wall to the right, smirking at her.

"Helen." The president sent her a sly grin. "You look like you've been playing in the rain."

Meeker glanced into the huge mirror on the wall to her right. Her shoes and stockings were splattered with mud. Her suit was damp and wrinkled. Her face was dirty, her makeup smeared, and her hair wet and stringy. "Sorry I'm not at my best, sir."

Roosevelt chuckled. "Winston, this is the beautiful young woman I was telling you about."

Churchill lifted his eyebrows. "Your definition of beauty and mine seem a bit different."

The President and Barnes laughed. Meeker failed to see the humor.

"Sit down, Helen," her boss suggested. As she took a seat in a high-backed leather chair, Roosevelt picked up the phone. "Could you bring us some coffee, please?"

With all eyes still on her, Meeker avoided everyone's stares by looking around the study. By estate standards it was small, not more than fifteen by fifteen feet. Besides the door she'd come in, the only other one was at the back of the room. One wall was nothing but bookshelves. A print of Washington crossing the Delaware, framed in brass, was the highlight of another wall. The chairs and couches were covered with green leather, and the room's end tables were dark walnut. The paneling appeared to be cherry. The light-green carpet was plush. The filled ashtrays and lingering smell of cigars proved the men had been taking advantage of Cuba's most famous export.

Roosevelt lifted his eyebrows high enough that they rose above his glasses. "I know I invited you to come to this meeting, but I'm guessing there's a reason behind your late-night arrival."

She nodded. "Wilbur Shellmeyer was executed tonight."

The president shook his head. "I'm sorry."

"He was a spy." Fister pushed off the wall. "People who work against their countries must pay the ultimate price, especially during times of war."

A steward, dressed in a white jacket and black pants, entered through the back door. He carried a silver tray with five coffee cups, a pitcher, creamer, bowl of sugar, and plate of cookies. Without a word, he set them on a table in front of the two world leaders, then stepped away until his back was against the bookshelves.

With everyone else's eyes on the tray, only Meeker noticed the man reach under his coat and yank a pistol from his belt. She unsnapped her purse and pulled out her Colt. Fister produced a gun as well … with a silencer screwed onto the barrel.

"Andrews," the Scotsman snarled.

"Nigel?" Meeker couldn't believe she hadn't recognized him.

"You can't stop me," Andrews answered. "I can easily get off at least one shot before anyone takes me down."

"Nigel, what are you doing?" she asked.

"This has to end. Someone has to stop the needless slaughter and all the lies."

"You don't have what it takes to end it, son," Fister replied.

"Put the weapon down."

Andrews shook his head and aimed at the men in the room.

Fister fired first.

The blast caught Andrews in the chest. He looked down at the blood spreading across his white coat for a moment before dropping his weapon and falling forward.

"Good job, Reggie!" Churchill exclaimed.

Barnes bent over the wounded victim. Meeker aimed her gun at the English army hero.

"You can relax, Helen," Fister said. "We nailed the traitor. Thanks for coming here to warn us he was in the area."

Meeker kept her Colt pointed at Fister's face. "Lower your weapon, Reggie."

"You first."

"What's this all about?" Roosevelt demanded.

Meeker stared Fister down. "Shellmeyer's last words were about an imposter. Somehow he figured out that the Nazis had a spy in our midst."

"It was Nigel." Fister pointed at his wounded comrade. "He hated war and was willing to sell out his country to end it. He wormed his way into a job where national security information would be at his fingertips, and he passed it along to Hitler. When he heard about this meeting, he must have figured he could cripple our war efforts by assassinating both Mr. Churchill and Mr. Roosevelt." Reggie shook his head. "I have to admit, passing himself off as my best friend to grab the spotlight and then turning it into a chance for revenge was brilliant."

"Yes," Meeker said, "it was brilliant. But Nigel isn't the only Brit Shellmeyer knew. You lived in his home as an exchange student."

Fister nodded. "Yes, he knew both of us. But he must have recognized Andrews's lack of character."

She narrowed her eyes at Reggie. "Last Tuesday at Rigatti's, how did you know I was in danger in New York the day before?"

"Your secretary told me."

"She couldn't have. She didn't know. And later that same night, you told me to forget the Shellmeyer case. But I hadn't shared anything about it with you."

"I overheard you and Reese," Fister argued, his gun still aimed at her.

Meeker shook her head. "Shellmeyer didn't leave a message about a spy. His final words were about an imposter."

"Clearly, he was referring to Andrews. Helen, why can't you accept that we got the bad guy?"

She allowed herself a grim smile. "The real Reggie Fister was an orphan who lived with the Shellmeyers for a year before going off to school in Austria. That's where you met him. You'd grown up in an orphanage too, and you looked enough like him to fool Shellmeyer into believing you were him."

"This is preposterous," Fister countered. But Meeker detected beads of sweat forming on his forehead.

"The deception worked … until the American newspapers ran a picture of you. That was when Shellmeyer grew suspicious. When the Nazi agents you were working for discovered he had arranged to meet an old friend from the attorney general's office to discover your true identity, they put a plan in action to keep the family quiet. And it almost worked."

"What are saying, Helen?" Roosevelt asked.

She pointed at Reggie. "This man, not Andrews, is the Nazi plant."

Chapter 37

Helen Meeker kept Reggie in the sights of her gun, waiting for him to either flinch so she could shoot him or admit she had him dead to rights. After more than a minute of uncomfortable silence, the unmasked hero finally spoke.

"You're smarter than I thought you were, Helen."

"You're not the first person to misjudge me," she assured him. "It must have been painful to be intentionally shot three times as a cover for injuries you supposedly received that night in France."

"Not as bad as you might think," he admitted. "They put me under, and the flesh wounds didn't do any real damage."

Meeker nodded at her boss and his guest, her gun still trained on Reggie. "Was this why they planted you—to kill two world leaders?"

"Not originally." He grinned. "I was only supposed to work my way inside Churchill's inner circle and then feed information back home. This opportunity fell into our laps."

"Put the gun down, Fister," Churchill ordered.

"No way. I'm walking out of here."

Meeker raised an eyebrow. "Not likely. You're either leaving this room a captive or dead. Either way is fine by me."

Fister grinned. "We have Henry Reese, Helen. He's alive. But if you want to see him again, you'll have to let me go."

Meeker swallowed the panic that threatened to close her throat. "Your plan won't work," she replied as calmly as she could. "Henry would rather die than let you go free."

His grin broadened. "We also have your sister."

Meeker felt weak. Her hands shook. "You're bluffing."

"We yanked her out of her dorm earlier today. Room 201. Her roommate's name is Rachel. Nice girl."

Apparently, he wasn't bluffing. Meeker wished the phone lines were working so she could call the school and confirm it.

"If I'm not at the pickup site before ten o'clock on Friday night, both Reese and Alison will be killed."

Meeker glanced at the President. Roosevelt nodded, then looked at Barnes. "Lower your gun." The agent did as directed.

"Smart move," Fister said. "Now it's your turn, Helen."

Duty or love? It was a question she never believed she would have to answer. Was she willing to sacrifice her sister for the good of the country? Alison was young, innocent, and the only family Meeker had left. The kid had her whole life in front of her. And they'd just found each other. How could she give her up?

But the country was at war against a foe that was killing thousands each day. Was Alison more important than all the other innocent young people being sacrificed every minute, simply because she was the sister of someone who worked for the President?

"I'm not dropping my gun," Meeker finally said. "If I did, you'd have a clear shot at the President and the Prime Minister."

"I would expect no less from you, Helen." Fister made his way across the room toward the back door. "You are a worthy opponent, my dear. I am sure we will meet again."

She certainly hoped not.

At the door, he looked at the others in the room. "No one had better follow me, or those two hostages will die."

"How do we know you won't kill them anyway?" Barnes asked.

"I give you my word as a Scottish gentleman."

As his left hand found the doorknob, Meeker squeezed the trigger. Smoke and noise filled the room. The bullet penetrated Fister's right wrist. He screamed. As soon as the Scot's gun fell to the floor, Meeker kicked it away.

Holding his right wrist with his left hand, the fallen hero stared up at her. "Why did you do that?"

"You're not Scottish, and you're certainly not a gentleman. So, your word means nothing."

Other agents rushed into the room as Meeker hurried to the President. "We've got less than a week to find them."

Roosevelt nodded. "Do you have a plan?"

"I need to head to Arkansas before the trail goes cold. Can you get me a special plane?"

"Of course."

"In the meantime, have our men work Fister over and see if he'll talk. He probably won't, but try it anyway."

Meeker glared at Reggie. The Secret Service agent had him in handcuffs and was wrapping a handkerchief around his wrist to stop the bleeding.

Fister leered at Helen. "You won't find her."

"Never underestimate an American woman—especially this one."

While her words were honest and filled with grit, Meeker wondered if she had the time, resources, and intelligence to find the two people she cared for most in the world before it was too late. She was sure of only one thing: if she failed, it would probably kill her.

BEST SELLING AUTHOR

ACE COLLINS

The

DARK POOL

IN THE PRESIDENT'S SERVICE : EPISODE 2

To Alison

CHAPTER 1

Monday, March 16, 1942
10:45 p.m.

The man's arms moved in piston-like fashion as he raced across an open field. Though he was tall and ruggedly built, his rapidly beating heart rumbled like a kettledrum, and his lungs felt as though they were being yanked through his chest. The bitter-cold March wind tore into his face, causing his cheekbones to all but cut through his skin. Yet, in spite of his mind pleading with him to stop, he kept going. He had to run. He had no choice. He had to either get away or die.

Glancing over his left shoulder into the night, he noted four figures with flashlights moving toward him. Were they getting closer? He thought so, but perhaps fatigue was just playing games with him. After all, he'd been sprinting for at least a mile.

His need to flee was almost overruled by a longing to slow down—maybe even give up. But he couldn't do that. Death was better than going back into the hole. So, he kept his legs moving across the flat prairie landscape. Even if his heart burst and he instantly fell dead, that would be better than the fate that awaited him back there.

Up ahead, he saw headlights moving from left to right. A highway! If he could get to it, maybe someone would pick him up. Then the monsters chasing him couldn't drag him back and continue beating him or filling his body with more of the mind-numbing drugs.

The hope of escape from his pursuers enabled him to push himself even harder. As he got within half a mile of the road, he saw more cars. Sweet freedom was almost in his grasp!

His breathing ragged, his chest heaving, he felt more like an old plow horse than a sleek thoroughbred. But victory would not be earned by the contestant with the best form. No, the blue ribbon was reserved for those who had the heart to battle until they broke the tape. And tonight he was going to give everything he had to achieve his goal.

In the dim light offered by the sliver of moon, he didn't notice the pool of shallow water until it splashed up into his face. And then it was too late. He lost his balance and fell forward into the mud. Pushing his torso up, he glanced back. His pursuers were closing fast.

Fighting tears of anger and disappointment, he rose to his feet. Soaked, cold, and exhausted, he glanced at the highway. So close but still out of reach.

When he turned back, the four men who'd been chasing him stood close enough he could see the whites of their eyes in the dark night. He could also make out the rifles in their hands.

"Go ahead and shoot me," he growled. "Put me out of my misery."

The quartet stopped at the edge of the pool. They said nothing. He knew they wouldn't.

A tall man walked up beside them. "Go get him," he ordered. "But don't beat him. We need him healthy and in one piece."

As the four mute warriors waded toward him, the defeated runner fell into the mud and wept.

CHAPTER 2

Monday, March 16, 1942
11:05 p.m.
Ithaca, New York

Helen Meeker turned her gaze from President Roosevelt back to Reggie Fister. Sometimes during times of war, doing the right thing for your country often meant going against every emotion in your heart. By shooting this man, had she sealed a death sentence for her partner and the sister she barely knew? And would she be able to live with herself if those two special people died thanks to her seemingly rash decision? With the clock ticking and both Reese and Alison in the hands of Fister's unknown confederates, she sensed that question would haunt her the rest of her life.

She turned her attention from FDR to the room's main door when six more Secret Service agents rushed in with guns drawn. They had taken long enough. She'd pulled the trigger of her Colt more than two minutes ago.

To these trained professionals, the scene must have looked like something out of a poorly scripted B movie. The smell of gunpowder hovered in the air, and two men lay bleeding on the floor. Yet in the face of all the violence and chaos, the leaders of the free world seemed calm. Roosevelt leaned back in his chair, and lit a cigarette, while Churchill scowled like an angry bulldog at the wounded and bleeding man on the carpet.

Secret Service agent Clay Barnes jerked the onetime British army hero off the floor and shoved him into a wooden chair. After handcuffing the man's left wrist to the arm of the antique, he turned toward the other agents. "Get the doc."

One agent left, but the others stood there with perplexed expressions.

"The fun is over, so you can put those guns away. Helen seems to have the situation well under control."

Before Meeker had a chance to even blush, the White House physician rushed onto the scene. He charged past the agents like an Olympic sprinter headed toward the finish line.

"What have we got here?" he asked breathlessly, medical bag in hand.

Meeker knew the dry-witted doctor well. A short, blocky, gray-haired man in his fifties, Cleveland Mills had been the head surgeon at New York Mercy before being asked to look after the President and his staff. Now, the father of three served as a fourth in bridge more often than as a medical caregiver. But at the moment, his top-notch skills were needed, and he was eager to knock off the rust and use them.

"The hero turned out to be a louse," Barnes explained, pointing to Fister. "But he needs some medical care before we haul him off to a jail cell."

"What about that man?" Mills gestured toward Nigel Andrews.

"The British scoundrel shot him." The agent soberly shook his head. "Probably dead before he hit the floor."

The doctor rubbed his chin. "Well, if you're sure the living one is properly restrained, I'll take a look."

Barnes scoffed. "If he tries to run away, he'll be dragging a heavy, century-old chair with him."

After collapsing onto the couch in exhaustion, Meeker watched the White House doctor examine the wrist she'd shot. Though she had no medical training, she'd seen several injuries like Fister's and knew his wasn't fatal. After all, she hadn't intended to kill him, just render him harmless.

Still, she doubted his wound would heal completely before he faced the gallows. In times of war, justice was dealt out quickly and with no mercy. Still, unless she worked some kind of miracle, Fister probably had more time to draw breath than Alison or Reese did. The innocent were not favored over the guilty in the game of life.

Though anxious to begin her search for her sister and partner, Meeker felt obligated to hold her position until this matter was fully cleared up.

As her eyes were glued on the doctor's efforts to clean and dress Fister's wound, she heard the British leader whispering to her boss.

"We can't let this little drama leak to the press. If newspapers in the UK or the US reported that a British hero tried to kill me, that would upset everything we English stand for."

"It wouldn't look good for a war hero to be exposed as a Nazi spy either," the President replied flatly. He took a long draw from his cigarette holder. "Besides, neither one of us is supposed to be on an estate in New York. As far as the world is concerned, I'm in Washington and you're in London. We can't blow this cover. So what story do you suggest?"

Churchill shrugged. "I'm certain my people can come up with a reason for Colonel Fister to disappear. Perhaps a plane crash or some such thing. And Corporal Andrews could be on the same flight." He looked at Nigel and shook his head. "Shame about the lad. He saved our lives."

FDR nodded. "Helen gets a large part of the credit for that too. After all, if she hadn't shot your hero, our wives would be planning our funerals."

Pretending to ignore the chatter, Meeker kept her eyes on Nigel Andrews's still body. His precious Becky would never see him again. And the cause of his death would be forever masked in a lie. Andrews had put his life on the line for his country. But no one would ever know.

"Wonder if we'll ever find out what really went down," Roosevelt mused.

The British leader sighed. "I doubt it. Colonel Fister talked my ear off as we drove up here, but I'm sure he'll clam up now."

As Meeker waited for the President's response, she thought she saw Andrew's right hand twitch. Could Fister's shot have missed its mark?

She hurried across the room, bent over the fallen Brit and grabbed his wrist. She felt a faint pulse.

"Doctor," she yelled, "Andrews is still alive!"

The physician looked up from his work. "Finish wrapping this up," he barked to a Secret Service man. After handing him a roll of gauze, Mills picked up his bag and rushed to the man he'd been assured was dead. After a quick examination, he ordered, "Get him on the couch."

Two agents who had been waiting for something to do lifted Andrews to the spot where Meeker had been sitting a few minutes before. The doctor ripped open his jacket and shirt and examined the chest wound. Andrews's eyes fluttered and opened.

His gaze locked onto Meeker. "Are Churchill and Roosevelt all right?" he croaked out.

"They're fine," Meeker assured him. "And we got Fister."

Andrews breathed a sigh and closed his eyes. "I'm not a spy. I couldn't turn on Great Britain."

"Everyone knows that now."

The doctor turned back to the agents. "We need to transport this man to the nearest hospital. Have you got a wagon?"

Barnes nodded. "We always have an ambulance on call. It's behind the house. What about Fister?"

Mills shook his head. "Just have your man finish wrapping that wrist. His wound is nothing a prison doc can't handle."

As the physician went back to cleaning the gunshot wound, Andrews lifted his head. "I need to talk to Miss Meeker."

"You need to rest, son," Mills advised. "You've lost a lot of blood. You could fog out on us at any moment. Save your talking till later."

"No," Andrews hissed. "A man's life is on the line."

The doctor peered at Meeker. "You can listen to what he has to say, but don't get in my way."

"Yes, sir." She knelt beside the couch and leaned close to the injured man's ear.

"Find the Lord's Rest," Andrews whispered, his voice faint but steady.

"I did. It's an old house in Jerusalem, New York. I've been there."

"Good." He sighed. "So you got him away from them."

"Got who away from whom?"

"The FBI agent."

"Henry Reese?"

"Yes. I heard two guys say they were taking him to the Lord's Rest."

A cold chill ran down Meeker's spine. She'd set that place on fire when she rescued the Shellmeyer girl. If Henry was in there, he would have been burned alive.

She drew closer to the Brit's face. "When did they grab Henry?"

"Just before dawn."

"Where?"

"Just outside of Elmira. I had a flat tire and Reese caught up with me. Before I could tell him my story, a car pulled up, and two men jumped out and started shooting."

Andrews took three shallow gasps before continuing. "I ran

off. Hid in the woods. When Reese ran out of ammunition, they knocked him out and threw him into their vehicle. That's when I heard them talking about where they were going."

Meeker's heart lurched. Elmira was close enough to the Lord's Rest that they probably got Reese there before she arrived and torched the place. She hadn't checked all of the rooms before she found the girl. Had she left her partner to die in that fire? The thought chilled her to the bone.

Andrews's breathing became more labored. The doctor shot Meeker a warning glare. But she had to get as many answers as she could.

"Were the men who got Henry German agents? Did one of them have a tattoo just above his hand?"

Andrews's eyes closed as he slipped out of consciousness.

Meeker gasped. "Is he—?"

"He'll be fine," the doctor assured her. "But I don't expect he'll wake before tomorrow night."

That wasn't soon enough. Vaulting to her feet, Meeker whirled around and glared at Reggie Fister.

He grinned at her. "What's wrong, Helen? You look as though you've seen a ghost."

Meeker marched across the room to the recently unmasked enemy spy. "What do you know about the Lord's Rest?" she demanded.

"I have no idea what you're talking about." He shrugged. "Sounds like a funeral home to me, which is most likely where Reese should be. Let me know when the services are and I'll send flowers."

Meeker drew back her arm and brought her palm and fingers full force against Fister's cheek. To her deep disappointment, he didn't even flinch.

"My, don't we have a temper?" He raised an eyebrow at her. "You certainly didn't act this way when I held you in my arms and whispered those tempting lies in your ears."

Blood rushed to Meeker's cheeks.

Fister chuckled. "That's right. You were just part of the assignment. My job was to shift your attention. So I fed you lines to get your focus off the case. And you wanted me. I saw it in your eyes and heard it in your voice. One more romantic night and I would've had you."

"You're disgusting," she spat. "And if anything happens to Henry or Alison, I will make sure you pay!"

Fister winked. "I look forward to you trying to do that."

Her heart pounding, Meeker bit her tongue and moved back to where Barnes stood. She grabbed his arm and yanked him out into the hall, where Fister couldn't overhear her. "We don't have much time if we're going to save my sister."

"And Reese."

Meeker choked back a sob. "I'm afraid we might be too late to save Henry."

The Secret Service agent crossed his arms. "What do you mean?"

"I need you to check out a house that burned down earlier today just outside Jerusalem, New York. It's called the Lord's Rest. You'll find at least two bodies in the ashes: men who were working with the Germans and likely Fister. But you may find a third one too.

"Henry?"

"Get an FBI team up there as soon as possible. Take control of that crime scene and dig through every piece of debris."

The agent nodded. "As soon as the phones come back up, I'll take care of it." He smiled. "But I'll bet we don't find Henry in the rubble. He's a pretty crafty guy. He can get out of pretty much anything."

"I hope you're right," she replied softly.

"You need anything else?"

"Yeah. Keep after Fister until he breaks. Pound him and pound him, and don't let him sleep. Anything he says, no matter how insignificant it might seem, write it down."

"What if he doesn't break before the deadline? He said if he wasn't at the pickup site before ten o'clock on Friday night, both Reese and Alison would be killed."

Meeker groaned. Like she needed to be reminded of that little detail.

"Maybe we should let him keep his appointment. We've made trades in the past for spies."

She rubbed her hands over her arms in an effort to shake a chill. "The government can't let Fister go, even if it means saving Alison's life. That's not the way things work, and you know it."

Barnes nodded.

"Our only hope is to find my sister—and Reese, if he's still alive—before the deadline. And Friday night will be here all too fast, so you need to get moving."

"You got it." Barnes took off down the hall.

Meeker hoped her old partner would forgive her, but since blood was thicker than water, she was going after her sister first.

CHAPTER 3

Tuesday, March 17, 1942
12:01 p.m.
Ten miles south of Springfield, Illinois

Fredrick Bauer knocked on the back wall of the sixty-year-old frame barn. As he gazed at the empty horse stall to his right, the hardwood floor in the stall dropped a few inches and slid open. After glancing over his shoulder to make sure he was not being observed, Bauer walked down the steep stairs.

Fifteen steps later, he entered a brightly lit twenty-by-sixty-foot chamber that looked more like a laboratory than a cellar. He had taken five years to design and create this place. A wide variety of testing equipment sat on a half dozen tables. With a full surgical center on the far side and a gun range at the back, he had everything he needed here. Outside of the FBI, this was likely the finest crime lab in the country. That thought brought him a tremendous sense of accomplishment and pride.

The most remarkable facet of this operation was that only a

handful of people knew of its existence.

A woman with high cheekbones and wide shoulders looked up from behind a desk as he crossed the room. She wore dark-framed glasses, a straight black skirt, a simple white blouse, and flats. Her blonde hair was tightly secured in a librarian's bun, and there were no signs of makeup on her pale skin.

Her expression was even more severe and detached than her appearance. If she felt any emotion, she disguised it well.

After closing a file she'd been reading and placing it to one side, she ran her long, thin fingers over her starched collar and stood. Her stance was almost military—two-by-fours were more pliable. Though her eyes studied him, she remained mute, showing she knew her place.

"Emma," Bauer asked, "how is our prisoner?"

"He is fine, sir."

Good. They would be needing him very soon. And he'd have to be in perfect shape.

Bauer strolled past the woman toward a cell in the far wall. This captive was his ace in the hole, the centerpiece of a plan that would finally be put into operation. After pulling a key from his coat pocket, he opened a windowless door and glanced in. The room's tall, ruggedly built guest looked up from his bunk, his eyes glowing in the light.

Emma came up from behind. "Is there something I should know?" she whispered.

Bauer shut and bolted the door. "Our operation last night did not go as planned," he explained.

"What do we do now?"

He walked around Emma and returned to the room's entry. When he arrived at the stairs, he stopped. "The less you know the better. You just make sure our guest stays healthy."

"Yes, sir."

He marched up four steps, then turned. "Once we get all the information we need, a team will come here to prepare him."

"Dr. Snider?"

"Yes, and two others."

Bauer climbed the remaining steps. Once back on the barn's main level, he stepped aside and waited for the secret panel to close. Once it was secure, he walked to one of the building's side doors.

As he stepped out into the sunshine, he looked across the snow-swept landscape. He'd warned Fister that a woman would be his undoing. Thankfully, he'd set a plan in place just in case Helen Meeker figured things out. The meddlesome woman would be busy in Arkansas while Bauer and his team went to work springing Fister from FBI custody. All things considered, this would make for an interesting challenge. Those were good for keeping the mind sharp.

Pushing his hands into his pants pockets, Bauer walked to the century-old farmhouse where Abraham Lincoln had once spent the night. After pouring a cup of tea, he turned his console Zenith radio on, tuned it to a classical music station and smiled as the sounds of Wagner filled the room. He picked up the copy of *Gone with the Wind* that he'd left on top of the radio, found a dog-eared page, settled into a chair, and escaped into another time and place.

CHAPTER 4

Tuesday, March 17, 1942
2:05 p.m.
Albany, New York

After the warden at the city jail made sure Fister's right wrist received a second examination, a bit of treatment and a fresh bandage, he took the spy to a small conference room and handcuffed his left arm to a table. Clay Barnes followed every step of the way.

This was new territory for the tall, dark-haired, thirty-five-year-old Secret Service agent. He wasn't used to either looking after a prisoner or being asked to pull information from him. But with the power and communication issues caused by the storm, Barnes had to fill that role until an FBI agent arrived and took Fister off his hands.

As the cocky and seemingly relaxed Brit settled into a chair, Barnes sat across the small table from him. Crossing his arms, he began his interrogation.

"This will go easier if you just give me the information I need now."

Fister raised an eyebrow. "You know that's not going to happen." His tone was not defiant, but assured and confident. He grinned and leaned back in his chair. "So I guess it's your move."

Two people's lives were on the line. Barnes had to get beyond that smug attitude and make this traitor uncomfortable enough to talk.

"Okay, Reggie … Can I call you Reggie?"

"Fine with me."

"Well, Reggie, here's what's going to happen. I'm going to pester you with questions. Incessantly. You're not going to eat, sleep, or even lie down. You won't be allowed to go to the bathroom without a guard at your side. Those handcuffs will start chafing. You'll get drowsy. Your muscles will beg for fuel, and your mind will start to fog over. You'll begin to want sleep more than anything in the world." Barnes lifted his bushy eyebrows. "No one can hold out forever. Even the strongest man breaks at some point."

"But I'm not a normal man," Fister bragged. "That's why I have this job. My skin is thick, my will strong, and my brain sharp. But, if it helps you pass time, you may go on with your lecture."

Barnes ignored the taunt. He looked the prisoner in the eye and leaned forward over the table. "Just for sport, I'll make the first question an easy one. Where is Alison?"

"Which Alison?" Fister shot back. "I've known a number of Alisons. There was a lovely blonde in Dublin, with the voice of a meadowlark and the morals of an alley cat. Then there was Alison in Paris. She was dark and sultry, and she loved my accent."

Taking a deep breath, Barnes forced a smile. "If you're so smart, I shouldn't have to explain which Alison I'm interested in."

Fister grinned. "If you mean Helen's sister, I don't know where she is. I've never even met her. But I do know we have her. And Henry Reese too."

"So where are they?"

Fister laughed. "All you have to do to save them is let me go." He shrugged. "Two for one sounds like a pretty good deal to me."

Barnes slammed his right fist on the metal table so hard that the dull ringing echoed for several seconds. "I can get tough if I need to. I could bring my fist down on the back of your head and drive your nose into that table, and I would enjoy it thoroughly."

The thought of working over the handsome face of this traitor appealed to Barnes more than he wanted to admit. In fact, the only thing keeping him from beating the man to death was his professional resolve and his personal faith. As the son of a Methodist preacher, he couldn't allow his burning rage for this individual to dictate his actions. If he did, he would never be able to face his father again.

But he couldn't let Fister know that. He had to convince him that he would break his neck on a moment's notice.

A flicker outside the window drew Barnes to cross the room. The clouds had lifted, and lights glowed in the buildings below. The phones would probably be working again within hours. That meant Fister would soon be the FBI's problem. And they wouldn't just ask a few questions. With one of their own having been kidnapped, their interrogation would get ugly.

Turning to face the prisoner, Barnes dropped his arms to his side and slid his hands into his trouser pockets. "So you put into motion a plan that included killing the free world's greatest leaders, but you don't even know what happened to the two people who got kidnapped?"

"Who said I put the plan in motion?" Fister shot back. "I just knew about it." His drumming fingers on the table caused the handcuffs to rattle on the surface. "Do you think I'm the brains here? I don't call the shots."

"Then who does?"

"Someone I've never met. I'm just a player in all this. I have no more power than you do. We both just do what we're told. The difference is, this game is fun for me. I enjoy playing with people's hearts and lives."

Barnes pointed his index finger at the prisoner. "You honestly expect me to believe you're powerless?"

Fister shrugged. "You believed I was a hero, didn't you?"

Barnes hated to admit that Fister was right. But everyone had been fooled. They'd all been awed by this handsome man, even bragged to friends and family that they'd met him. But he couldn't give Fister the satisfaction of knowing he'd hoodwinked them.

"My job was to take out Churchill and Roosevelt. I failed. But the people who tell me what to do had a backup plan in place just in case things didn't work.

"How long have you been working for the Nazis?"

Fister looked toward the ceiling. "Isn't there supposed to be a single overhead light shining directly into my eyes?" He leveled his gaze at Barnes. "You're not very good at this, are you?"

"I'm leaving the tried-and-true stuff for the FBI. My approach is different. I'll treat you like a man and not a stray dog, even though placing that label on you would insult a flea-bitten hound."

"Was that supposed to hurt?" Fister laughed, then rested his elbows on the table. "Let me tell you what you should be saying. 'Okay, Reggie, I'm going to get out my knife and slowly peel back the skin from your body. I'll begin at your toes and work my way up to your head. If that doesn't make you talk, I'll fillet you like a trout. But no matter how much pain you're in, I won't let you die.' That's how this game is played. You need to get with the program, Clay."

"Maybe they play that way on your side," Barnes growled. He stood and leaned against the wall. "You want to know how I figured out what side you were playing for?"

"Could be interesting." Fister shrugged. "Besides, you might as well talk, since I'm not going to."

"Reason number one. You were fighting the Nazis in France when your unit was attacked. All of your men escaped. You were left behind, but somehow you weren't killed. The Nazis would've skinned you alive if you'd been captured."

"Interesting. Go on."

"Reason number two. You tried to kill the President and the prime minister, then shot the man who figured it out. The fact that your supposed best friend turned on you speaks volumes."

"Don't forget the part where I turned Helen Meeker's head," Fister cut in. "Have you ever kissed her, Barnes? She's a real good kisser. There's passion burning in that woman. She's like a volcano ready to explode."

Barnes knew the prisoner was trying to get under his skin and cause him to lose focus. He was experienced enough to let the jabs roll off his back and move on. "So clearly, you were working for the Germans."

Fister blinked. "Really? I don't seem to recall that. You'll have to show me my official Nazi employment records."

Barnes walked back to the table, retook his seat, and leaned toward his guest. "You do know you're going to die, right?"

"So are you," Fister noted, almost gleefully. "We all die at some point."

"Your date with the grim reaper will be determined by your value and the information you share. If you want to continue breathing, you need to help us get Reese and Alison back safely. If you don't, I wouldn't be surprised if old Winston himself did the honors of ending your life. I understand he was a pretty good marksman during the first world war."

Fister grinned. "Having Winston take me out personally. Not a bad way to go." He said it as if the thought brought him some kind of sick joy.

Fister sighed. "Clay, you bore me. Everything's black and

white to you. You think this is all about good and evil. If I'm not on FDR's side, I must be on Hitler's payroll."

"You have just defined the times we live in."

"What if I'm on neither?"

"No one can be neutral. You're either on the right side or the wrong side."

Fister smiled. "You're wrong, Clay. War offers tremendous opportunities for profit. Poor men die so wealthy men can become even wealthier."

"What are you saying?"

"There are profiteers in your midst. You work with them. You think they're all draped in the American flag. But the people I'm talking about are draped in green dollars rather than red, white, and blue patriotism. They'd sell their souls and their country for what you Americans call bucks. But they're not Nazis."

What was Fister talking about? Was he just killing time? Or hinting at something profound?

Either way, the cocky prisoner had just revealed his Achilles' heel.

Barnes pushed back his chair and exited the small room without another word to Fister. If he was right, he had to track down Helen Meeker. And fast.

CHAPTER 5

Tuesday, March 17, 1942
4:07 p.m.
St. Louis, Missouri

Helen Meeker drove her yellow Packard to New York, where she caught a military plane to St. Louis. At just past four in the afternoon in the "Show Me" state, she booked a commercial flight to Little Rock. While waiting in the airport for the plane to arrive, she used a pay phone to call her office at the White House, grateful that phone service was back up.

"Good to hear from you, Miss Meeker," said Rose, the receptionist on duty at this hour. "The president told me to expect your call."

"Any messages for me?"

"Just one. Clay Barnes. He's in Albany."

Meeker grabbed a pen and paper from her purse. "Did he leave a number?"

"Jupiter 2-7500."

"Got it. I need to call him right away. Please tell the President I'll check in when I have news."

"Will do."

Meeker pushed the lever down on the pay phone, then let it back up. When she heard a dial tone, she pressed the O key. When the Bell Telephone operator came on the line, Meeker provided her identification, call authorization code, and the number in Albany. Three operators and four minutes later, the Secret Service agent answered.

"Is that you, Helen?"

"Yeah." Considering the recent storms, the connection was surprisingly good. "You have some updates for me?"

"I called the college. Your sister isn't there, but the school doesn't consider her to be missing. She's on a geology field trip at a state park. She's with four other students and a professor. They checked into a lodge yesterday. So apparently Fister was bluffing."

"Did you speak to Alison?"

"No. But the official at the college told me they're probably out on trails, looking at rock formations. Most likely won't come in till after dark."

"Until I hear her voice, I won't be convinced. Where is this park?"

"About an hour and a half northwest of Little Rock. It's called Petit Jean."

"I'm at the St. Louis airport right now, waiting for a flight to Little Rock. Can you have a car ready for me at the airport so I can drive up there tonight?"

"I'm a step ahead of you. There's a vehicle the FBI grabbed in a recent raid just waiting for you. It's not a new model, but they claim it runs good."

As long as it got her to the park, she'd be happy. "What's the name of the professor in charge of this outing?"

"Dr. William Manning."

After jotting down the name, Meeker asked, "You get anything from Fister?"

"He talks a lot, but not about anything that matters. The FBI has him now, but I doubt they'll get much either. To him this is all a game."

"Spying is hardly a game."

"Oh, he refuses to admit he's working for either the Germans or the Italians. He talked about some organization he's a part of, but he didn't name it. Just kept rambling about money and power and how we're all blind as to who is really running the show."

"He can lie with the best of them." Meeker knew that from personal experience. "Did the FBI find anything at the Lord's Rest?"

"They dug four bodies out of the rubble. But the lab can't identify who they are. Until they identify one of them as Reese, I'm going to assume he's alive."

"I hope you're right. You got any other leads?"

"Well …" Barnes paused. "There is something unique about this whole mess."

"What's that?"

"The FBI checked into the medical workup Fister had when he was examined at Walter Reed a couple of weeks ago. All the chest wounds checked out just as he said they happened in Germany."

"That's not a shock. I would expect his cover to match in every detail."

"More surprising is Fister's blood type. He's B negative. Very rare."

Meeker shrugged. "That's what I am."

"Well, the two of you are in less than two percent of the world population. But it gets stranger."

"Go on."

"Fister's blood is unlike anything the doctors have ever seen. It seems almost supercharged to enhance healing. The place where you shot him looks like it's a few weeks old, not hours."

A chill raced down Meeker's spine. "That is odd." She wondered if the Nazis were on the verge of creating some kind of new super-warrior.

"The FBI doctors have taken blood samples. Rebecca Bobbs is studying them in the lab now."

"I suggest you alert the President to that news."

"Will do."

A series of loudspeakers droned, "Flight seventy-seven to Little Rock is now boarding."

"I've got to go. But first, tell me who's meeting me in Little Rock."

"An FBI agent named George Wheeler. He knows the area and the people. Used to work as a state patrolman. I informed him that you will be driving to the park."

"Good." Meeker smiled. "Call him if you get any new information while I'm on my flight."

"You got it."

Meeker dropped the phone into the cradle, grabbed her bag, and rushed to the gate. After presenting her ticket, she climbed the portable steps into the DC-3's cabin, found a seat and all but fell into it. She needed sleep, but sleep didn't come easily. After thirty minutes of tossing and turning, she finally dropped off into a fitful slumber where she was haunted by the image of Reggie Fister's sly grin.

CHAPTER 6

Tuesday March 17, 1942
5:10 p.m.
Ten miles south of Springfield, Illinois

Fredrick Bauer strode down the steps into the barn's underground chamber. At the bottom of the stairs he stopped, the air causing his nose to burn. The lab reeked of a bizarre combination of ether and gunpowder. The strange mishmash of odors made him smile. The work he'd ordered was being done.

Emma sat behind her desk, dressed in her usual straight black skirt, simple white blouse, and flats. She didn't look up from the file she was reading until he reached her desk.

"Snider is operating now," she reported.

"Good." Bauer glanced toward the surgical area, which was surrounded by a series of pulled curtains. The plan was on schedule. That was all that mattered.

"He brought a man and a woman with him. I was not introduced to them."

"You don't need to know who they are." Bauer glared at her.

Emma cringed, but she did not argue. "The man set up the shooting, and the woman assisted the doctor, but neither of them said a word the whole time. I found it unnerving." She paused, as if hoping for an explanation, which he did not provide. "So many people who come here never say anything. They just look at me with mournful stares."

"Those people are paid well to do a specific job, and they do it," he snapped. "The world would be a far more efficient place if everyone took their work as seriously as those who visit this facility."

"They could at least exchange a greeting," she muttered. Catching herself, she lowered her gaze. "I'm sorry. I shouldn't have said anything."

"Emma, there are times when too much knowledge is a dangerous thing. By not telling you more than you need to know, I'm actually doing you a favor."

"Yes, sir. I appreciate that. But ..."

"But you still want to know why so many of our visitors say nothing when they're here."

She nodded.

Bauer sighed. "They don't speak because they can't."

Her face contorted into a look of utter confusion.

"If they could speak, I wouldn't be able to use them."

Emma gazed toward the curtains as if thinking over what she'd just heard. After more than a minute of quiet contemplation, her expression still indicated that she didn't fully comprehend.

"They are mute, Emma."

Her eyes remained locked on the curtain. "All of them?"

Before Bauer could answer, one of the curtains was pulled back. A short, hunch-shouldered, balding man in his sixties emerged, wearing a white surgical gown and cap. He stopped by a trash can, removed the gloves from his long, thin fingers, and lumbered over to the desk. "Would you like a report?"

Bauer touched Emma's shoulder. "Please go to your quarters for about fifteen minutes."

She nodded and climbed the stairs. When he could no longer hear her footsteps on the barn floor, Bauer turn his attention back to the doctor. "You may talk freely now."

Snider sat on the edge of the desk. "Everything is as it should be. Parker and Sullins did their jobs perfectly."

"When can we move him?"

"Within a few hours."

"Good. We should have a location targeted by tonight."

Snider glanced back toward the operating room. "I've heard a rumor," he whispered.

"Rumors are for bored housewives," Bauer snapped. "You are neither bored nor a housewife." Seeing Snider's hurt reaction, he softened his expression and tone. "How long have we known each other, Eric?"

"Twenty years."

"Then don't beat around the bush. Ask me what you want to know."

With a sigh of relief, the doctor leaned close. "I heard we lost the facility in New York."

"It burned down," Bauer said without emotion.

"And the men there?"

"They died."

"I see."

Bauer patted the man's shoulder. "Those we lost were expendable. Better that they died than to fall into the hands of the FBI."

"But I knew one of those men."

"I hired all four of them. But they performed a service, like soldiers on a battlefield. You need to keep your eye on the big picture."

Snider shook his head. "The older I get, the harder that is to do."

Bauer patted his friend's back. "Go back to your mansion in Chicago and relax. Spend some time with your friends at the club. I'll take care of the issues."

Snider wrung his hands. "But what if someone talks? It would ruin me."

"Who knows about your work on this project?"

"The two people who assisted me today."

"And they can't speak. We brought them here blindfolded, so they don't know where this place is. And they don't know your name."

"What about the woman?" Snider shot a glance at the stairway.

"Emma is just another piece of machinery. If she gets too curious or looks like she might reveal us, she will be replaced. And she will never tell her story, I can assure you of that. You have nothing to fear, Eric. So just sit back and enjoy the spoils of your work."

"I guess you're right."

"Of course I am. Now, get out of here. In an hour, two of my associates will arrive to deliver your patient to our handlers in the east. And it would complicate their lives and yours if you were still here when they arrived. You see, they can talk."

Snider stripped off his surgical coat, dropped it on the desk, picked up his jacket, and raced up the steps.

After the doctor was gone, Bauer turned his gaze back to the curtains. He smiled. It was almost time.

CHAPTER 7

Tuesday, March 17, 1942
6:33 p.m.
Little Rock, Arkansas

As soon as Helen Meeker walked out of her plane and into the small airport lobby, she spotted a tall, wide-shouldered man with a broad chin and dark hair. With his black suit, white shirt, and studious glare, George Wheeler looked like Dick Tracy come to life.

When he spotted her, his grimace turned into a grin. "You must be Helen Meeker," he said in a deep voice as he stepped forward and extended his hand.

"And why do I *have* to be Helen Meeker?" she cracked.

"Because Barnes told me you'd be the most beautiful woman on the plane."

She rolled her eyes. After only a few hours of sleep over the last three days, she doubted she looked anywhere close to her best. But she accepted the compliment and his hand with a smile.

"You hungry?"

"I had something on the plane."

"Then I'm guessing you want to head for that park. Let me take your bag."

Meeker pulled on her coat over her dark-blue suit as they headed for the exit. Emerging into the cool evening air, she glanced up at the clouds. They looked ominous. "Where's our car?"

Wheeler pointed to the third vehicle along the curb. "It's the black Auburn sedan with the red trim and wheels. Sorry it's such an old model, but my assigned car was in an accident yesterday, so I had to take what I could get."

"Accident?" She raised her eyebrows as he moved toward the driver's side of the Indiana-built car.

He shrugged but didn't bother explaining until they were out of the airport parking lot. "I was tracking a couple of robbery suspects. They held up a bank in Hot Springs and used a stolen Texas car for the getaway. I got them almost to the state patrol roadblock when they opened fire on me. Pretty much destroyed my Ford's lights, radiator, and front tires."

"Did they get away?"

"'Fraid so."

"At least you weren't hurt."

"Not a scratch." He shook his head as if he were disappointed not to have been injured.

She glanced into the wide, deeply padded backseat. "What's

the story on this car?"

"It was used by some hoods that were running a backroom casino in Hot Springs. They were doing pretty well until they tried to muscle in on some of Lucky Luciano's friends."

"Luciano has been in prison for years."

"He still runs things from behind bars."

That didn't surprise her. "His lawyer came to the White House a while back, offering Luciano's service to the war effort. He claims he has the connections in Europe to get several crime families involved in the war against the Axis powers."

"He probably does have some pull. He's got his fingers in all kinds of things in Hot Springs. And his New York operation may not be as strong as it once was, but it's still bringing in the cash."

Whoever said crime doesn't pay clearly didn't know what he was talking about.

Wheeler downshifted and made a right turn. "The men who owned this car made the wrong guys mad, and they ended up at the bottom of the Ouachita River. The FBI gathered up the spoils, including this beauty. It might not look modern, but I like the art-deco styling, and the car handles nicely. Takes the curves as well as any car I've ever driven."

"Pull over," Meeker ordered.

"Why?"

She grinned. "I want to see what this thing will do."

He parked on the side of the road. "Barnes warned me about you."

"Then get ready to hang on," she suggested.

After they switched seats, Wheeler asked, "Hey, aren't you

supposed to be catching me up on why you're here?"

"Don't worry. I can do that and drive at the same time."

CHAPTER 8

Tuesday, March 17, 1942
7:00 p.m.
Petit Jean State Park, Arkansas

The trip to the lodge should have taken about two hours, but with Helen Meeker driving, she and George Wheeler arrived in just under ninety-five minutes. They left a lot of Goodyear rubber on the Arkansas curves, and the FBI agent seemed to have aged at least five years.

Meeker was at the check-in counter by the time the woozy agent had pulled himself together and entered the rambling one-story, rock-and-log building. She ignored Wheeler's ashen face and focused on the short, thin, gray-headed park ranger. "My name is Helen Meeker. I'm with FDR's office. My associate is with the Little Rock branch of the FBI. His name is George Wheeler."

"I'm John Stacks. Do you need rooms?"

"No, we need information. Some students from Ouachita College are here on a field trip. The man in charge is a professor named Manning."

"Dr. Bill." Stacks grinned. "We love that guy. He brings students up here all the time."

"Are he and his group here now?"

"Haven't seen them since supper last night." The ranger rubbed his jaw. "But their car is here, so they must be in the park. Is something wrong?"

"I hope not. Could you take us to their rooms?"

"Sure." Stacks grabbed a set of brass-plated keys and stepped out from behind the counter. "Follow me."

Meeker and Wheeler followed their guide out the front door of the main lodge, across a native-stone patio, to the lodge's far wing. When they got halfway down the hall, he stopped at room 11 and knocked. No one answered. He repeated his efforts at 13 and 15, with the same results.

"Guess they're out." He shrugged. "You want me to open one?"

Meeker nodded.

Stacks unlocked the door to a small, cedar-walled, simply furnished room with a bed, dresser, small desk, and two chairs. "Dr. Bill must still have them out on the trail."

"They aren't out there," Meeker said.

"How do you know?"

She pointed to the far side of the room. "Those shoes are covered with mud. So are the clothes on the dresser. Clearly the girls came back from the hike, cleaned up, and changed clothes."

"What about the guys?" Wheeler asked.

They checked the other two rooms and found work clothes and muddy boots there as well.

"They're not in the dining room," the ranger noted. "I would've seen them walk by the front desk." He looked at the clouds. "With rain threatening, I doubt they'd be outside. Not in their good clothes."

"Where is their car?" Meeker asked.

"It's in the same parking space it's been in since they arrived two days ago. You want to see it?"

She shook her head. "If it hasn't moved, that would be a waste of time." Meeker ran her fingers through her dark auburn hair, took a final look around the room, and stepped back into the hall. With the men following, she exited the building and marched back to the main lodge.

She glanced into the dining room. A half dozen people, all over forty, sat in the large open area, enjoying a game of cards. A pot-bellied, balding man with twinkling eyes and a broad smile sported a six-sided silver star on his chest.

Meeker was about to cross the room to talk with this local sheriff when the phone on the counter rang.

Stacks picked it up. "Hello?" After a short pause, he said, "Yes, he's here. Just a second." The ranger walked to the dining room entrance and yelled out, "Paul, it's for you."

The lawman nodded to his friends, dropped his cards on the table, and lumbered to the desk. After silently acknowledging Meeker and Wheeler, he took the phone from Stacks. "This is Sheriff Faulkner. What do you need?" After a few moments, he said, "I'll be there in half an hour to pick him up. Keep your eye on him and try to keep him calm."

As he set the receiver back into the cradle, the ranger asked, "Something wrong?"

"Not really." Faulkner shook his head. "Old Jed is at the sauce again. Seems he barged into Mable Landis's house acting like he'd seen a ghost. She got him settled down, but I need to get over there and take him to the jail to sleep it off."

"Excuse me, Sheriff," Meeker said, taking a step toward the large man. "Could I ask you a few questions?"

Faulkner raised his eyebrows and smiled. "Been a long time since a pretty young thing like you asked me for anything. What can I do for you, ma'am?"

"My name is Helen Meeker. I work for the President. This is George Wheeler. He's with the FBI. We're looking for a group of students from Ouachita College. We have reason to believe foul play might be involved."

"Oh, I doubt that." The lawman shot her a smile that was probably meant to be comforting. "Kids get lost on hikes all the time when they want to, uh … have a good time. What with the war going on, a lot of them are trying to get their good times in now, because they don't know how many they'll have. I'm sure your group will turn up eventually."

"I'm not so sure." Meeker bristled at the man's insinuation and lack of concern. "One of those kids is my sister, and there are some people who might be trying to use her to settle a score with the President."

"I see." Faulkner's easygoing demeanor turned serious. "I

haven't seen anything suspicious. But if you want to follow me to Morrilton, I'll be happy to do what I can—once I get Jed squared away."

"Thanks." She turned to Sparks. "Don't let anyone into those rooms. They need to stay locked until we have a chance to fully investigate them."

CHAPTER 9

Tuesday, March 17, 1942
7:35 p.m.
Ten miles south of Springfield, Illinois

Fredrick Bauer watched the two big men push his prisoner into a 1938 Oldsmobile sedan. They weren't as gentle as Bauer would have liked, but as long as they got the human parcel to its destination alive, it didn't matter.

"When do you need him in New York?" the taller one asked.

"Things are moving faster than I figured they would," Bauer replied. "They're transporting our man tomorrow night. So I need this cargo to be outside of Albany by five in the afternoon. You got that, Mr. James?" Bauer sneered, using the man's pseudonym.

"Yes, sir."

"The address of the safe house is in the packet I gave you when you and Franks arrived. So is half the cash. I'm sure I don't have to remind you of the price you'll pay if you fail me."

The broad-shouldered, dark-headed man stood straighter. "You've made that clear every time we've worked together. But we haven't missed yet."

"Clearly not, or you wouldn't be standing here," Bauer stated. "Now, listen closely. There will be two men in the safe house. You'll call them Smith and Jones. They will respond by saying, 'You must be James and Franks.' If you don't hear those names, they're not the right men. Got it?"

The man nodded.

"After the introductions, you will say a sentence that includes the words 'Boston Red Sox.' They will respond by saying something about Babe Ruth. You will answer with a phrase that includes 'Worst trade ever.' If you mess up on any of that, they will kill you—no questions asked. If they mess up, you kill them, and then call me for further instructions."

"That's a lot of checks and balances."

"There have to be. The FBI and the Secret Service are in on this now. We need to make sure they haven't captured Smith and Jones and substituted someone else for them."

The man grinned, his open mouth showing a gap between his front teeth. "Are their real names actually Smith and Jones?"

Bauer raised a brow. "Are you two really James and Franks?" He stuck his hands in his pockets and shook his head. "Look, I don't care what their real names are, and I don't want to know. It's safer for everyone that way. But I know where to find them if I need to get rid of them."

War was a cold business. It had to be conducted without

emotion and with little regard for human life. Loyalties couldn't shift. And though Bauer realized that James and Franks knew that, he still felt a need to emphasize that they were always one mistake away from the grave.

He turned his attention to the two men standing beside the massive automobile. "If all of the passwords are delivered perfectly, you turn your package over to them."

James shrugged. "Wish all the jobs you gave us were this simple."

Bauer gave him a cold stare. "Getting the package to the destination in less than twenty-four hours won't be easy."

James chuckled. "We have a plane waiting on the outskirts of Springfield. We'll make it with time to spare."

"Is the pilot someone you trust?"

"Without question." Franks stood tall. "I'm the pilot, and it's my plane. And as far as the Feds are concerned, I'm delivering materials to an industrial plant in New York. And since I picked up a shipment of radio tubes in St. Louis this morning that has to be in New York tomorrow, our cover is perfect."

Bauer narrowed his eyes at Franks. "Just make sure no one sees our package."

"They won't. I have a hidden baggage area just for special items like this."

Bauer yanked his hands out of the pockets of his overcoat and ambled to the car. He glanced through the back window at the bound and gagged man lying on the floorboard. He wasn't ready to write Reggie Fister off yet. It was time to play his trump card.

CHAPTER 10

Tuesday, March 17, 1942
11:44 p.m.
Morrilton, Arkansas

"They're back, I tell you. They want their money, and I don't have it!"

Helen Meeker stared at the disheveled little man sitting in an old wooden chair in front of the sheriff's desk. If ever someone fit the term *loony*, this poor guy was it. The sad human being had slipped into a world where nightmares were real and daily life was a fantasy.

"Two of them held a gun on me today. They're really serious now. You have to believe me!"

Jed Tanner, dressed in worn-out brown dress pants, a tattered and dirty white shirt, scuffed black shoes, and a shiny tan suit jacket, could not sit still. He was dripping with sweat in spite of the chill in the air. His wild green eyes constantly dashed from one side of the room to the other. His thinning blond hair looked as though it hadn't been combed in weeks, and he was three days beyond needing a shave.

The last time Meeker had seen someone like this was in a psych ward. And that was where this poor man needed to be.

After crossing and recrossing one leg over another, and slapping at some unseen creature that he seemed to believe was hovering in the air just above his head, Tanner continued his rant. "I wanted to give them their money. I really did. But we ran out." His eyes found Faulkner. "They trusted me, Paul, and I failed them. And they won't let me forget it. They'll never leave me alone!"

The heavyset sheriff crossed the room and switched on a 1937 console-model Aircastle radio. After it warmed up, he moved the dial until he found a station playing big-band music. As the strains of Kay Kyser's version of "The White Cliffs of Dover" played, the wild man in the chair began to calm down. Within seconds he was relaxed and humming along with the band.

With the situation now under control, Faulkner signaled for Meeker and Wheeler to follow him outside. Once the door was closed, the sheriff pulled a pack of Camels from his pocket and tapped one out into his hand. "Want one?"

Meeker shook her head.

Wheeler said, "I don't smoke."

After putting the cigarette between his lips, Faulkner pulled out a lighter, flipped the top, and lit the rolled tobacco. After a few puffs he looked at the nearly vacant downtown street. "Jed was the president and owner of State Bank when the Depression hit." His voice had the cadence and tone of an undertaker. "There was a run on the bank. He kept his people until there was no cash left. A lot of his customers lost everything they had. Most of them recovered eventually. Jed never did. He spent some time in a mental hospital, but after he was released, his nightmares continued to haunt him. He started drinking almost nonstop. But there isn't enough booze in the world to allow him to forgive himself."

"What kind of nightmares did he have?" Wheeler asked.

"Mostly about a farm family coming into the bank with their three little kids and their elderly grandmother, pleading with him for their money. See, the Bakers left town not long after they came into the bank asking for their money. Since Jed couldn't give them any, they headed to California to hopefully find work. They were all killed in a traffic accident in Oklahoma. When Jed heard about their deaths, he fell apart. Even tried to kill himself, but the doctor got the poison pumped out in time."

The sheriff glanced in the window. "Music is about all that calms him down these days." He took a few more puffs, then tossed the cigarette butt onto the sidewalk and watched it burn for a few seconds before stepping on it with this boot. "I thought he'd sobered up. I would've sworn he hadn't had a drink in months. But it looks like he fell off the wagon."

Meeker tapped her toe on the sidewalk. While this was a mildly interesting story, the clock was ticking. It was almost midnight and she hadn't found her sister. "Sheriff, we need to find out if anyone in town saw the missing students."

As if he hadn't even heard her, Faulkner's eyes remained locked on a corner a block to the south. "The old bank building's down there. It looks pretty much the same as it did on the day of the run. No one ever bought it. Not surprising. I mean, what can you do with a bank building?"

The sheriff shook his head. "Even though he doesn't own it anymore, Jed still has the keys. He goes in there when he's having one of his spells. Countless times I've found him inside the vault on his hands and knees, trying to find money. So sad. And I think he's actually getting worse."

"How so?" Wheeler asked.

"His hallucinations are becoming stranger and more vivid. Instead of ghosts from the Baker family, now he's claiming to see two men with guns." Faulkner continued to study Tanner. "No one ever held a gun on him in real life. Guess he's just slipping deeper into the fantasy world he calls home."

Meeker strolled over to the window and glanced in at the little man. "You say these episodes are triggered by alcohol?"

Faulkner's sad eyes reflected his deep concern for his friend. "When he's sober, he's still haunted, but not delusional."

"I stood right next to him," Meeker said. "I didn't smell any booze."

Leaving the two men to puzzle over her observation, she opened the office door and returned to Tanner's side. She leaned close to the man's face and took a deep breath. Satisfied he hadn't been drinking, she turned off the radio, ending Woody Herman's "Blues in the Night" before it finished. The puzzled man glanced up at her. "Mr. Tanner," she said softly, "my name is Helen. Did you go to the bank tonight?"

He shook his head. "Not tonight. Earlier today."

"And was the Baker family there?"

"No. Got some new customers this time. I guess they wanted to open an account. I told them we didn't have any money. Tried to direct them to the National Bank. But they never said a word."

"Did they have guns?"

"Two of them did. And one of them tried to shoot me. But when he pulled the trigger, the gun didn't fire."

"What happened then?"

"They shoved me into the safe with the others."

"What others, Jed?"

"There was an older gentleman and four young people. Two girls and two boys."

"How did you get away?"

After swatting at something only he could see, Tanner closed his eyes.

"Jed, what happened to the other people? Do you know where they went?"

Jerking his shoulders from side to side, the little man rubbed his hand over his face. Then he looked off into the distance. "The two men with guns came into the vault with us. While one of them aimed a gun at us, the other one started beating up the kids. I wanted to make him stop. And then I realized I could. And it was easy too."

Meeker gently touched Tanner's shoulder. "Jed," she whispered, "how did you stop the man from beating on the kids?"

He shook his head. "I thought it was a nightmare. I figured if I couldn't see it, it wouldn't be real."

"What did you do, Jed?"

"When they weren't watching me," he explained with a sly

grin, "I snuck out of the vault and closed the door. But it didn't work. Even after I shut it, they were still in my head." He stood and yelled, "They won't leave me alone!"

"You locked them in the safe?" she shouted over the man's screams.

"Yes."

Meeker looked to the sheriff. "The students and the men who took them are locked in the bank vault. We have to get them out before they run out of air." She returned her attention to Tanner. "Jed, you have to open that vault."

"I can't," he cried. "I don't know the combination. They changed it after the bank failure."

Meeker glanced at the sheriff. "Is that true?"

"Sure is. And the man who had it changed died in 1939. Nobody knows how to open that vault."

"My Lord," Tanner sobbed, his eyes wide. "They were real people. And I killed them." Falling to his knees, he grabbed his head and screamed loud enough to wake the dead.

CHAPTER 11

Wednesday, March 18, 1942
12:09 a.m.
Morrilton, Arkansas

After climbing the five twenty-foot-wide concrete steps of the State Bank building, Helen Meeker used Jed Tanner's key to open the deserted bank's ten-foot-tall, windowed door. As she entered the dark, cold building, her heels echoed on the marble floor. While not frantic, she was deeply concerned. If she was going to save the people Tanner had locked in the vault, she'd have to move quickly. Based on what the deranged man had said, they'd been in there at least six hours.

The sheriff and the FBI agent followed her inside.

"I don't suppose there's any power in here," she muttered.

Faulkner ran his hand up the plaster wall to the right of the door and pushed a button. Three bulbs dimly lit the interior of the fifty-year-old brick building.

With its thirty-foot ceiling, brass light fixtures, and etched walls, this must have been one of the most impressive small-town banks in Arkansas at one time. Now it was a ghost of what had been … and perhaps a tomb to what could be.

"The city pays the electric bill," the sheriff explained as Meeker and Wheeler looked around the lobby. "It's safer to have power than not to. Besides, we're still trying to find a buyer for this place."

"Where's the vault?" Meeker asked.

"Through the main room and to your right."

She marched past six teller cages and a large table sporting pens, deposit slips, and complimentary calendars for 1929. Toward the back of the lobby were two offices. Tanner's name was painted on the frosted glass of the room to her right. Just beyond that office was a fifteen-by-fifteen-foot metal door with what looked like a large ship's wheel in the center of it.

"That vault is bigger than my office on the inside," Faulkner said. "When I was a kid, I thought it could hold all the money in the world."

"That's good," Wheeler noted. "The larger the area, the greater supply of air for the people inside."

Meeker grabbed the large metal wheel and pulled. The door didn't move. She made a fist and banged it against the door.

"They can't hear you," the sheriff said. "The door and walls are almost two feet thick."

She stared at the round lock in the center of the wheel. "And no one knows the combination?"

"Not anyone who's still alive," Faulkner said. "And there's

not a locksmith in the state who could open this thing. Drills would wear out before doing any real damage."

Wheeler stepped into the office beside the vault and studied the adjoining wall. "Is the chamber as deep as this room?"

"They're exactly the same depth," Faulkner said.

After strolling back to the lobby, the agent pulled a pencil from his pocket and grabbed a deposit slip from the table. He jotted something down, studied his notations, then announced, "Based on my calculations, they can likely stay alive for another seven to ten hours."

"How do you know that?" the sheriff asked.

Wheeler shrugged. "I actually had a question about people locked in an airtight room in one of my college algebra classes. I was the only one to get it right."

Meeker turned to the sheriff. "Maybe the people who made this safe could tell us how to open it."

Faulkner sighed. "The manufacturer was in San Francisco. But they're out of business now."

She raked a hand through her hair, trying to stay focused. She couldn't lose her head just because her sister was likely inside. She had to treat this as objectively as any other problem or she'd go crazy.

"I can't imagine what they must be going through in there," Wheeler mumbled. "Locked in a soundproof room, with no idea whether anyone even knows they're there. The situation must seem hopeless."

Ignoring the ominous thought, Meeker studied the vault door's smooth, cold metal. "When you can't do something yourself," she whispered to herself, "you go to an expert." She looked back at the sheriff. "Is your office unlocked?"

He nodded.

"Good. You two stay here and try to come up with a viable idea. I'm going to go make a phone call."

Meeker rushed out of the bank, barreled down the steps, and ran the block to the sheriff's office as fast as she could in high heels. Not bothering to close the front door, she raced across the room and sank into the seat behind the desk. Panting, she lifted the receiver and dialed zero. When the operator came on she asked for Long Distance. Ten minutes later FBI agent Collins answered.

"Do you know what time it is?" he moaned after she identified herself.

Meeker was all too keenly aware of the passing of time right now. "I need to talk to Stan, the lock expert from the robbery we foiled at the Continental Bank on March fifth."

"But he's in the city jail right now—thanks to you."

"I know. But there are some people trapped in a locked bank vault, and I need a pro to get them out."

"Is it on a time lock?"

"No. The bank closed up shop more than a decade ago, and the man who knew the combination is dead. I've got to get this thing open or seven people will die."

"Even if Stan Weiss could handle the job, he couldn't get there in time."

"I realize that," Meeker snapped, "but he might know someone in this area who could. I'm at the sheriff's office in

Morrilton, Arkansas. The number is Madison 4-6551. Have Stan call me here as soon as possible."

"Will do," Collins replied.

"And just in case Stan doesn't know anyone good in Arkansas or Oklahoma, call the office and get them digging through the files to find a safecracker."

"I'll call them on my way to the jail." Collins hung up.

CHAPTER 12

Wednesday, March 18, 1942
1:29 a.m.
Morrilton, Arkansas

As she sat in the sheriff's swivel chair, impatiently waiting for the call from Collins about a safecracker, Helen Meeker considered her limited options. Beyond what she had just put into motion, she could think of none.

As the Seth Thomas wall clock ticked minutes away, she tried to remain calm and focused. But with lives hanging in the balance, time seemed to be racing by.

At half past one, the phone finally rang. She snatched up the receiver and jammed it to her ear. "Helen Meeker."

"Long-distance call from the Washington DC city jail."

"Put it through."

"Miss Meeker, this is Stan Weiss. Agent Collins told me what's going on. He said if I help you I can get a break in my sentence. Is that true?"

"I work for the President, Stan. I can make it happen."

"What do you need?"

Meeker brought the man up to speed. "No one knows the combination to the vault. And the company that made it is out of business."

"Was the company located in San Francisco?" Weiss asked.

"How did you know?"

"Safetylock is the only major safe maker that's no longer in the game. They went under in 1933. Their machines are hard to crack. Guys like me hate them."

"Not what I wanted to hear," Meeker muttered.

"That doesn't mean I can't do it. But it would take me a good hour or so. Most safes I can open in less than ten minutes. But even if I got on a plane right now, I couldn't get to where you are in time to save those people."

"I realize that. Is there anyone in this area who could do the job?"

"Only one that I know of. Casper Light. Folks call him Fingers. He's serving a twenty-year stretch in Malvern, Arkansas. He's got a lot of talent, but he's as mean as a snake. Don't ever turn your back on him. I did that once."

Meeker searched through the sheriff's desk drawers for a map. Finding one, she unfolded it. After thirty seconds she spotted Malvern. Doing some quick math, she figured Fingers could get to her location in about three hours.

"Thanks, Stan. I'll see you get a break."

"I appreciate that. At my age, there's no telling how much longer I'll last in stir."

"Is Agent Collins with you?" she asked.

"Yeah."

"Put him on, please."

A few seconds later the FBI agent was on the line.

"Collins, I need you to get the prison to transport Casper Light here to do the job."

"I'll do what I can."

"You can't drag your feet on this. Seven people will die if we don't get them out by six o'clock."

"Got it."

"Call me at this number in one hour. In the meantime, I'll go back to the bank and fill in Wheeler and Faulkner on what's going on."

"Good luck."

"Thanks. We'll need it."

Meeker figured it would take Collins at least a half hour to spring Fingers from the Malvern unit of the Arkansas Penal System. But that was only the beginning of the process. Would the state troopers be able to bring the safecracker to Morrilton, and would the convict be able to free the seven vault prisoners from a sure date with death?

Never had the clocked ticked so loudly or the minutes moved so quickly.

CHAPTER 13

Wednesday, March 18, 1942
5:55 a.m.
Morrilton, Arkansas

"What time is it?" Helen Meeker asked George Wheeler as she paced in front of the vault.

The agent, who was sitting in an old chair near the bank's front door, checked his watch. "A few minutes before six."

She inhaled a quick breath. "How much time do we have to open the vault before it runs out of air?"

He shrugged. "Somewhere between one and four hours."

That was far too big a gap. Meeker preferred clear facts over vague estimates.

At the sound of a car outside, the agent glanced out the large plate-glass window that overlooked the streets of the town. "Sheriff's back. Has someone with him."

Meeker held her position. It was too soon for the safe-cracker to arrive, and right now the only person she wanted to see was Fingers.

Faulkner strolled into the building accompanied by a black man in a denim jacket, white shirt, bib overalls, and a St. Louis Browns baseball cap. "Helen, George, this is Alf Greene. He runs the garage about a half block behind this building."

"Nice to meet you." Wheeler extended his hand.

"Alf, tell these two folks what you saw yesterday."

The short, thin man crossed his arms over his chest. "About three o'clock, a man walked into my place and handed me a note. It said that he and some friends were having car trouble and he'd pay me a hundred bucks, plus the cost of the parts, to get their vehicle running. So we hopped into my tow truck and drove out to a spot on Highway 154 near Perry, where an old Hudson was pulled over to the side of the road. Two girls, two boys, an older man, and a young, tough-looking guy stood in the woods nearby. As I got out of my truck, I waved, but none of them waved back."

Meeker narrowed her eyes. "You didn't talk to any of them?"

"Nope. And they didn't talk to me."

"Go on," Faulkner said. "Tell the story just like you told it to me."

"When I looked under the hood, I realized the water pump had seized up. Then the belt broke and flew into the radiator, which caused a leak. I told the man with the note that I'd need to get the car back to my shop. Then I'd see if Western Auto had the pump and belt. The guy didn't say anything, but he nodded. I took that as a yes."

Greene ran his hand over his slick head. "After I got the car hooked up to my truck, the guy handed me another note. It said they wanted me to tow the car with all the passengers riding in it. I told him it'd be better for my truck if the Hudson was empty, but the guy shook his head and pulled out a fifty-dollar bill. So, I did it their way."

How odd that someone would communicate everything through written notes. Perhaps the man was mute. But were all of his friends unable to speak as well?

"When we got to my garage, the man helped me push the car into my building. The rest of the group walked down the alley. I figured they were going to get something to eat."

Meeker doubted that. More likely they needed a place to hide out for a couple of hours. Probably picked the first vacant building they could get into.

"The man waited at my shop while I went and got the parts. After I came back, he gave me a note asking how long the repair would take. I told him the car would be ready by six, and he walked out my back door. That was the last I saw of him. The car is still in my shop."

"Why do you suppose they didn't speak?" the sheriff asked.

"Maybe they were foreigners," Wheeler suggested.

"But the notes were written in English," Meeker said.

"You need anything else from me?" Greene asked.

"No," Meeker replied. "But thanks for the information."

"You're welcome," the mechanic said with a smile.

Moments after Greene left, another car pulled up to the curb just outside the bank building. Three men got out of the backseat. Two were state patrolmen. The other was a short, thin man in prison stripes. He was pale, skinny, about six feet tall. His gaunt face was pockmarked, his eyes dark and menacing, and his hands cuffed.

As soon as the three men came through the front door, Meeker led them to the back of the bank. When they reached the vault door, she said, "Get the cuffs off him and let him go to work."

Fingers smiled as one of the lawmen unlocked his hands. After rubbing his bony wrists, he examined the vault door. "Been a while since I've seen one of these. June of 1926, to be exact. In San Diego. We got away with fifty grand on that job."

Meeker ignored his bragging. "Think you can do it again?"

The convict grinned. "I'm one of only five men in the country who can talk to this baby and get it to listen. Assuming you got a stethoscope."

Wheeler reached into his coat pocket, retrieved the medical instrument, and handed it to the safecracker. Fingers cradled it in his hands. "Rene Laennec sure made my work a lot easier."

"Who?" Wheeler asked.

"The Frenchman who invented the stethoscope." Fingers positioned the small tubes into his ears.

"How long?" Meeker demanded.

He knelt before the vault door and placed his right hand on the dial. "Might be less than a minute. Could take an hour."

"Make it closer to a minute, okay?"

He raised an eyebrow. "I need everyone to be as quiet as a church mouse. Just sit back and watch an artist at work."

Holding the stethoscope's bell to the door, Fingers fixated his attention on his work, seemingly unaware that anyone else was in the room. As the minutes passed, everyone but Wheeler found a wall to lean against. He sat in a chair, crossed one leg over the other, popped his neck, and closed his eyes.

Time dragged. Six ten became six thirty and then six fifty. For Meeker every minute was an eternity. Each moment brought those in the vault closer to death.

As she waited, she thought of the few memories she and Alison had created since they reunited. There should have been many more. Why had she let her work get in the way of bonding with her only living relative?

If, by the time the door opened, everyone inside had died, their deaths would be on her head. This wasn't crazy Jed's doing. She bore the full responsibility.

As Meeker mentally beat herself up, the thin man in stripes continued to play with the locking mechanism on the door, his face never changing expression.

At just before seven o'clock, Fingers rose to his knees and smiled.

"Is it done?" Meeker asked.

"There's just one number left."

"Then do it," Meeker demanded.

"As soon as everyone hands me their guns."

"What?" Faulkner barked.

"I want a get-out-of-jail card for opening up this can."

The sheriff pulled out his Smith & Wesson and aimed it the grinning con. "You get back to work or I'll shoot you."

"Then the seven people in this vault will die."

"How do we know you'll finish the job and let them out?"

Meeker asked.

"All I'm asking for is the chance to get away. Just drop your guns at my feet. While you're rescuing the folks inside, I take off."

"We'll catch you before you get very far," one of the troopers taunted him.

"Probably." Fingers shrugged. "But if I get even an hour or a day or a week of freedom before you do, it'll be worth it."

The lead trooper turned to Wheeler. "It's your call."

The FBI agent reached into his coat, pulled out his service revolver, and slid it across the dusty marble floor to the safe-cracker. The two troopers and Faulkner followed suit.

Smiling, Fingers picked up all but one of the weapons and emptied the chambers. The last gun he stuck in his belt.

"Where are the keys to your car?" Fingers asked the sheriff.

"In the ignition."

"You parked right in front of the one they brought me up here in?"

"Yep."

The safecracker looked at the lead trooper. "And where's your car key?"

"In my pocket."

"Slide it over to me."

The cop did as instructed.

"You got what you wanted, now get on with it," Meeker growled.

Fingers turned back to the vault's massive door. He spun the large wheel, then pulled the lever. A second later he yanked the door open about three inches. "It has been a pleasure serving the FBI."

As Fingers made his escape, gun in hand, Wheeler pulled the vault door wide open. Two young men and two women sat in the center of the large, open area.

"Alison," Meeker whispered.

The beautiful college student smiled as she stood. "It took you long enough."

After hugging her sister, Meeker asked, "Are you okay?"

"I'm fine. But one of the two men who kidnapped us died a couple of hours ago. I think he had a heart attack. And Dr. Manning is kind of sick."

Meeker followed her gaze to a pale older man, his eyes red and his shoulders hunched. Behind him stood a large, solidly built young man with a gun in his hand.

When the remaining kidnapper realized his rescuers were unarmed, he darted past them to the main exit and raced out the door.

As the lawmen retrieved their weapons and ammunition, Meeker ran to the lobby, pulled the gun out of her purse, and hurried to the front door. She stepped outside just as the young man was about to enter a grocery store. She aimed her Colt at his left knee. "Stop or I'll shoot."

He turned and raised his gun. Before he could squeeze the trigger, Meeker fired. He fell face forward onto the street. A second later, the two troopers emerged from the bank, brandishing their weapons. One ran toward the downed man. The other got into the patrol car and sped in the direction Fingers had gone.

Meeker stepped back into the bank.

"The man in the vault is dead," Wheeler announced. "I recognize him. His name's Richard Barton. He worked for Lucky Luciano in Hot Springs." The agent scratched his head. "Moving from organized crime to working for the Nazis seems like a strange career choice."

"I clipped the kidnapper so he couldn't fly. Maybe he can explain what's going on."

Wheeler shook his head. "Not going to happen. Barton has no tongue, so I imagine this guy doesn't either."

"Excuse me?"

"Barton's has been cut out," he replied matter-of-factly. "Probably the same with all of them."

Meeker shuddered. That explained the notes. But who would do such a thing?

"Too bad the safecracker got away," Wheeler said.

Faulkner chuckled. "He won't go far. My car was running on fumes. I was going to fill it up this morning. Glad I didn't."

Meeker forced a weak smile as she turned to her sister. "Alison, you're coming home with me."

"What about school?"

"We'll work something out. But until we find Henry Reese, I don't want you to be alone. You understand?"

"Yeah. I'll miss my friends, but I wouldn't want anyone to have to go through something like this."

"What's your next move?" Wheeler asked.

"I'm going back to New York," Meeker explained. "I'm hoping the man the FBI is holding can give me the clue I need to find the best partner I ever had."

CHAPTER 14

Wednesday, March 18, 1942
3:11 p.m.
Rural New York

At just past three in the afternoon, James and Franks drove up to the two-bedroom, white-frame home just outside the small Hudson River town of Cedar View, New York.

"You wait in the car with the package," James ordered as he slipped out from behind the wheel of the rented 1938 Ford sedan. After glancing over his shoulder toward the all-but-deserted highway, he ambled to the house's front stairs. Even though the cold north wind was biting into his cheeks, he climbed the four steps slowly, unsure as to who might be inside.

Once on the stoop, he rapped on the door. A few seconds later it was opened by a mountain of a man more than six and a half feet tall and likely two hundred fifty pounds. His dark complexion and deep black eyes hinted at Native American origins. Behind him stood a man who was six inches shorter but who looked equally strong and menacing.

"I'm looking for Smith and Jones."

The huge form blocking the door replied in voice deep enough to shake a large building, "You must be either James or Franks."

"I'm James. Franks is in the car with the package." He adjusted his tie, then added, "He's a Boston Red Sox fan."

"I always liked Babe Ruth."

"Franks still thinks sending the Babe to the Yankees was the worst trade ever."

Smith relaxed a bit, but his expression remained guarded. "Bring the package in. We'll take over from here."

James motioned to Franks, who got out, opened the passenger-side back door, and yanked the human cargo off the floorboard. The guy's mouth was gagged, his hands were bound, and he wore a blindfold.

After standing him up, Franks pushed him across the yard, up the stairs, and to the front door. Smith grasped the captive's shirt collar and pulled him into the house. Jones then led the man out of sight.

Smith reached into his pants pocket, pulled out an envelope, and handed it to James. "You can count it if you want, but it's all there."

Their work done, the men returned to the Ford. James didn't know what was going to happen to the prisoner. But with ten thousand dollars to split with Franks, he didn't much care.

CHAPTER 15

Thursday, March 19, 1942
8:09 a.m.
American Airlines Flight 39

Helen Meeker and her sister limited their conversations to small talk until after their plane lifted off the runway at the Little Rock airport.

"What's this all about?" Alison asked when the noise in the plane made eavesdropping impossible.

"I can't really tell you very much."

Alison nodded. "But what happened at the park when those men took us has something to do with your work with the President, doesn't it?"

"Yes."

"Do you know who they were?"

"Hired hoods from Cleveland. I interrogated the one who lived. He had no idea why they were doing the job. It was all about a paycheck for them."

Alison shook her head as if she found it hard to believe anyone would make a living like that.

"He told me that after the deadline passed he would have set you free, but I didn't believe him. You could identify them. So whoever hired them probably would have ordered them to kill you if things hadn't worked out the way they did."

"Not a very cheery thought." The girl sighed as she let her head fall back against the plane's seat.

Meeker shrugged. "It's a cruel world. Especially these days. Human life is as cheap as it has ever been. People seem to trade life with as little emotion and far less thought than folks on Wall Street trade stocks and bonds."

A stewardess walked up from the back of the plane and leaned over toward Meeker. "Nice to see you again, Helen."

She introduced the woman to Alison.

"The pilot just received a radio message that there will be a military plane in St. Louis for you two. A man will meet you at the airport gate and take you to your flight to New York."

Meeker smiled. "Thank you."

"My pleasure." The young woman straightened. "Love your suit. Where'd did you find it?"

"I didn't pack enough clothes for the trip, so my sister and I did some shopping yesterday. I found this in a store in downtown Little Rock. I think it was called Kathryn's."

"Next time we have a layover there, I'll have to check it out. Would you ladies like anything to drink?"

Meeker looked to Alison, who shook her head. "We're fine."

As the stewardess returned to the back of the plane, Alison leaned close to her sister. "Those men who kidnapped us never said a word, not to us or even to each other. Did you get the one you captured to talk to you?"

"Not exactly. He explained through written notes that they'd agreed to be made mute as a requirement for getting jobs. They each got twenty-five thousand dollars in exchange for having their tongues cut out." A shiver raced up her spine. "They didn't even know where the surgery was performed. They were blindfolded the entire time."

"Who would let someone take their voice away?"

Meeker took a moment to formulate her answer. "It happens all the time. But usually the people who let someone take their voices can still talk. They just stop doing it."

Alison's forehead puckered. "What are you saying?"

"If you don't read, study, and think for yourself, then your words are just a reflection of what other people tell you. That's what happened in Germany. The people lost their voice to Hitler. In fact, they freely gave their voices to him. They allowed him to call the shots and they did nothing but cheer. The ideas they embrace, the words they systematically repeat, are nothing more than directives placed in their minds and spewed out of their mouths, with little connection to their own thoughts. People like that might as well have their tongues cut out, because they've fallen into a cult-like mentality that feeds them slanted views and assures them that those opinions are the only ones that have substance."

Alison stared at her with wide eyes. “I just wanted to know why someone would allow someone else to cut out their tongue.”

“I know.” Meeker locked eyes with her sister. “But, please promise me you’ll find out what all sides think about an issue and then make up your mind based on what you believe, not what others tell you to believe. Because that’s basically what this war is all about. We’re fighting for the right to think and speak about and believe whatever we want. Having a press that gives a voice to all sides of an issue will prevent monsters like Hitler from rising to power.”

The startled look on her sister’s face made Meeker realize she’d been preaching. “Let’s talk about something else. Why don’t you tell me about the boys you like at school.”

While she tried to focus on Alison’s story about a young man named Cliff, her mind drifted to a man whose kiss still lingered on her lips. If Henry Reese died, she would never forgive herself for not telling him how she felt about him.

CHAPTER 16

Thursday, March 19
7:55 p.m.
Albany, New York

"You still have time to tell me what I need to know," Clay Barnes announced as he walked into the small, stark, brick cell at the Albany Police Station. "After all, your house of cards is falling apart."

Reggie Fister, dressed in prison stripes, grinned at the Secret Service agent. "Oh, I think it's your house that needs repair. Mine is still pretty strong. Especially since I'm holding two powerful wild cards. After all, you Americans are pretty sentimental when it comes to human life. I don't see you allowing Alison Meeker or Henry Reese to die just to keep me in custody."

Barnes looked at his watch. It was almost eight. Though Fister hadn't slept in days, he was nowhere near breaking. Still, since the man was going to be transported to a maximum-security unit soon, he decided to take one more shot at rattling the prisoner.

"You don't hold either of those wild cards anymore, Reggie."

Fister's head jerked and his eyes locked onto Barnes. "You're bluffing."

"Nope." He folded his arms and leaned against the cold brick wall. "Alison was freed earlier this morning and we have one of the two men who snatched her. The other one is dead."

For the first time, Fister actually looked surprised. "He won't talk."

"Obviously not." Barnes laughed. "But from what I hear, he's pretty prolific with a pencil. The FBI agent in Little Rock was even impressed with the guy's spelling."

Fister studied the tabletop for a few moments before returning his gaze to his interrogator. "You said I lost both of my cards."

"Several bodies were found in the rubble of the Lord's Rest. Henry and I were good friends. I hated to lose him. But at least he died doing what he loved."

The prisoner shrugged. "Those cards didn't mean anything anyway. They were merely diversions. And the man you caught can't give you anything you need."

Barnes pushed himself off the wall and strolled toward the door. "We have you, Alison is alive, and Reese died for his country. Game, set, match."

The guard opened the cell door to let Barnes out. Before he left, he added, "Oh, and Nigel Andrews is doing fine. Your shot missed all the vital organs. You can chew on those facts on your trip south."

As he savored his parting shot, a quartet of FBI agents brushed past Barnes. They marched into the cell, snapped handcuffs onto Fister, and led him out the door, down a hall, through a back entry, and to a waiting car. Barnes followed and watched the black Buick depart with someone who had once been considered a hero.

As the car faded from sight, he heard the clicking of high heels behind him. Turning, he looked into the beautiful eyes of Helen Meeker.

"Am I too late to see him off?" she asked.

"Yeah. Reggie Fister is on his way to a place so far removed from freedom that he might never see the sky or feel the warmth of the sun again."

She gazed down the now-vacant alley. "Too bad. I had a couple of questions I wanted to ask him."

"He wouldn't have given you straight answers. I know that from experience. But I did shake him up a little when I informed him that his two trump cards are void."

"We found Henry?" she asked, her voice infused with hope.

"No. But I let Reggie think his body was discovered in the ashes of that old house."

Disappointment clouded Helen's face and made her shoulders sag. "How are they transporting Fister?"

"You'll love this." Barnes chucked. "He's going by freight train, locked in a box car."

Helen chuckled. "Well, I'm heading back to Washington on Highway 9. Maybe I'll wave at the train as I drive by."

He put a hand on her upper arm. "You ought to take a day off. I doubt you've slept much this week."

Helen shook her head. “No days off until after we find Henry.”

That didn’t surprise Barnes a bit. “How’s your sister?” he asked, eager to change the subject.

“She’s okay. That girl is a real trooper. She’s in the front office right now. I’m planning to keep her close until we get this mess cleared up.”

“Good thinking. I’m sure you can find something for her to do at the White House. Can’t get much safer than that.”

They stood there for a few silent moments, staring down the alley Reggie Fister had just traveled. It was filled to overflowing with trash cans, loose newspapers, and empty bottles. That seemed an appropriate end to the man’s saga. He might never tell what he knew. But at least now he could no longer hurt anyone.

CHAPTER 17

Thursday, March 19, 1942
10:18 p.m.
US Highway 9 West

Helen Meeker's yellow Packard hummed along the highway on a clear night with temperatures in the low forties. Her sister sat in the passenger seat, gazing out the window at the rural countryside. They'd visited enough on the two flights to New York that they no longer needed to talk. Instead they hummed along with the music coming from the car's eight-inch radio speaker.

When familiar strains of a new tune came on the radio, Meeker said, "I know that song. But I don't recognize the singer. Do you know who he is?"

Alison smiled. "You really don't know the dreamy guy who sings 'Night and Day'?"

"Should I?"

"Do you remember the Tommy Dorsey Band's hit 'I'll Never Smile Again'?"

"Of course. I love it."

"Well, this guy was their singer on that record. He sang with Harry James for a while too. But now he's out on his own. The bobby-soxers all think he's dreamy."

"Dreamy?" Meeker laughed.

"Yeah. His name is Frank Sinatra. Frankie is what's buzzin' now."

"Buzzin'?"

"He's been on the radio a lot the past few weeks. He's leading the way and setting the trends."

"If you say so."

Alison giggled. "Really, Helen, you have to catch up on the lingo, get to know the glitterati."

"Glitterati?"

Alison rolled her eyes. "The people who are grabbing the spotlight and making waves. I can't believe you don't know that."

Meeker resisted telling her sister that she'd been too busy saving the free world to keep up with slang terminology. "So, are there other glitterati you like to listen to?" she asked, hoping she'd used the word right.

"Gosh, yes. Freddie Martin, Glenn Miller, Sammy Kaye, Benny Goodman. If it swings, I'm with it."

None of the names rang a bell with her. "Sounds like I might have to buy some new records."

"What's that?" Alison pointed to something up ahead.

Seeing a half dozen police cars, Meeker gently applied her brakes. The uniformed officers were stopping each car and searching seats and trunks.

"What do you think they're looking for?"

"I don't know. But hand me my purse. If I've already got my identification out, maybe we can get through this quicker."

As Meeker pulled up behind three other cars, a state trooper approached, holding a flashlight. When he got to her vehicle, she rolled down the window. "Something wrong?"

"A train derailed just ahead. The Feds had a prisoner in one of the cars and he escaped. We're looking for him."

Meeker's heart skipped a beat. She handed the cop her ID. "Was the prisoner's name Fister by any chance?"

"They didn't give us a name, just a description."

"Did the description include a bandage on the man's right hand?"

The trooper's eyes widened. "How did you know?"

"I'm a part of this case." She nodded at her identification.

The man glanced at the papers. "Holy cow, you work for the President."

"Yes. And I know the escaped prisoner, probably better than any of the FBI agents who are running this thing."

He handed the papers back to her. "I'll get on the radio and tell them you're here." He took off at a sprint.

"What's going on?" Alison asked.

Meeker took a deep breath. "The man who escaped from that train is one of the most dangerous people on earth. He's the reason you were kidnapped."

Alison gasped.

The uniformed man returned to the car. “About a mile up the road, there’s a two-story, red brick home just off the highway. That’s the temporary command center. I told the troopers to let you through.”

“Thanks.”

Since the cars in front of her had already gone through inspection, Meeker drove up to the roadblock. The officers waved her past the barricade.

Quickly pushing her vehicle up to fifty, she kept her eyes peeled for the meeting point. Seeing a group of men in suits standing at the end of a gravel lane, she turned in. They nodded as she passed.

As she pulled alongside about forty other cars, Meeker saw dozens of men rushing off into the woods and fields in several directions. The chaotic scene looked more like panic than plan.

She shut off the motor and looked at her sister. “I want you to go in with me. But you need to be quiet. Just follow me and try to stay in the background.”

“Got it.” Alison’s tone held excitement. To the college kid, this must seem like the adventure of a lifetime. To Meeker it was a nightmare.

Grabbing her purse, she stepped out of the vehicle. With her sister by her side, she crossed the yard and walked onto the porch. Barnes stood there, waiting for her.

“What happened?”

“The rails were disconnected at a spot in the middle of the woods, just before a bridge. About twenty cars ended up on their sides. The engineer and three firemen are dead."

"And what about Fister?"

"The car with him in it was near the back of the train, so it stayed upright. As soon as one of the FBI agents opened the door, someone tossed in a gas bomb. Before anyone knew what had happened, Fister was gone."

"How can I help?"

"You can identify Fister. So I'd suggest you go with one of the teams and look through houses in the wooded area."

"Sounds good." Meeker glanced at her sister. "What about Alison?"

"She can stay in the house with me."

"You're not joining the search?"

Barnes curled his lips. "The FBI doesn't want Secret Service involved."

Meeker bristled. The ridiculous rivalry between the two agencies caused many irritating delays.

"I'll take care of Alison. You go to the back of the house. Eugene Tyler's team is getting ready to take off."

After a quick hug, Meeker left her sister in Barnes's care.

Someone she knew had set up Fister's escape. Probably someone she talked to on a regular basis. But who?

There was no time to contemplate that right now. She had to help track down Fister before the man made a clean escape.

CHAPTER 18

Thursday, March 19, 1942
11:17 p.m.
Rural south central New York

Meeker studied FBI Agent Eugene Tyler as they left the command center to begin their search. The small man with a square jaw and dark eyes looked like a human Boston terrier. And his stern appearance fit perfectly with his no-nonsense approach.

He and his team of five men quickly and efficiently went through half a dozen homes and twice as many barns in a little over two hours. Fister was not in any of them.

The seventh home they came to was little more than a shell of a house. The broken windows and missing shingles indicated the building likely hadn't been lived in for at least twenty years.

"If it was a man, it would be a Republican," Meeker quipped.

The agent's brow furrowed. "What did you say?"

She shrugged. “The whole thing is leaning right.”

“There is no place for humor in the field,” Tyler growled.

Meeker disagreed. Humor was a requirement for sanity in a job like theirs. Clearly this man didn’t think so. “Most folks would walk right past this place without a second look. But if you wanted to evade a search party, this would suit you perfectly. Since no one lives here, there’s nobody to turn you in.”

Tyler turned to his men. “Go in with guns drawn. Search every inch of the place. If there’s an old can of beans in the pantry, I want to know about it.”

The men hustled to obey their orders.

Tyler looked at Meeker. “You coming in?”

“No. I’ll stay here and watch the yard.”

He shrugged. “Suit yourself.”

It took ten minutes for the men to explore every nook and cranny in the old house. As they reassembled outside the rear of the home, Tyler approached Meeker. “We didn’t find anything.”

“Not even a can of beans?” Meeker quipped.

Tyler glared at her. “I just hope the other groups are doing better than we are.”

The moment the words left his lips, a half-dozen shots rang out from the woods about twenty yards away. Two of the FBI agents fell to the ground, grabbing their shoulders. Everyone scrambled for cover.

After retrieving her Colt from her purse, Meeker crouched behind the south wall of the house, anticipating more fire. There was none.

“Why do you suppose he stopped shooting?” Tyler asked,

kneeling beside her.

"I want to know why he shot in the first place. We weren't onto him. Why would he call attention to himself?"

"Criminals aren't known for being bright," Tyler said, his eyes focused on the place where the gunshots had originated. "Most are impulsive. He probably just panicked."

Meeker shook her head. "I don't know about garden-variety criminals. But I do know Fister. He is anything but impulsive or stupid."

Tyler turned to his men, who were hiding behind nearby trees. "Cover me. On my signal."

Meeker chuckled. "Talk about impulsive and stupid …"

"I've got a job to do, woman," Tyler barked. "You just stay out of the way."

"It's your party."

Tyler groaned. Then he raised his pistol. "Now, men," he cried out.

The agent, gun blazing, stepped out from behind the house and sprinted toward the woods. The remainder of the team sprayed fire at the point where the shots had originated. Not a single round was returned.

When Tyler made it to the tree line, he stopped and peered into the eerily quiet darkness. He stepped into the woods, then reappeared a few moments later and waved for his party to join him. His team, even the two wounded ones, hurried to join their leader.

Meeker stayed put. "What did you find?" she hollered.

"Nothing," Tyler called back. "Just a few casings."

She shook her head. All those heroics for nothing.

The agents circled around their leader, likely planning their next move. Meeker sat on the ground and pondered the situation. Why would anyone shoot at them? And how had the shooter manage to elude the search party?

An idea hit her. “Tyler,” she yelled across the field. “Get over here.”

The man marched back to the abandoned house. “You got something?”

“How are the guys who were shot?”

“Lucky. Their wounds are little more than scratches.”

“That’s what I figured. I don’t think the shooter wanted them dead.”

Gun ready for action, Meeker crept toward a small, unnatural-looking hill in the otherwise level yard. Using her free hand, she pulled away some brush. “Looks like a root cellar to me.”

“Men,” Tyler hollered, “get over here.” They raced to his side. “Dobbs, open that door. Jenkins, shine your flashlight into the hole. Everyone else, prepare for action.”

Meeker put a staying hand on Dobbs’s arm. “We need whoever is in there alive. This could be the only person who could reveal whether there was a connection between those shots and the train crash.”

Dobbs, a blocky man of average height with coal-black hair and a round face, grabbed the door’s handle, swung it open, then quickly backed away. Jenkins’s light captured the form of a man huddled just inside the door. He was wearing prison stripes.

“Come out with your hands up,” Tyler ordered.

The man staggered forward, hands raised. He stopped ten feet in front of the agents. Though he lacked his usual swagger, Meeker immediately recognized the tall, rugged man with wavy hair and expressive eyes.

"Are you Reggie Fister?" Tyler asked.

"I am," came the soft reply.

CHAPTER 19

Friday, March 20, 1942
2:15 a.m.
Rural south central New York

Helen Meeker followed FBI agent Eugene Tyler as he escorted his prisoner back to the temporary command center. As they marched Fister into the house, Clay Barnes stepped out onto the porch. "You found him!"

"I did," Meeker acknowledged. "But I'm not sure why."

"What do you mean?"

"It was too easy. Why would someone wreck a train to spring a guy and then hand him right back to us?"

Barnes shrugged. "Maybe they needed something he knew, and after he gave them that information, they had no more use for him."

That made as much sense as anything else. And if it was true, perhaps Fister would roll over on those people now.

She stepped into the home and strode down a hall into the living room, where the captive sat handcuffed to a chair. In the room's bright light, there was no doubt this was Reggie Fister. The man who'd nearly charmed her into bed, and who'd planned on killing the president, now looked like a beaten dog.

"I need to talk to him alone," Meeker said.

"I don't think so," Tyler argued. "We're going to wait until the command leader gets here so he can work the guy over."

"You know, there are still killers on the loose out there. Why don't you and your men go find them?"

Tyler's face turned a deep shade of red. "I've had just about enough of you. I can do my job without the help of a woman. So why don't you just go back to your job as FDR's pet."

Meeker felt her blood boil. "You would never have found Fister if I hadn't discovered his hiding place," she growled. "The least you can do is step aside and let me have a few minutes with him. I've earned that much."

"You've earned nothing," Tyler shot back.

Barnes came into the room "Helen, the President is on the phone. He wants to know what information you've been able to get from Fister. I told him you haven't completed your interrogation yet. He sounded upset."

Meeker hid her satisfied smile and turned to Tyler. "Would you like to take that call and explain to the President of the United States why I haven't finished my job?"

Tyler's shoulders slumped. "I just don't understand why it's so important that you talk to him first."

"Because he might know where Henry Reese is. And since

I know this man better than anyone else, he's more likely to tell me than you." She caught the agent's gaze. "You do want Henry back on the force, don't you?"

"Of course."

"Then give me five minutes with Fister."

"Fine. But you can't talk to him alone."

"Okay. Then let Clay stay in here with me."

Tyler released a long sigh. "Fine. Have it your way."

Barnes smiled. "Let me go tell Mr. Roosevelt what's going on. I'll be right back." The Secret Service agent hurried off.

Meeker and Tyler waited, without making eye contact or conversation, until he returned.

"You've got five minutes," Tyler grumbled. He turned to his men. "Cover the door and windows. Make sure this prisoner does not get away."

After everyone but Barnes had left, Meeker faced Clay. "The President's call came at the perfect time."

Barnes grinned. "There was no call."

Meeker wanted to hug Clay. "Thanks."

She turned her attention to the prisoner. He sat listlessly in the chair, staring blankly ahead, as if unaware of anything going on around him. Seeing him look so disoriented, she almost felt sorry for him. "What is your name?"

"Reginald Fister." His words were slurred and his eyes unfocused.

"You already know who he is," Barnes whispered.

"Yes. But he's obviously been drugged. I asked that question to determine how aware he is."

Meeker lifted Fister's chin and peered into his pale-blue eyes. He didn't react.

Keenly aware of Tyler's five-minute time limit, she noticed blood had soaked through the bandage around Fister's wrist. She ripped off the tape and unwound the gauze. The wound had opened and was slowly dripping blood.

"It looks worse than it did this morning," Barnes observed. "He must have reinjured it trying to escape."

Meeker crouched before the prisoner. "Do you know who I am?"

He shook his head.

Meeker stood. Clearly, she wasn't going to get the information she needed from this shell of a man.

Tyler opened the door and marched in. "Time's up. He's ours now."

"You can have him," Meeker mumbled as she headed for the door.

"Where you going?" Barnes asked.

"Back to Washington." She glanced over her shoulder at Tyler. "When the drugs wear off, let the President know if he says anything."

"Oh, we'll make him talk." The agent's chest puffed with pride.

"We'll see."

CHAPTER 19

Saturday, March 21, 1942
9:07 a.m.
Washington, DC

Helen Meeker was already wide awake when her alarm went off. The President had demanded she get some rest, but her sleep had been fitful, to say the least. She dragged herself out of bed, got dressed, then sat on her bed, staring at nothing in an almost catatonic state.

When she heard a knock on her bedroom door, she croaked out, “Come in.”

Alison burst into the room, nearly clapping her hands in excitement. “Are we really going to the White House today?”

“Yes.” She took a deep breath and stood.

“I can’t wait to meet the President.”

“You’ll like him.” Meeker shuffled to the sink to brush her hair. “He has a dry wit and a quick smile.”

"I'm sure he's proud of you for helping to wrap up a huge case."

Alison perched on the edge of the bed and bounced on the mattress. Meeker stared into the mirror at the dark circles under her eyes. After covering them with a bit of makeup, she returned to her room, where her sister stared at her, wide-eyed.

"You caught the man the whole world wanted, but you haven't smiled once since we got home. You look like you've just lost your best friend."

"I may have," she whispered. Each hour that passed meant less of a chance that Henry Reese was still alive.

The ringing phone yanked Meeker out of her morbid thoughts. She picked up the receiver after the second ring. "Helen Meeker."

"This is the overseas operator. You have a call from London. The caller's name is Russell Strickland. Do you want to accept it?"

Meeker racked her exhausted brain, trying to remember where she'd heard that name. Then it came to her. He was the man the preacher was supposed to meet in Mississippi. Reese had told her he was in England now, working with the OSS. She'd asked Henry to track him down and see if he had any leads on Reggie Fister.

"Yes, please. Put him on."

Over a lot of static on the line, and strange noises in the background, she heard, "Miss Meeker?"

"Yes."

"I have a bit of information for you about Reginald Fister."

"Shoot," Helen pleaded as she grabbed a pencil and a scratch pad.

"He was born in a small town in Scotland. His father was Scottish and his mother German. They were both killed in a house fire when Reginald was two years old."

"And my theory about Reggie having an identical twin?" Meeker asked.

A tremendous booming noise sounded over the line. For a moment, she thought the call had been lost. Then Strickland's voice came back. "Sorry about that. The Germans are bombing us today. That last one came rather close."

"Are you safe?"

"I'll get to a shelter after I give you what you need."

"Then hurry, please."

"You were spot on. After the parents died, Alistair Fister was sent to live in a children's home in Germany. Reginald was shipped to the one in Edinburgh. I found no trace of what happened to either of them after that."

"Thanks." Another blast echoed through the phone line. "Now find someplace safe."

"I will."

As soon as Meeker set the receiver back in the cradle, Alison asked, "What was that all about?"

She gazed at her sister. "The FBI has Reggie Fister. But it's not the Fister they need."

"Huh?"

"The real Reggie Fister came to this country as an exchange student," she mused out loud. "But the Nazis nabbed him when they got his twin to spy for them. If the Fister who pretended to be a British hero was ever caught and unmasked, they would replace him with the twin. That was the plan all along. And it was brilliant! The train crash was staged to make the swap. That's why they shot at us … to make sure we found him."

Alison looked confused. "How did they know Fister was on that train?"

"We've got a mole. And I think I might know who it is. But I can't make a move until I'm sure." She grabbed her purse and coat. "You ready to meet my Uncle Franklin?"

"More than ready."

"Then get your coat and let's go."

The two women stepped out of the apartment and into a day that felt more like spring than late winter. When they got to Meeker's yellow Packard, Alison slid into the passenger side and immediately flipped on the radio and cranked up the volume. Tommy Dorsey's "Fools Rush In" filled the air.

As Meeker walked past the front bumper of her car, the voice she now recognized as Frank Sinatra's sang loud and clear. She paused and looked at the clear blue sky. In the face of all this beauty, and with the strains of a love song ringing in her ears, it was almost impossible to believe there was a war raging. Yet here she was, charging right into it.

As Frankie continued to croon about fools rushing in where angels were afraid to go, she shook her head. Was she a fool to live this kind of life, to chase these dreams? This was a dangerous game she was playing.

But if she hadn't been so foolhardy, Fister would have

accomplished his task, and Roosevelt and Churchill would be dead. And though she might have lost Reese, she did save her sister. And now she knew the truth about Reggie Fister.

No, Helen Meeker was no fool. And her "rushing in" had paid off. She was born to do this. And she would keep trying to save the world as long as she had breath in her body.

Feeling good about herself and the mission, she looked at her sister, who was staring at her, no doubt wondering why she hadn't gotten into the car yet.

Suddenly, two gunshots rang out. One bullet exploded through the windshield and buried itself in the cushion on the driver's seat. The second slammed into Meeker's chest, the impact pushing her into the sedan's massive grill.

For a second, she clawed at the hood, looking into Alison's bewildered face. As the strength oozed from her body, she slid down to the pavement. Her mind sank into a deep, dark black pool.

BEST SELLING AUTHOR

ACE COLLINS

Blood BROTHER

IN THE PRESIDENT'S SERVICE : EPISODE 3

To Alison

CHAPTER I

Saturday, March 21, 1942

9:19 a.m.

Washington, DC

The music blaring from the car radio was so loud Alison didn't hear the gunshot. So when her sister suddenly paused just in front of the car and then slowly dropped out of view, she had no idea why. But the pained and perplexed expression etched on Helen's face just before she fell told her something was horribly wrong.

Bolting upright, Alison yanked the door handle and scrambled out of the yellow Packard. Her black pumps barely touched the rubber-ribbed running board as she rushed around the passenger-side front fender. She found her sister awkwardly sprawled on the sidewalk, her right hand still grasping the sedan's massive bumper. Blood stained her jacket and blouse, and it was forming a dark puddle on the sidewalk.

"Helen!" Alison fell to her knees and placed her palm against her sister's face. "What happened?"

There was no response.

After taking a deep breath to steady her nerves, Alison pressed her hand against her sister's side. The rushing blood's wet warmth caused a chill to race down her spine. "Oh, Helen."

Someone must have shot her. But who would want to kill her sister? After all, the FBI had Reggie Fister in custody.

Her gaze jumped from the wound to Helen's face and back. *Think, girl! Get a hold of yourself. You took a first-aid course in college. What do you need to be doing?*

The most important task right now was to stop the bleeding. Alison ripped off her coat, balled it up, and pushed it against Helen's side.

Now she had to get her sister to a hospital.

She glanced around. The immediate area was void of life. There weren't even any cars rolling down the street. No one was walking a dog or riding a bike. Where was everybody?

Dear Lord, if ever you needed to send an angel, it's now. I need some help here!

Her head bobbed from side to side, scanning the surroundings. Not a soul appeared—human or angelic.

As the seconds rushed by, Alison fought an internal battle. Was she better off staying and continuing to press into the wound, trying to slow the bleeding, or should she race down the street and find someone who would call for help? She didn't know. But each moment that passed put her sister closer to death.

"Oh, Lord, please," she begged. "You have to help me."

From the corner of her eye, she caught movement. About

half a block down the street, a mailman emerged from behind a yellow-bricked apartment building less than a hundred steps away. The short, white-haired gentleman was sorting letters as if there were nothing else in the world that needed his attention.

When Alison cried out, he looked up. His face contorted in confusion, he froze in place, a half-dozen letters in each hand.

"Someone just shot my sister," Alison screamed. "Please get help."

As if hit by a bolt of lightning, the postman dropped the mail into his bag and hustled toward Alison. After taking a moment to assess the scene, he rushed across the street to a red-brick home. He raced up the house's six steps and rapped on the green wooden door until a portly, middle-aged woman pulled it open.

Alison couldn't hear the exchange between the two, but when the homeowner stepped out of the way to allow the postman in, she figured he must be calling for the police and an ambulance.

Turning her attention back to Helen, Alison pushed her hand more firmly against the coat, covering the angry wound. But were her efforts doing any good? Helen's eyes were closed, her mouth slightly open, her lips twitching. Blood was still pooling up on the sidewalk and now dripping off the curb.

Leaning close to her sister's face, Alison whispered, "Help's on the way. Just keep breathing." Yet her words rang hollow. Would help really get there in time? And was there anything they could do when they arrived?

This couldn't be happening. The danger was supposed to be over. The FBI had caught the only man who wanted to harm Helen.

Alison looked back at the house the postman had disappeared into. How long had it been? A minute? Five? She didn't know.

This was supposed to be a dream day. A few moments ago she was on her way to meet the President of the United States. Now she was watching the life drain from her only living family member.

With a start, she realized Helen was no longer moving. Even her lips were still. Gripped by panic, Alison touched her sister's neck. She couldn't feel a pulse. She moved her finger forward, then to the side. Still nothing.

Wait! Though the sensation was so weak she could barely feel it, it was definitely there. Helen's heart was still beating! At least for the moment.

As hopelessness transformed into a sliver of optimism, Alison heard running footsteps on the street behind her. A deep, out-of-breath voice said, "Help is on the way. How is she?"

Alison turned her eyes to meet those of the concerned postman. "I don't know. She's lost a lot of blood."

"What happened?"

"I'm guessing she was shot. But I didn't hear or see anything." Tears filled her eyes.

The sound of sirens brought Alison's attention to the street. A half-dozen blocks away, a police cruiser was closing in. A moment later, a red-and-white ambulance came into view behind it.

"Okay, Helen," Alison pleaded, her eyes still glued to the emergency vehicles, "stay with me. You're going to be all right."

As the two vehicles came to a halt, a pair of policemen and

three medical personnel leaped out. Alison's gaze fell once more on her sister. Helen's color was ashen, her lips blue, her hands limp.

CHAPTER 2

Saturday, March 21, 1942

9:19 a.m.

Washington, DC

Fister rose from his kneeling position at the open window, still cradling the rifle in his arm. He'd done his job. Time to get out of here.

He glanced over his shoulder to survey the one-bedroom apartment he'd broken into. He needed to make sure he hadn't left any trace of his presence here.

The latest issue of *Life* magazine sat on a small table beside the entry. On the far wall was a photo of a woman and a little girl, both cute in a wholesome Midwestern sort of way.

He briefly allowed his mind to consider who they might be and what their families were like. They were alone in the photo. Was the man in their lives serving in the military? Maybe he'd died in the war. Many men had already paid the ultimate price, and a lot more would do the same in the next few years. Countless women would be left behind to raise their children alone. Was that the case here?

To his right was a small kitchen. Two glasses and two bowls in the sink hinted at a breakfast of cereal and either milk or juice. A pair of small black shoes indicated the little girl in the photo likely lived here with the woman.

Walking into the bedroom, he noted a small twin bed pushed against the wall and a double bed on the other side. He opened the closet door. All women's clothing. No man called this place home.

After closing the door, he ran a gloved hand over the dresser. Not a speck of dust.

For a moment, he longed to know more about the pretty woman who was such a good housekeeper. What was her story? What did her voice sound like? What color were her eyes?

In truth, the identities of the pair who lived here were unimportant. The fact their home had provided the best position from which to accomplish his job, and the fortuitous coincidence they hadn't been home when he arrived, was all that mattered. It was time to move on.

He tossed the gun on the double bed, then strolled to the front door, unlocked it and stepped out into the sunlight. After glancing both ways, he pushed his hands deep into his pants pockets and sauntered down the sidewalk to a 1939 Chevy coupe parked at the curb. He opened the green car's passenger door and eased inside.

"Let's go," he muttered to the raven-haired woman behind

the wheel.

Grace pushed the starter button, and the vehicle's six-cylinder stovepipe engine roared to life. Easing off the clutch, she slowly pulled the hulking auto into the street.

Fister flipped on the radio, and the strains of a new release by Alvino Rey and His Orchestra filled the car. He turned up the volume and hummed along with the tune.

After the hit song had finished, he said, "Do you suppose it's true?"

"What's true?" Grace asked as she eased the car from second into third.

"What that song says about Texas? I mean, do you think the stars at night are really that much bigger and brighter than the ones found anywhere else?"

"I wouldn't know," she mumbled as she stuck her arm out the window to signal a left turn. "I've never been to Texas."

"Neither have I." He laughed. "But I have reason to believe I'll get there soon."

The two rode in silence for several minutes. After the coupe had crossed the state line into Maryland, Grace brushed her shoulder-length hair away from her face and ran her tongue over her ruby-red lips. "Did you have to kill her?"

He shrugged. "It was necessary."

"Why?"

He studied the driver, taking in her ivory skin, deep-brown eyes, high cheekbones, and slightly square chin. This woman was beyond perfection. She demanded attention without asking for it. When she walked into a room, everyone else faded into the background. There were likely men who made a hobby of just watching her breathe.

But like a cobra, she was also deadly. Grace had a hot body but a cold heart, made even more ruthless by her genius-level IQ. She was the kind of woman you wanted to lure into the dark. But few who stepped into the shadows with this creature ever lived to talk about it.

He forced his eyes back to the road, as much to regain his concentration as to check on their progress. "The phone tap revealed Helen was getting way too close to the truth. If she told the FBI what she found out this morning, the mission would have to be scrapped, and years of work would go down the drain. It's that simple."

"And you have no regrets?"

He shrugged and looked out at the meadow on his right. "Emotions have no place in our lives right now. There's business to be done and that means difficult decisions need to be made."

"That sounds pretty heartless. I mean, you knew her pretty well, didn't you?"

"Yes, I did. And she was even more dangerous than you are."

Grace opened her mouth to reply, but her words were cut off by the sound of a siren. She glanced into her rearview mirror. "What should I do?"

"Pull over. Running would alert the cop that his life might

be in danger."

She eased off the accelerator and steered the car toward the shoulder. "You think they're onto you?"

Fister slipped his hand into his coat pocket and felt the Lugar he considered his best friend. "You were driving too fast. This is likely nothing more than a traffic stop." But if someone had seen too much, he wanted to be ready.

Fister glanced over his shoulder at the 1940 Ford patrol car. After parking behind them, the uniformed trooper got out and strode toward their car. He hadn't pulled his gun, and his expression seemed more disgruntled than cautious, so there seemed to be no reason for concern.

Grace rolled down her window, and the state trooper nodded at her, as if to assure her there was nothing to worry about. "You on your way to a fire?" he asked as he leaned over and looked into the car.

"Just got to talking and wasn't watching what I was doing," Grace replied in a calm tone.

The officer studied her face for a moment, then smiled. "Hey, you're Grace Lupino. I've caught your show at The Grove. Took my wife there on our anniversary. Boy, the only thing more beautiful than you is your voice. It's like listening to an angel."

"Thank you," Grace replied with a smile that showed a perfect set of teeth. "I hope you'll come back. I sing there every week, Thursday through Saturday."

He sighed. "'Fraid I can't afford to go a place like more than once a year."

Grace opened her purse and pulled out a small brass case.

After unsnapping the latch, she removed a business card and handed it to the officer. “Give this to the doorman. The show and dinner will be on me.”

The officer whistled as he took the gift. “Wow. Thanks, Miss Lupino.”

“And make sure you come back to the dressing room after my show. I’d love to meet your wife.”

“I sure will.” The trooper’s grin nearly split his face. “Meg will go crazy when I tell her who I met today.” He tucked the card into his shirt pocket. “But please remember to drive a bit more slowly. The speeds limits are lower now due to the war.”

“I’ll do that,” she assured him.

As the policeman practically skipped back to his car, Grace turned toward her passenger and smiled. “You owe me one.”

“You saved his life,” he shot back, easing his hand from his pocket. “So the way I figure it, he’s the one who owes you. Now, let’s get moving. I have a plane to catch.”

CHAPTER 3

Saturday, March 21, 1942

10:30 a.m.

Washington, DC

"What do we have?" Spencer Ryan asked as he hurried into Washington General's emergency room. The tall blond doctor locked his deep green eyes on the barely breathing woman lying on the gurney, probably in her late twenties or early thirties.

"Single gunshot wound to the midsection," replied the gray-haired nurse in her mid-fifties. "Entered four inches below her left shoulder and exited between the vertebral ribs. She's lost a lot of blood and is hemorrhaging internally. Vitals are weak but steady."

"Get a blood type and then move her to surgery."

"We already have a blood type," Sally said. "She's B-negative. We only have a couple of units on hand."

Ryan shook his head. "We're going to need more than that."

As the hospital team pushed the patient out of the room

toward the surgical wing, Sally said, "I'll do my best to find some. This is one patient you really need to save."

He gazed at her. "What do you mean?"

"Her name is Helen Meeker. She works for the President. The White House has called twice in the past five minutes, asking for updates on her condition. This woman might well be the most important patient you've treated in your career."

Ryan rubbed the cleft in his square chin with his forefinger. If the President was keeping close tabs on this person, that likely meant the shooting had political implications. "Sally, call the White House and have them send Dr. Cleveland Mills over here to assist me."

"He's already on his way." She winked at him. "Apparently, FDR thought Mills was the right man for the job too."

"Then find me some more B-negative blood," Ryan barked as he pushed through the curtains and down the hall.

"Yes, sir."

As he marched toward the surgical wing, Ryan sensed he was about to face the most crucial moment in the thirty-five years he'd been alive. Regardless of the outcome, his life would likely never be the same after this. If he was successful, FDR would forever be on his side. If he failed … he didn't even want to consider that option.

CHAPTER 4

Saturday, March 21, 1942

11:22 p.m.

Washington, DC

Clay Barnes strolled up the sidewalk toward the FBI forensic scientist examining the scene where Helen Meeker had fallen. Dressed in gray slacks, a black blouse, and flats, the petite blonde in her early thirties stooped beside a dark pool of blood, studying the 1936 Packard parked at the curb.

"You need a coat," Barnes suggested as he noticed her trembling in the chilly air.

"Left it in the car." Her Southern accent gave away her Arkansas roots. "Why did the Secret Service send you over? This is an FBI crime scene. Even the local police have been pushed out."

Barnes shrugged. "FDR wants to make sure Hoover does a good job on this one. As a matter of fact, he's the one who told the director to assign you to the case. I'm glad old J. Edgar followed through."

Rebecca Bobbs stood. "I was wondering why they let me out of the lab." Her gaze focused on a window about a hundred yards to the east.

"Is that where the shooter was positioned?"

"Yeah. He broke into the lower-level apartment of a young widow named Jane Sims. She was working at a local department store, and her daughter was with friends. It was an easy lock to pick." She pointed toward the building. "Third window from the left. That's the apartment's living room. Evidence shows he only shot once."

"Any prints?"

"No," she replied, her gaze still locked on the window. "It was a professional job all the way ... except for one thing."

Before Rebecca could explain, two FBI field ops wandered near, taking measurements and jotting down notes. She remained silent until the pair had moved up the street.

"Helen's sister was in the car, but she didn't see anything. Didn't hear anything, either, which isn't surprising. No doubt the gun had a silencer."

"Any other witnesses?" Barnes asked.

"No." Rebecca shook her head. "How's Helen?"

"Out of surgery, but it doesn't look good. She lost a lot of blood, and there was considerable internal damage."

Rebecca frowned. "I figured that, based on the large pool of blood by the car."

"And she's a rare blood type. B-negative."

Rebecca's deep blue eyes shot to Barnes. "B-negative?"

"Yes."

"I need to get back to the lab." She turned suddenly and jogged toward her car.

Barnes chased after her. As she pulled the driver's door open, he caught her by the arm. "You said there was something that made you question this being a professional job. What was it?"

"I'll tell you later." She climbed behind the wheel. "There's something important I have to do now."

Barnes held his position between Rebecca and the open car door. "The President needs to know what you know."

She slipped the key into the ignition and hit the starter. The motor roared to life. "The rifle was left at the scene. Just casually tossed onto the bed."

"So?"

"It was a Karabiner 98." Rebecca reached for the door.

Barnes remained in her way. "Isn't that what German soldiers carry in the field?"

"You know your foreign weapons."

"But how did it get here?"

"I don't know. But Hoover thinks it means the Nazis put a hit out on Helen and one of their men pulled the trigger."

"Seems logical."

"That's the problem. It's too open-and-shut. No, something else is going on here."

"Why do you think that?"

"Writing it off as an enemy hit means the FBI will shut down the investigation. They'll figure he's dropped into the shadows and has been spirited out of the country. So they won't bother looking for him. I'm guessing whoever did this knows that."

Barnes nodded, impressed with Rebecca's keen mind. "I'll make sure the President sees through the blind."

"You better." She reached around him and grabbed the interior door handle. "Now can I get back to the lab?"

He took a half-step back. "What's the big rush?"

She glared at him. "Helen Meeker is my oldest and dearest friend. We've both been so busy lately we haven't seen each other as much as we'd like. But she needs me more now than ever." She swallowed a lump in her throat. "I just hope I can deliver in time."

CHAPTER 5

Saturday, March 21, 1942
3:30 p.m.
Chicago, Illinois

Stepping out of the 1938 Plymouth, Fredrick Bauer wrinkled his nose as the unique aroma that defined the stockyards filled his senses. Turning up the collar on his dark overcoat, the tall, thin man strolled over to a fence and looked out at the livestock. With his hands pushed deeply into his pockets, he considered the events of the day.

A U-boat had sunk a tanker within twenty-five miles of the North Carolina coast. That attack had shaken millions to the core. As Nazi subs attacked again and again off the American East Coast, nervous throngs wondered how long it would be until Hitler landed troops here.

The fools didn't realize that Germany cared nothing about America. They wanted to control Europe. The U-boats were simply taking the nation's focus off the main prize.

Bauer heard a car roll into the gravel lot behind him. Rather than turn around to see who had joined him in this lonely part of the Windy City, he continued to look out over the sea of cattle.

Footsteps crunched in the gravel behind him. "They came a long way to die," the visitor noted wryly.

"Not as far as Americans have traveled to fight in a war and probably die." Bauer turned to face his guest. "I see you're still wearing black suits."

"As are you," the man replied.

Bauer shrugged. "Somber colors fit our job. After all, we decide who lives and who dies." He turned back toward the cattle pens. "How long have we known each other, James?"

The short, stocky man ran his hand through his closely cropped red hair and shrugged. "Maybe five or six years."

"It's actually been seven," Bauer corrected him. "You'd been with the FBI for just five months when I gave you your first tip."

"Melvin Purvis was impressed with the information."

Bauer yanked his hands from his pockets, leaned his elbows against the fence, and intertwined his fingers. "And Purvis made sure Hoover knew he could depend on James Killpatrick. A few dozen tips later, you pretty much started calling your own shots. I hear folks call you Bloodhound Jim for your ability to sniff out clues."

The small man smiled. "If you want me to admit I owe you big time, I do. I just don't understand how you get all this information about gangs and Nazi agents."

Bauer eyed James. "There's a lot of things you don't know

about me, Jim." Bauer gave a wry smile. "Not that you haven't tried."

"What do you mean?"

"You've dug everywhere you can, trying to figure out who I am. You've even tried a half-dozen times to have me followed." Bauer pointed his finger into Killpatrick's face. "If you ever tail me again, I'll be sending flowers to your funeral. Do you understand?"

James nodded meekly.

"Good. Now, I asked you here to give you the goods on a doctor in Chicago who's a Nazi agent. In fact, he was behind the mess with Fister trying to kill FDR and Churchill."

"You know about that?"

"I knew before you did. Now, do you want the information or not?"

"Of course." James looked at his right foot, which was pawing at the dirt.

"All right, then. This doctor has been working with the Nazis for years. He funnels information and money to agents, and he's the conduit to getting the information they gather back to Germany. Walk back to my car with me, and I'll give you the file containing all the information you need to arrest and convict him."

Bauer ambled to the Graham sedan, reached in through the open driver's window, pulled out a folder and handed it to the agent.

James's eyes widened as he reviewed the first page of material. "Dr. Eric Snider is one of the most respected men in

Chicago social circles."

"True. But he has no real practice. And yet there are millions of dollars in his bank account. Makes you wonder, doesn't it?"

"But—"

"The information in that file links Snider to everything, including the shooting of that woman in Washington this morning."

James's gaze shot up to Bauer's face. "You mean Helen Meeker?"

He smiled. "I knew about that before you did too. According to this material, Snider ordered the hit as a personal favor to Hitler."

"My Lord," James whispered.

"Snider is out of town right now, but he'll be back tomorrow night. Make your raid then. I would suggest after dark. I'm sure you'll uncover evidence linking Snider to a host of open espionage cases."

James narrowed his eyes at Bauer. "What do you get out of this?"

He grinned. "A chance to live an adventurer's life and help my country in the process."

"Won't you let me tell Hoover about your contributions this time?"

Bauer chuckled. "I've never wanted the spotlight. I'll leave that to you. I just want the satisfaction of seeing my work carried out." Bauer opened the car door and slid in. "Goodbye, James."

He smiled as he pulled out of the parking lot. One possible broken link in his chain was about to be eliminated. A second meeting this evening should prove just as fruitful.

CHAPTER 6

Saturday, March 21, 1942

6:30 p.m.

Washington, DC

Carrying a sealed metal box, Rebecca Bobbs strode into the hospital. Pushing through the waiting room and past the front desk, she continued down the hall until she reached the critical-care nurses' station. Behind the desk sat a white-clad woman, perhaps forty, with dark hair and a stern expression.

"You aren't allowed to be in here," the nurse barked.

Rebecca ignored the gruff warning. "I need to see the physician in charge of the Helen Meeker case."

"Why?" The large woman rose from her chair and crossed her arms over her ample bosom.

"I'm a forensic expert, and I'm working with the FBI. I believe I have something that will aid in Miss Meeker's recovery."

"You aren't a doctor."

"No, I'm not." She placed the metal case on the counter. "Now, I'm going to ask you again, who's in charge of this case?"

"Spencer Ryan," came the blunt reply.

"I need to talk to him."

"He's on rounds."

"Get him over here. Now."

The nurse stood straighter. "You have no right to make demands of me."

Rebecca exhaled a frustrated sigh. "Helen Meeker, who happens to be my friend, is in grave condition. Every minute we waste could cost her life. I have something here that might at least buy her some time."

The nurse gazed at her as if considering the strong words.

"You know, in my line of work I've learned about all kinds of foolproof ways to murder someone and never get caught."

"Is that a threat?"

"Nope, just a fact. Now, are you going to call the doctor or not?"

The nurse glanced at the metal container, then finally picked up the phone. "Dr. Ryan, you're needed at the critical-care nurses' station."

Rebecca crossed her arms over her black coat and tapped her foot. The bulldog in the nurse's uniform sat down and began leafing through files.

A few moments later, heavy footsteps sounded down the hall. A man in white jogged their way. "What is it, Nurse Kelly?"

The woman stood and pointed at Rebecca. "This person claims to be from the FBI. She's demanding to speak to you."

The doctor turned his attention to Rebecca. "What's so important?"

She picked up the metal container and nodded down the hall. Once they were out of earshot of the nurses' station, she stood close enough to Dr. Ryan to whisper. "I worked the crime scene where Helen Meeker was shot. I know she lost a great deal of blood. I also know her blood type is B-negative. I doubt you have enough on hand."

Dr. Ryan frowned. "You know a great deal about something that supposedly had a lid on it."

She nodded. "I have a supply of B-negative blood from the FBI lab."

"That's very kind of you, but we have a sufficient amount for Miss Meeker. Now, if you'll let me get back to my job—"

Rebecca grabbed his arm to stop him. "This blood was taken from a Nazi agent who infiltrated the British military. It's … for lack of a better word … supercharged."

"I beg your pardon."

"The man was shot, and his wounds healed so quickly we couldn't fathom it. We don't know if it's a natural phenomenon or if he was part of some kind of German experiment. But I have a pint with me. I think it might give you the edge you need to save Helen."

Dr. Ryan rubbed his hand over his mouth, glanced down the hall toward a closed door, then slowly moved his gaze back to Rebecca. "How can I be sure you aren't some crackpot?"

She whipped out her badge and showed it to him. "I know this case inside out. I've already shared information that hasn't been released to the newspapers. And you can call the FBI and check out my story. But that would take up precious time. Besides … they don't know that I borrowed this blood from them."

His eyebrows shot up. "You stole it?"

She shrugged. "They can get more. They have the man in custody. If I knew where he was, I would've brought him down to serve as a live donor."

The doctor pinched his lips together. "I don't know about this."

"What have you got to lose?"

"My license." He glared at her. "Look, even if I tested the blood and found it to be a suitable match for Miss Meeker, I'm not the only doctor involved in this case. Another guy is calling the shots now on orders from the President. He never leaves the patient's side. He's even posted a guard inside the room."

The guard didn't come as a surprise. But who was this second doctor? "How well do you know this man?"

"I just met him today. But I've known about him my entire career. He's a legend. I've always wanted to work with him. He's the President's personal physician."

Rebecca smiled. "Dr. Cleveland Mills."

"You know him?"

"Quite well, actually. He operated on me before he went to work for FDR. And I've asked him a host of questions over the years about cases I've worked on. He likes me. More important, he'll believe me."

Ryan nodded. "All right. I'll take you to him. But this whole thing still sounds squirrelly to me."

"I'm sure it does," Rebecca said as she accompanied the doctor down the hall. "But in times of war, new discoveries are made more quickly than during periods of peace. In the next few years, we'll no doubt see medicine advance almost as quickly as we see advances in man's inventions to kill."

CHAPTER 8

Saturday, March 21, 1942

10:30 p.m.

Gary, Indiana

Fredrick Bauer opened the small wooden chest and examined its contents. He ran his hand over a million dollars in faceted white diamonds before shutting the lid and looking back at his host.

"Will that do?" the man asked.

Bauer smiled at the tall, athletically built man in his forties. Ralph Mauch was not someone to mess with. A generation before, he had been a heavyweight boxing champ in Europe. Even now, it appeared the blond man with the piercing blue eyes would have no problem going at least five rounds against the likes of Joe Lewis.

"Where did they come from?" Bauer asked.

"If you're asking if they can be traced, the answer is no. These gems were looted when the Nazis marched into Paris.

They have no connection to anything in this country. You can do whatever you want with them."

Bauer nodded, shut the lid and put the box back on the table in Mauch's small study. "Have one of your men take the chest to my car. I'll trust your assessment on how much they're worth."

Mauch leaned back in the oversized leather-backed chair and crossed his muscular arms over his dark-green sports coat. His expression was a strange mix of admiration and disgust. "You would have earned a great deal more if you'd delivered on the big job."

Bauer shrugged. "Who would've thought the woman would figure things out? She wasn't even supposed to be there. We had her on a wild goose chase. She simply got lucky."

"I don't believe in luck," Mauch replied, his voice harsh and cold. "You plan, you prepare, and you execute. That's how it works. Your problem was Fister. Still is. He simply can't be controlled. He's too unpredictable."

"I didn't pick him," Bauer shot back. "Your people delivered him to me."

"We don't like that business in Washington this morning either," Mauch warned. "Shooting Meeker serves no purpose."

"You didn't order that?" Bauer asked.

"No."

"I didn't either."

Spotting a copy of *Gone with the Wind* on Mauch's bookshelf, Bauer stood and retrieved it. Running his fingers over the spine, he turned to Mauch. "Have you read this?"

"No, but my wife has."

"I'm partway through it now." Bauer returned to his chair, still holding the book. "I hear it's an all-time best seller. I think that says a great deal about this country, don't you?"

Mauch smoothed his hair with his right hand. "Fredrick, if you didn't order the hit on Meeker, who did?"

Bauer frowned. "I have no idea. But I have a contact who might."

Mauch rubbed his brow. "Let me know what you find out." He glanced at a newspaper sitting on a table to his right. It was filled with the latest images and stories of battles on both fronts. "Who do you think is going to win this war?"

"We are," Bauer asserted. He let his response linger for a moment before pulling an envelope from his coat pocket. "This microfilm contains plans for a new American plane. It's experimental, so who knows if it will ever go into production? But there might be elements of it that Berlin could take, refine, and put to use."

"Doesn't sound like a game-changer to me," Mauch argued. But he plucked the envelope from Bauer's hand anyway. "Hitler has two other things he wants more. And you have promised to deliver them."

"I'm close on both counts. It's just a matter of finding the right moment to get them." He sighed. "But as far as I can tell, they're worthless. The words on those papers are nothing but myths."

"Try telling that to Hitler," Mauch scoffed. "He's bought into all that mystical stuff. I mean, he actually believes De Soto stumbled onto something of great power during his 1541 exploration of America."

"If it was that powerful, why did the guy who found it die on the trip? Shouldn't his discovery have kept him safe?"

"What you and I believe isn't important. The only thing that matters is what that crazy man in Germany believes."

Bauer stared at the microfilm in Mauch's hands. "At least, that will buy us some time until I can get what the old fool really wants. But playing with the occult is not going to cancel out his stupid decision to invade Russia."

"Time will tell."

"Well, time is money, so have your people put that chest in my car. I need to get back home."

"And where is home for you, my friend?"

"That's something you'll never know. And take my word for it, it's far better that you don't."

CHAPTER 9

Sunday, March 22, 1942

8:33 p.m.

Chicago, Illinois

James Killpatrick and three other men, all dressed in dark suits, tan overcoats, and hats, stepped out of the black 1940 Lincoln Zephyr and walked to the gates of the palatial white-stone mansion owned by one of Chicago's most respected citizens. A long driveway winding through a half-acre of manicured lawn led up to the home's main entry. Except for two lit windows on the far right side of the ground floor, the two-story structure appeared lifeless.

"You sure this is the place?" asked a tall man in his late twenties.

Killpatrick looked back over his shoulder into the man's eyes. "You read the file. This is Snider's home."

"Yes, sir," came the apologetic reply.

He gathered his team close and outlined their mission in hushed tones. "We've been here for an hour, and no one has entered the home except Snider. He's not expecting us, so he likely won't be armed. I'd rather we do this without fireworks, but have your guns ready just in case."

His men nodded.

"Now, listen up. Hoover wants this guy alive so we can find out what he knows. These men are like a cancer—you have to find it all if you want to be healthy." Killpatrick paused, studying his team. "Any questions?"

"How do we get through the gate?"

Killpatrick smiled. "Follow me." He led the trio to the iron entry and pointed at the latch. "Notice anything?"

"It's not locked," said the agent who'd asked the question.

"Good observation, Price."

The young man lifted the latch, and the gate swung open. "How do you know all this stuff? No one at the Bureau gets dirt on folks like you do."

"It's a gift. Now, let's go."

Killpatrick crept up the lane toward the entry, his team following close behind. When they reached the porch, he climbed the two steps and raised his finger to the doorbell. But he didn't press it.

"Something wrong?" Price asked.

"The door is slightly ajar." He turned to his men. "Keep out of sight, but have your weapons ready. Better to blow a hole in your coat pocket than to have someone blow one in you." He grinned wryly. "Ruins your coat either way."

He punched the buzzer. No response. He repeated his action

with the same results.

Pulling his revolver, he eased the door open with his foot and stepped inside a large, dark foyer. "This is the FBI. Come out with your hands up."

Hearing nothing, he reached to the right of the door and felt along the wall for a light switch. Finding one, he flipped it on.

To his right was a living room; to his left, a dining room. Both extravagantly furnished. And apparently empty. But a light shone through an open door on the far side of the living room.

"You think he's in there?" Price whispered.

"He could be anywhere. But my old Sunday school teacher always told me to follow the light. So that's where we're going first."

As he moved toward the living room, he whispered, "Green, you move to the right. Price, you take the left. Johnson, watch our tail. We don't want anyone coming up behind us."

Killpatrick moved slowly past a large couch, a huge stone fireplace, and a Zenith console radio, keeping his eyes on the partially open door. Taking a position just to the right of the entry, he peered inside.

The room was small, no more than fifteen by fifteen, and likely used as a study or library. A lit brass lamp sat on an oak desk in the middle of the room. Two padded red leather chairs flanked the floor-to-ceiling bookshelves to the left. The door hid everything to his right.

Killpatrick signaled Green and Johnson to cover both sides of the entry. Keeping his gun at waist level, he pushed the door with his left hand. As it slowly opened, he noted a small yellow love seat. A man lay sprawled awkwardly against one of the arms, blood dripping from a wound in his forehead. His limp right hand held a gun.

"One victim," Killpatrick announced in a hushed tone. "Move in together on my signal." He waited a second, then nodded.

As Killpatrick approached the man on the love seat, Price walked to the desk and looked behind the large oak rolltop. "Got another one. And he's alive."

After knocking the gun away from the first victim's hand, Killpatrick moved to Price's side. The man on the floor had been badly beaten. His face was cut, swollen, and bruised; both eyes were black. While his breathing was steady, he appeared to be unconscious. A pistol rested on the floor about a foot from his right hand.

After slipping his weapon back into his shoulder holster, Killpatrick dropped to one knee and turned the man's face toward him.

"Either of these guys the one we're looking for?" Price asked.

"They both are."

"What?"

"The one on the couch is Dr. Snider. This man is Henry Reese."

"The missing agent?" Green asked.

"That's right." Killpatrick checked Reese's pulse. "Henry, can you hear me?"

The beaten man's eyes fluttered and opened. "Bloodhound?"

Killpatrick chuckled. “Yeah, it’s me, buddy.”

“Where am I?”

“In Chicago. More specifically, you’re in the home of Dr. Eric Snider. My guess is you killed him.”

A concerned look filled Reese’s battered mug. “I did?”

“Don’t worry about it. He was a spy. He deserved it. Now, rest easy. We need to get you to a doctor. A real one.” He turned to his men. “Green, call an ambulance. Price and Johnson, you two go through the house and see if anyone’s hiding somewhere. If you find anybody, shoot first and ask questions later.”

After his men rushed off, Killpatrick glanced at the dead doctor. So much for delivering Snider to Hoover for questioning. But at least Henry Reese was alive.

CHAPTER 10

Monday, March 23, 1942

9:30 a.m.

Washington, DC

Rebecca Bobbs strolled by the nurses' desk and smiled at the stern-looking woman behind the counter. The woman shot back a hateful glare.

"Nice to see you again, too, Nurse Kelly," she said, then made her way down the hall to room 172. She knocked lightly. The door opened and a uniformed man appeared in the entry.

"Rebecca Bobbs. The doctors are expecting me."

The muscular, six-foot-tall policeman stepped to one side, allowing her to enter. The room was just like a thousand other critical-care units. Helen Meeker, pale but breathing steadily, lay in the bed in the center of the room, eyes closed and lips slightly open.

"She's much better," said one of the two doctors standing on the far side of the bed. "I wouldn't have believed it was possible, but there was something in that blood transfusion that accomplished a lot more than we could do through our best medical procedures."

"That's what I figured." She turned from Dr. Ryan to the older man. "Give it to me straight, Doc."

Cleveland Mills shrugged. "She's not out of the woods yet. But a day ago I didn't give her one chance in a hundred. Any way you can get us some more of that blood?"

She nodded. "I convinced the FBI to draw more from the prisoner we got the first batch from."

"Great." Mills smiled.

"There's just one problem."

"What's that?" Ryan asked.

"This batch is normal B-negative. There's nothing special about it."

"How is that possible?" Mills asked.

"I don't know. Neither does anyone else at the lab. But the wound on the man's hand isn't healing at a faster rate than anyone else's would. Maybe he was exposed to something just before we drew blood the first time. Or perhaps he was taking some kind of drug before we picked him up, and he's no longer taking it. All I know is that incredible healing factor isn't there anymore."

Dr. Ryan placed his hand on Rebecca's chin and lifted her face until their eyes met. "You saved her life with what you gave us. She experienced a week's worth of healing in a single day."

She forced a smile. "I hope you're right. But now the only supply of blood that might have saved countless other lives is gone." She looked at the other doctor. "In saving my friend, did I doom a million others?"

Cleveland Mills touched her shoulder. "You did what you felt was right at the moment. Given the choice, I would have done the same thing. And so would the President."

Rebecca closed her eyes for a few moments, trying to relish the realization that her friend might live after all. Her justification did little to remove her overriding sense of guilt.

She turned back to the men. "I'm a scientist. Even though my expertise is in solving how people died or committed crimes, I've always considered myself a part of making the world better for the living. Somehow we stumbled on something that had more potential for healing than anything on this planet. Given time and thorough study, we might have found a way to re-create it. But rather than think of future generations or the men on the battlefield, I selfishly thought of my friend and how much I'd miss her if she died." She gazed at Helen. "I don't think she'd respect that kind of thinking."

The doctor walked up to the guard. "Would you mind stepping outside a second?" He turned to Dr. Ryan. "You as well. I need a moment alone with Miss Bobbs."

"Of course." The younger doctor shuffled toward the exit. After the two men left, Mills closed the door and then signaled for Rebecca to join him by the window.

"Becca, you and I know this blood came from Reggie Fister. But the President doesn't want anyone else to be aware of that fact."

"I wasn't going to give away his identity. Most people at the

FBI don't even know he's still alive."

The doctor nodded. "I spoke with the President today. Apparently something's happened to Fister. He seems confused and lost. He's like an addict whose mind has been deeply affected by a long period of drug use. The doctor in charge described it as going through withdrawal. Perhaps he's coming down from the drug that supercharged his blood."

"Is that what you think?"

"I don't know what to think. But if the Nazis managed to arrange for Fister's medical miracle, they might be able to do it on a huge scale. The Germans could put together an almost invincible army."

Rebecca stared at her shoes. "I really messed up, didn't I?"

"I don't see it that way. And neither does the President. Fister's blood fix was temporary. And now he's a physical wreck. So there are obviously problems with the process."

Rebecca turned to stare at Helen. "Will she go through withdrawal too?"

"There's no way to tell at this point. But while we're waiting to see what happens, we need to figure out who tried to kill her. Since this seems to be a matter of national security, the President has come up with a plan. I've convinced him to include you in it. He wants you to return to the White House with me."

"I'll need to inform my superiors at the lab."

"They've already been told."

"What about Helen?"

"Dr. Ryan will take good care of her. And he'll let me

know if there's any change in her condition." Mills caught her eye. "This mission is dangerous, Becca. You could end up like Helen ... or worse. It's your decision whether to accept it or turn it down."

Rebecca smiled grimly. "I'm more than ready to do my part. I want to pick up where Helen left off."

"That won't be necessary." Mills steered her toward the door. "We already have someone to do that job."

CHAPTER II

Monday, March 23, 1942
10:18 a.m.
Chicago, Illinois

Henry Reese's head was beginning to clear, but his memory remained as foggy as a fall night in London. He simply couldn't explain where he'd been or what he'd done in the last several days. Even after a good night's sleep and two meals, he was still drawing blanks. He felt as if he'd been sleepwalking for a week.

This was more frustrating than anything he'd ever known. He was failing, not just as a person but as a professional.

His fellow agents had been sitting in his hotel room with him for hours, but he was unable to provide them with any leads. They'd have been better off talking to a three-year-old.

"Ballistics tests prove you fired a gun," Killpatrick said for the tenth time. "And a bullet from the gun you had in your hand killed Snider. You must remember firing it."

Reese raised his palms. "How many times do I have to tell you? I don't even know who Snider is. I have no idea how I got into that house, and I sure don't remember shooting him."

He ran his hands through his hair, doing his best to unearth whatever memories he could. "I can remember things that happened two weeks ago as clear as day. And I remember everything from this morning." He moaned. "I could tell you the names of every kid in my grade-school class and even give you most of their birthdays. I can give you details on my investigation of the January sixteenth plane crash in Nevada. I know how many folks were on the flight, where it took off, the names of the crew. But for the life of me, I don't remember anything about Snider."

"What's the last thing you recall before waking up here?" Killpatrick asked.

Reese dredged his disheveled memory banks. "Being in a gunfight while chasing a guy named Andrews. Someone slugged me. I don't know anything after that."

Killpatrick paced the small hotel room, clearly trying to get some mental traction.

"Can't you fill me in on what happened to me?" Reese finally asked.

The agent sat in a desk chair and loosened his gold tie. "That guy you were chasing, Andrews, ended up in the same room with FDR and Churchill."

"Did he try to kill them?"

"No. He tried to save them. It was Reggie Fister who tried

to kill them."

"Fister?" Reese stared at the other agent in disbelief.

"Would have done it too, but Helen shot him first."

"Is he dead?"

"No. But we have him in custody and he won't talk."

Reese pushed out of bed and walked to the mirror. The dark circles under his eyes almost met his lips. His skin was pale, his eyes bloodshot, and a week's worth of beard growth covered his face. He'd seen corpses that showed more life.

Reese turned away from the glass. "What else can you tell me?"

Killpatrick took a deep breath. "Somebody shot Helen."

Reese's breath caught in his throat. "Is she alive?"

"Last I heard, she was hanging on. But she's unconscious. And since Fister's in custody, no one knows who tried to gun her down."

"Who else would have a reason to kill her?"

"We don't know. But we suspect Dr. Snider ordered the hit. Now that he's dead, we can't interrogate him. We were hoping you could give us a lead."

Reese groaned. "I wish I could."

"Maybe something will come to you."

"I hope you're right."

"Why don't you get cleaned up? We'll catch the next flight back to DC. Hoover wants an update on what you were working on just before you were abducted." He paused. "Do you remember what that was?"

"Yeah, I do," Reese answered. "And he's not going to like what I found out."

CHAPTER 12

Monday, March 23, 1942

11:19 a.m.

Washington, DC

Clay Barnes eased down on the corner of his desk and studied the three guests seated in front of him. They hardly seemed qualified to capture a killer. But Alison Meeker, Rebecca Bobbs, and Dr. Cleveland Mills were the players the President wanted on the team.

Who would've thought he'd be depending on a trio of civilians to apprehend the person who'd tried to kill one of his closest friends? But the FBI was too busy to put their full weight behind it, and the local police had nothing to go on. He was not about to let this case grow cold, like so many other murders in this country. And neither was the President.

His guests were bright, willing, and even eager, but they were not trained. One of the women was a college kid, the other a person who knew her way around a lab. Neither of them weighed more than a hundred fifteen pounds. The old doctor was a good man in surgery, and he'd fought in World War I. But how good would he be in a knife fight?

These people had lives. Friends. Hobbies. Family. Unlike him, they likely turned their radios on for something other than news once in a while. And unlike him, they probably had something to live for. Was it fair to put them in harm's way?

None of that mattered. FDR had approved the plan, and there was no turning back now.

He tossed a newspaper into Rebecca's lap and waited for her to read the headline: "Helen Meeker, FDR Aid, Shot. Out of Surgery and Expected to Be Released Tonight."

The woman looked up. "I was just in her room. She wasn't even conscious. She's in no condition to be released."

"No, she isn't. But we need whoever shot her to believe she is. According to that article, you and Dr. Mills will be accompanying Helen to her apartment, where you'll both monitor her recovery."

Rebecca handed the paper back to him. "I don't understand."

Barnes dropped the copy of *The Washington Post* on the desk and made his way to a window overlooking the White House's north lawn. He jammed his hands into his pockets and studied the gray sky. "Here's the plan. The three of you will go to the hospital at separate times during the day. Alison, you'll put on your sister's clothes. Tonight, you'll all leave together. A police escort will lead you to the apartment. Shortly thereafter, the protection will seemingly disappear. If the assassin comes out o hiding to finish the job he started, we'll capture him and gain the inormation we need in order to find out why Helen was shot and who ordered it."

"Why am I involved?" Rebecca asked.

"You're one of Helen's closest friends. People would expect you to be with her during a time like this. Also, you know how to handle a gun."

"True." Rebecca crossed her legs and smoothed her skirt. "But I'm no match for a hired killer."

"He won't know that." Barnes winked.

"Look, I'm fine with being there," she said, "but Alison's a kid. Why risk her life?"

"Actually, this was my idea," the young woman said. "If whoever shot my sister thinks I got a good look at him, my life is in danger as long as that wacko is out there."

"Exactly my point." Rebecca raised an eyebrow at Barnes. "Couldn't we bring in some pros from the Secret Service for this charade? Alison should be taken as far away from here as possible. You could even put a guard on her."

Alison clenched her trembling fingers. "I think I'd be saer in the apartment with you and the doctor than anywhere else."

"So does the President," Barnes added. "But there's another issue at work here. Helen has long believed there's a mole at the White House. If we use our regular staff for this job, the mole may find out this is a setup."

Rebecca sighed. "So you've leaving it up to the three of us to catch this menace?"

"Actually, there'll be another man in the apartment with you.

He's flying back to Washington right now. We'll make sure he's in place before you leave the hospital. He's volunteered for the job, he has a vested interest in seeing it through, and he knows Helen well."

Rebecca narrowed her eyes at him. "And who's that?"

Barnes straightened. "Henry Reese."

A collective gasp filled the room. "He's alive?" Rebecca shrieked.

"He's a little rough for wear. But he wants to nab the guy who shot Helen, and the President wants to give him that chance. The doc said he's in good enough shape to pull this off. And since we haven't announced that Henry's been found, no one at the White House will know he's there."

As the trio digested the surprising bit of news, Barnes moved back to the window. There was something else at play here too, something that directly involved Rebecca Bobbs. But he'd wait to reveal that until after this assignment was finished.

CHAPTER 13

Monday, March 23, 1942

5:15 p.m.

A farm outside Springfield, Illinois

"Why'd you do it?" Fredrick Bauer demanded.

Fister, outfitted in a blue suit, white shirt, and gray tie, smiled. "Two reasons. First, she was onto the truth. The phone taps you instigated proved it."

"You should have let me take care of that." Bauer got up from the divan of his rural home and stood directly in front of his cocky guest, who'd parked his keister in an overstuffed green chair.

"I was the better man for the job. After all, how can the FBI suspect someone they already have in custody?"

"And what was your second reason?"

"She embarrassed me." Fister scowled. "No woman does that to me."

Bauer glared at the disgusting excuse for a human being.

"Well, she might just do it again."

"What are you talking about? Helen Meeker's dead."

"She's getting out of the hospital tonight."

"That's impossible. I hit her with a kill shot."

"But your blood, engineered in my labs, enabled her to recover."

Fister shook his head. "I need to get over there and finish her off."

"Oh, no, you don't. You're staying right here."

"But—"

"I've got a man in DC who can do the job. And he's not some self-absorbed spy who lets his emotions override his good judgment. He has a long and perfect track record with organized crime."

"And what if your Mr. Wonderful doesn't get the job done?"

"Then I have a backup plan, of course. I *always* have a backup plan." Bauer shook his head. "You know, for a man Germany invested years of training in, you can be a real idiot. You couldn't have done this job on your own. Who helped you?"

Fister sneered. "A friend."

"Give me a name."

"Grace Lupino."

"Oh, that's just great." Bauer threw his hands up in disgust. "I spent years getting her into the perfect spot to gather information and go unnoticed, and you go and do something that might expose her."

Fister grinned. "I didn't expose her. She's still a Washington club singer."

"If she's compromised," Bauer barked, "I will never be able to replace her." More than once that woman had managed to get information no one else could. And he had a very important assignment for her down the road. "I don't want you to ever contact her again. You got that?"

"Sure," Fister chirped. "Now, when are you going to take out Helen Meeker?"

"Tonight." After inhaling a deep breath to calm his emotions, Bauer returned to his chair. "I do have a job for you, one that's more up your alley."

"What's that?"

He grabbed an eight-by-ten photo off the end table and tossed it into Fister's lap. "That man is Jacob Kranz. He's one of the world's top economists. He escaped from Germany in 1935. He's living in New York now, and Hitler wants him back."

"Why?" Fister asked, studying the picture.

"Kranz is using his wealth to help fund the resistance in Germany. He even underwrote a failed assassination plot on Hitler. The Nazis want to put him on trial and then publicly execute him for treason."

Fister sneered. "There's no way to kidnap a man like that and smuggle him back to Germany. Not when there's a war going on."

"Hitler doesn't want excuses. He just wants the job done." Bauer tapped his fingers on the desk. "Besides, this will buy us some time on the bigger things the Nazis are expecting me to accomplish."

Fister leaned back in his chair and crossed his right foot over his left knee. "So, how do we do the impossible?"

"Kranz has a daughter who goes to school at the University of Texas. She's enrolled under a false name: Suzy Miller. Kranz has been careful never to be seen with her in public, so few people know about their connection. You nab the girl and take her to our base in south Texas. Once she's safely there, we'll contact Kranz and give him a choice. Either his daughter is smuggled back to Germany, where she'll be placed in a concentration camp, or he changes places with her."

Bauer handed Fister a photo of the coed.

He grinned. "She's kind of cute."

"Her mother was an actress, and the girl inherited her looks."

Fister's eyebrows rose. "Can I take some … liberties with this job?"

"There won't be any chaperones, so feel free to enjoy yourself. Just make sure she's alive to talk to her father when the time comes."

"When do I leave?"

"We'll get you on a train tomorrow. You'll be staying in the Texas Inn, just off campus. One of our mute friends will meet you there with a car. Take your time scoping things out. When you have the girl, your connection will provide you with a plane and a pilot to fly you to a ranch close to Brownsville." He crouched in front of Fister, his nose inches from the man's face. "And Reggie …"

"Yes?"

"Don't shoot anyone. Is that understood?"

"I promise, this will be clean."

"It better be. If it's not, you're going to end up in a concentration camp or in front of a firing squad."

CHAPTER 14

Monday, March 23, 1942

9:30 p.m.

Washington, DC

Alison, wearing a large floppy hat and an oversized trench coat, was wheeled from the hospital to Helen Meeker's yellow Packard. After taking her place in the backseat, she was joined by Dr. Cleveland Mills. Rebecca Bobbs slid behind the wheel, then followed the 1941 Ford police sedan to her sister's apartment.

Once everyone else was inside, two uniformed policemen helped Alison to the door. Ater speaking briefly with the doctor, the pair got back into their squad car and roared off into the night.

"How's Helen?" a deep voice asked.

Alison switched on the lights, revealing a man in a dark suit, light blue shirt, and black tie.

"Henry," Rebecca said with a smile, her blue eyes lighting

up. "It's good to see you alive. I should have known nothing can harm you."

He opened his arms to the blonde. After a long hug, he stepped away, nodded to Alison, and reached out his hand to the doctor. "I'm Henry Reese."

"Cleveland Mills. But you can call me Doc."

"What can you tell me about Helen?"

"When I looked in on her this morning, she seemed slightly improved. She's been moved to a remote room that only three people are aware of, including the young doctor who's taking care of her. She should be perfectly safe there."

"I hope so."

"What do we do now?" Rebecca asked.

"We wait." Reese shrugged. "At some point, one of the bad guys will likely try to enter this apartment with the intention of overtaking Dr. Cleveland and kidnapping the woman they believe to be Helen Meeker." He nodded at Alison. "What they won't know, hopefully, is that I'm here too." He pulled a gun out of his shoulder holster. "And I'll be ready for them."

Alison gulped. Part of her hoped these guys would make their move soon so this could all be over with more quickly. She didn't know how long she could sit and wait, imagining everything that could go wrong.

CHAPTER 15

Monday, March 23, 1942
10:30 p.m.
Washington, DC

Louise Kelly crept down the dimly lit hallway, glancing left and right to make sure she wasn't being observed. When the white-clad nurse reached the right room, she paused in the doorway. Seeing no one in either of the chairs or beside the bed, she entered, silently closing the door behind her.

She was hours later than planned, but this was the first time the room hadn't had someone in or near it. Dr. Ryan had been pulled away less than an hour ago to perform emergency surgery on a car-wreck victim, finally giving her the chance she'd been waiting for.

Well, as her mother always said, better late than never.

Louise reached into her pocket and pulled out a syringe as she moved quietly to the bed. She hadn't been fooled by the deception. She'd known Helen Meeker was in no shape to go home. And now the woman never would. That knowledge caused her both a twinge of guilt and a great sense of relief.

In the dark room, she reached out her gloved hand and felt for the patient's arm. Finding it, she pushed the tip of the needle into the shoulder area and engaged the plunger.

After dropping the instrument back into her pocket, Louise headed back toward the door. No one would ever suspect her. The cause of death would be listed as complications due to a severe gunshot wound. It was the perfect crime. By the time Spencer Ryan came back to check on Meeker, she'd have been dead for at least two hours.

As she reached for the door handle, a low voice whispered, "Why did you do that?"

Whirling to her right, Louise tried to penetrate the darkness in a far corner, but she saw only shadows. "Who's there?"

"You have a long tenure of service at this facility, without a single blemish on your record."

Louise shuddered. Who was the person behind those haunting whispers? She couldn't even tell if it was a man or a woman. But clearly whoever it was knew something about her.

"Why would you try to murder a patient?" the soft voice asked.

Louise wanted to run, but fear held her in place, squeezing her heart and stealing her breath.

"You must have been paid a lot of money."

"That's not true," she blurted out. "Someone else's life depended on it."

"Whose?"

Beads of sweat dotted Louise's upper lip. "I—I can't tell you."

"You'd better. If you don't, you'll be on your way to jail within minutes."

Louise sank into the nearest chair, fighting both fear and tears. "They have my daughter. They told me they'd kill her if I didn't do as they asked. Hannah's only sixteen. She's all I have. If she dies, I might as well die too."

"Are you supposed to call them when you've finished the job?"

"No. They told me they'd know by midnight whether Helen Meeker was dead, and if so, they'd let my little girl go. They must have someone watching."

The hidden voice sighed. "Go back to your station and stay there until someone discovers the body."

"My shift is over."

"Then go home and wait for your daughter."

Feeling as if she'd been freed from a cage, Louise stood quickly and opened the door. She barreled out of the room and down the hall without looking back.

As she scurried through the lobby, a beautiful raven-haired woman nodded to her before disappearing into a stairwell leading to the basement.

CHAPTER 16

Tuesday, March 24, 1942
1:30 a.m.
Washington, DC

Henry Reese was listening to the radio playing Glenn Miller's "A String of Pearls" and flipping through an issue of *Life* magazine when a knock on the front door brought him to high alert. After grabbing his gun from where it rested on the coffee table, he signaled for Rebecca Bobbs to answer. As she moved toward the entry, the agent backed into the dark bedroom.

"Who is it?" Rebecca asked.

"Clay Barnes," came the muffled reply.

Rebecca glanced back to Dr. Mills on the far side of the room, then at Alison seated in a chair at the kitchen table, and finally turned toward Reese, standing mostly out of sight behind the bedroom doorway. He nodded.

Ater flipping the latch, she eased the door open. A second

later three men pushed hard against the entry, knocking the woman to the ground.

"Nobody move," the tallest one barked, aiming a Luger at the doctor.

"Who are you?" Rebecca demanded as she pushed off the floor into a kneeling position. "And what gives you the right to barge into my friend's apartment?"

The man grinned, his pallid complexion revealing he'd spent little time in the sun. "That's none of your business," he announced, his voice gruff and coarse.

The intruders closed the door behind them, then scattered throughout the room, each of them picking out a target. Noting the silencers on the guns and the gang's composed nature, Reese realized this was not a fly-by-night raid. These men were seasoned and prepared, and the leader was an experienced hit man Reese recognized. Even if he surprised them, he wouldn't be able to take out all three before they at least winged a victim or two of their own. And if he shot too quickly, he might hit one of his own people.

Time to play a bit of poker.

Reese emerged from the shadows, his gun aimed at the leader. "When did Rusty Cline start working for the Germans?"

The trio's gaze collectively flew to the agent.

"If any of you moves, Cline gets it between the eyes."

"Don't drop your guns," Cline ordered. "We've got him outnumbered." He peered closely at Reese, keeping his gun sighted on Alison. "Do I know you?"

"My name is Henry Reese, and I'm with the FBI."

Cline shrugged.

"I thought you were muscle for the New York mob. You freelancing for the Nazis now?"

"I don't know anything about Nazis. But I do know you could only get one of us before we shot you, the woman, or the old man."

"I've got backup," Reese bragged.

Cline cackled. "We've been watching this place for hours. You're the only one here." He smiled. "I, on the other hand, have a fourth member on my team, and he has a gun aimed at you through the bedroom window."

Was Cline bluffing? Reese couldn't afford to look behind him to find out. If there really was a guy out there in the darkness, the outcome of this lethal game was already decided. And since he'd told the FBI and Secret Service not to get too close so as not to scare anyone off, he was to blame.

The only question was who would shoot first—and how many would die before the gunfire ended.

"Drop your weapon, G-Man," Cline ordered.

"I don't think so," Reese growled. "I can at least get you, and likely one more."

"But you'll die too."

"I die either way. You're not going to let anyone walk out of here alive." That was Cline's MO. And why he'd never served time or been killed. "I have you in my sights. If the guy behind me makes a sound, I'll blow your brains out. So your side may win the war, but you'll lose the battle. Have you considered where you want to be buried?"

Cline swallowed hard, but didn't take his gun off Alison.

Reese inched a bit closer. "Even if you somehow survive, you won't get paid. Helen Meeker's not here."

Sweat appeared on the man's brow as he took a closer look at Alison.

"That's her sister."

"What are you trying to pull?"

Reese pointed to the newspaper on the table. "Helen's picture is right there on the front page."

"Keep him covered," Cline shouted to the unseen man behind Reese. He compared the photo in the paper to the young woman he had targeted. Then he fixed his gaze on Reese. "What's going on here?"

"You're the one who fell into a trap, Cline."

The hood shook his head. "I knew this job was too clean."

"Look, there's no reason anyone has to die here. If you tell me who sent you, I'll let all of you walk away. If you're ever caught by the cops, you'll have a chip you can play because you helped the FBI today."

"It's not that simple," Cline muttered. "I was told to leave no witnesses. If I do, I won't live long enough to get caught for anything." He cocked his gun.

From the corner of his eye, Reese saw Rebecca push off the floor and reach for the light switch. A second later, the room went black.

In the sudden darkness, Rebecca bolted at Cline. Her shoulder slammed into him, and he tumbled forward as she grabbed for his weapon.

With catlike reflexes, he jabbed an elbow into her chin and rolled to his right. He was rising to one knee when a flashlight beam caught his chest. A shot rang out, and Cline crumpled to the floor.

The beam found one of Cline's men, and another shot rang out, catching the man in the wrist and knocking the gun out of his fingers. He collapsed with a scream, writhing and clutching his hand.

The flashlight went dark.

"Let me hear your weapon hit the floor," demanded a gravelly voice a few feet to Reese's right.

A moment later, the sound of something heavy hitting the carpet echoed through the room.

"Put your hands on your head," the voice ordered.

"They're there."

The flashlight came back on, proving the man's claim.

"Becca," Reese said, "give us some light."

When the room was once again illuminated, Cline lay in a fetal position on the floor, his blood staining the green carpet. One of his men stood in the corner, his hands on his blond mop of hair. The other intruder was trying to stop the profuse bleeding coming from his right wrist.

Beside the door, Rebecca held a gun she'd retrieved from one of the men. Dr. Mills still sat in his seat, observing Cline's wound. Alison leaned against the kitchen sink.

On Reese's right, holding a flashlight in one hand and a gun in the other, stood Helen Meeker, her dark eyes shining and a grin framing her pale face.

CHAPTER 17

Tuesday, March 24, 1942

1:50 a.m.

Washington, DC

Helen Meeker surveyed the room. Ater confirming that the bad guys were all incapacitated, she caught her sister's adoring gaze. "Alison, you okay?"

"Yeah."

Meeker turned to Rebecca. "It's great to see you again, my friend. It's been far too long."

"I thought you were in a coma," Reese said with an ear-to-ear smile.

"And I thought you were dead," Meeker quipped. "You look terrible. If you've taken up boxing, you should quit now, while you still have a somewhat straight nose."

While Reese gathered up the rest of the thugs' firearms, Meeker watched Dr. Mills ministering to Cline's wounds.

"How's he doing?"

"He won't live very long."

After handing her Colt to Rebecca, Meeker stooped beside the dying gunman.

"You're good," he murmured.

"Are you the one who put the bullet in my gut last Saturday?" she asked, hoping he'd want to clear his conscience before his time ran out.

Cline shot her a painful grin. "If I'd done it, you wouldn't be here."

"Then who did?"

"I don't know. I was just sent in to clean things up."

"Who sent you?"

He shook his head.

Reese knelt beside Meeker. "You working for the Nazis?"

"I'm not that low." Cline's eyelids fluttered and closed. A few second later he stopped breathing.

Meeker stood and turned to Rebecca. "Call the Bureau. Let's get these others in custody."

Reese rose beside her. "I take it you found the guy outside the bedroom?"

She shrugged. "I put him to sleep, then opened the window and climbed in to save your bacon."

"I saw her," Rebecca said. "She signaled me, then stepped back into the shadows. I'm just glad I figured out she wanted me to turn the lights out."

Dr. Mills walked up to Meeker. "When you came out of your coma this afternoon, I told you not to leave your room."

"And if I'd followed your orders, the President would be looking for a new doctor."

"All this blood for nothing," Reese grumbled, gazing around the room.

"Maybe not."

"What do you mean?" Mills asked.

"There was another attempt on my life today."

Alison gasped.

"I managed to foil it with the help of a good-looking doctor named Spencer Ryan. He put a rather lifelike mannequin in my bed. When the nurse who was forced to try to kill me came in, she was wearing rubber gloves, so she couldn't tell it wasn't a real arm she injected poison into. Spencer is with her now. Once her daughter is returned home safely, he should be able to get the rest of the story out of her. Maybe even the telephone number for her contact."

"Spencer, eh?" Reese asked, a hint of jealousy in his tone.

"Yes." Meeker winked. "Did I mention that he's really good-looking?"

"You did," the agent grumbled.

Meeker clapped her hands. "All right, folks. Let's get this mess cleaned up."

CHAPTER 18

Tuesday, March 24, 1942

7:30 a.m.

Springfield, Illinois

Fredrick Bauer parked his car outside the train station and studied the passengers walking into the depot. Most were young men in uniform, strolling toward an adventure that would soon take them into harm's way.

Bauer glanced at Reggie Fister, sitting in his passenger seat. "Those boys have no idea what's in front of them. Most of them aren't coming back. This might be the last time they see their folks or their hometown. They may never have another date or even drive a car."

"Who cares?" Fister sneered. "They're just war machinery. They can be replaced."

Bauer raised an eyebrow. "Like you?"

Fister's lip curled. "Oh, I'm special, don't you know."

Bauer ignored Fister's bragging, still focused on the

servicemen waiting on the platform. "Look at those expectant faces. They think they're off to do God's work."

Fister frowned. "You know better than that."

"Of course. But the war promoters have to sell it as something noble. I mean, the Nazis have rewritten the entire Christian faith to make Germans the chosen race, the only ones who truly represent God. That's how they justify their actions. Since it was Jews who killed Christ, that makes every Jew the enemy. So murdering them by the millions is touted as divine."

Bauer watched a young man in an Army uniform kiss his crying sweetheart good-bye. "Do you think Hitler really believes that Jesus was the Son of God, thereby making his crucifixion such a heinous crime?"

"I doubt it." Fister shrugged. "But as long as the men fighting his wars believe it, that's all that matters."

Bauer pulled his gaze away from the group of deluded soldiers. "America and Britain aren't much better. They're saying that Germany represents Satan, and that their countries are the world's moral voice. They wrap up the Bible in a red, white, and blue flag and send their children off to die, as if this war is a holy crusade. They quote Scripture and preach sermons on patriotism, claiming that killing millions of Germans is furthering God's plan for this world."

Fister eyed him with curiosity. "And what about the Japanese?"

"They believe God is behind them as well, and that the rest of the world is heathen and therefore doesn't deserve to live."

"And do you consider yourself any better?"

"At least I don't evoke God's name to justify my actions. I know what I do is selfish and evil. But I don't kill randomly. I do it with purpose."

"So that makes you the noble one?"

"No." Bauer chuckled. "It just makes me practical."

"Who do you think will win the war?"

Bauer considered the question carefully. "The Germans and the Japanese have the will to win, but the Americans have the resources. And the wisest leaders."

"You think they're smarter than Hitler?" Fister asked in a low voice.

"Instead of staying focused on a war he could win, he invaded a country that offered him nothing but stubborn resistance." Bauer pulled a cigarette out of his pocket. "Still, Hitler might have survived his ill-advised attack on Russia if Japan hadn't drawn the United States into the war. Neither country can win against an enemy with the resources the US has."

Fister turned his gaze to the depot. "Then what are we doing here?"

"I think you're in this because you're an adventurer. When the Germans were training you, you bought into their beliefs, to a certain extent at least." Bauer narrowed his eyes at Fister. "There's no doubt in my mind that they removed your soul. You have no hint of a thread of morality, which makes you perfect for this work."

"And you?"

Bauer pushed in the car's cigarette lighter. "I have no allegiance to any flag, country, or leader. The war offers me opportunities to make money and gain power off the misfortune of others. No matter who wins, I will not only survive, I'll thrive."

Fister rubbed his jaw. "Is it too late for me to join your team?"

Bauer laughed. "I doubt Hitler would let you work for me. Within a few days, you'll be taking either Kranz or his daughter back to Germany. You'll be a hero in Hitler's eyes. He'll probably keep you by his side until the bitter end. And then you'll likely die in a hail of bullets. Won't that be glorious?"

For the first time, Bauer detected a hint of regret in the tough man's eyes.

The lighter popped, and Bauer touched it to the end of his cigarette. Reggie Fister wasn't much different from those new recruits on the train platform. Just like them, he was headed off into the unknown. And Bauer didn't envy him one bit.

He took a long draw and exhaled a curl of white smoke. "It's time for you to go."

Fister brushed a speck of dust off the gray suit he'd been given to wear on his journey south. "I wish you could have come up with something better for me than this. Looks like it came from a second-hand store."

"It did. The last thing you need is to stand out in a crowd. And you'd better drop the British accent. You need to be just another American businessman."

"I know my cover." Fister straightened in his seat. "My name is Bill Johnson. I was born in Boston in 1915. Due to an injury suffered in a car wreck in 1938, I am not eligible for military service. I work at a law firm in Chicago." He shook his head. "Could I be more boring?"

"Just follow the script and don't ad lib this time."

Fister grunted, then reached into the backseat, grabbed his suitcase and stepped out of the car.

As Bauer watched his operative climb onto the platform, he made a mental note. It was time to recruit a new adventurer.

CHAPTER 19

Tuesday, March 24, 1942

5:00 p.m.

Thurmont, Maryland

On FDR's orders, Helen Meeker and the rest of the people involved in the shootout at her apartment were flown to the presidential retreat at Camp David. After being checked out by Dr. Sterling Ryan, they were fed, shown to a bedroom and told to get as much rest as possible.

When Meeker finally pulled her sore body out of bed, it was late afternoon. After dressing in dark slacks and a yellow sweater, she rummaged through the kitchen, made herself a turkey sandwich and joined Henry Reese in the main living room. She sat in a leather chair, looking out over the expansive grounds.

"What happened to you after I was kidnapped?" she asked.

He shrugged. "I'm not sure. They tell me I was drugged. And that I might never remember what happened on those days."

Meeker pulled her aching feet up onto a stool. "I heard they found you in some doctor's house in Chicago."

"Yeah, with a gun in my hand. Apparently, the one used to kill Snider. The files indicate he set up the hit on you and that he was Fister's boss. Guess that makes me a hero."

She studied his handsome but bruised face. "At least the swelling is coming down. You almost look human now."

He frowned. "I'm sure I'd remember shooting a guy. It had to be a frame."

"So who did kill Snider?"

He stood. "I don't know." Reese shoved his hands into his pockets and walked to the large window overlooking a small lake.

Helen joined him, pushed her arm through his, and leaned her head on his shoulder. "I'm just glad you're okay."

She was enjoying the warmth of his body against hers when she heard ootsteps on the wooden floor. Releasing Reese, she turned and spotted a smiling Clay Barnes.

"Hope you two rested well," the Secret Service agent said.

"I hate that word," Reese grumbled. "Whenever anyone mentions *rested,* there's always a big job that needs to be done."

Barnes chuckled. "Helen, Dr. Ryan tells me you're fit for duty already. I hope if I ever get shot there's some of that blood around for me too."

"Better to just avoid being shot," she said. "I'm not proud of having Reggie Fister as my blood brother."

"Can't say I blame you there," Barnes quipped. "Now, if you two will follow me into the dining room, there are some things we need to discuss."

Reese and Meeker followed Barnes into the retreat's spacious dining room. Already seated around the large table were Alison, Rebecca Bobbs, Dr. Cleveland Mills, and Dr. Spencer Ryan. Meeker grabbed the open spot beside her sister. Reese took the chair between the two doctors.

Barnes walked to the head of the table and remained standing. "People, let me start by saying that each one of you possesses unique skills that make you valuable to your country. But those talents are yours. None of you has to volunteer to use them in the President's service."

Meeker shot a look at Alison. Her own job required that she do whatever was needed to help her country and the President. But her sister was a civilian, with no such demands on her.

Barnes glanced down at the files spread before him, tapping one with his index finger. "Except for Dr. Mills, none of you has any dependents. Your parents are dead, and except for Alison and Helen, none of you has siblings. I apologize for the harshness of this statement, but if any of you die, there won't be anyone to mourn the loss."

Meeker glanced across the table at Reese. When their eyes locked, he shrugged, apparently just as clueless about all this as she was. "Get on with it, Clay," Reese said. "What's going on here?"

Barnes looked up. "We have a couple of delicate problems that we need to address off the books."

"What do you mean?" Bobbs asked.

Barnes sat, resting his elbows on the table and folding his

hands. “If we do this, Rebecca and Henry won’t be working for the FBI, Helen will not be aligned with the Secret Service, and Dr. Ryan will no longer be a practicing physician.”

Murmurs filled the room.

Barnes picked up a photo and slid it down the middle of the table. “Can any of you tell me what that is?”

Reese glanced at the image. “Fort Knox.”

“Exactly. And there’s supposed to be more than twenty thousand metric tons of gold bars in that facility.”

Meeker peered at Barnes. “What do you mean by ‘supposed to be’?”

“Recent tests have proven that some of the gold bars transferred to Fort Knox over the past two years are not solid gold but gold-plated. We estimate there may be a couple of million tons missing.”

“How is that possible?” Reese asked. “Those shipments have all kinds of security checks. And the trains are heavily guarded from beginning to end.”

“We believe the exchanges were made before the bars arrived at the train station. But we can’t find any proof. Whoever did it covered their tracks well.”

“No pun intended, right?” Meeker rolled her eyes.

“Only a handful of people know about this,” Barnes continued. “Obviously, the team involved in testing at Fort Knox knows. I’m the only one in the Secret Service the President has told. He also shared it with Dr. Mills a couple of weeks ago.”

No wonder the good doctor didn’t seem surprised at the news.

"Not even Hoover is aware of what's going on here. If this were to get out, it would shake the confidence of our entire country, not to mention all the Allied nations."

"Do you think the Germans are behind this?" Alison asked.

"No. This started before we got into the war."

"Organized crime?" Reese suggested.

"Possibly. Three weeks ago, two men disappeared from their duty posts at Fort Knox. We haven't been able to find them."

Meeker's head was spinning. She couldn't imagine how all this was affecting the others in the room, especially Alison.

Barnes opened a file and pushed two more photos toward the middle of the long table. "The picture on my left is of Captain Ellis McCary. He's thirty-five, divorced, and has a spotless service record. The other is Master Sergeant Buster Rankin. He's twenty-eight, has no children, and his wife was killed in a hunting accident three years ago."

"And you think these two guys could pull off something this big?" Ryan asked.

"No. But they might be connected with the people who did." He took a deep breath. "At the same time McCary and Rankin disappeared, something else disappeared that's worth even more than the missing gold."

Meeker wondered what could be more valuable than all that gold.

Barnes moved to the side of the room and leaned on a large china cabinet. "On December 27, 1941, in anticipation of a possible attack on Washington, the original Declaration of Independence and the Constitution of the United States were removed from the National Archives and shipped to Fort Knox for safekeeping, along with the Magna Carta and many of the crown jewels of Europe."

Reese whistled.

"A recent examination of those documents proved that the Declaration of Independence and the Magna Carta that we have in our vaults are not authentic. They're copies."

The gravity of the theft sent the room into a deep silence for several minutes.

"The press cannot get wind of this. Not even Congress can know about it. Since we likely have a mole in the White House, we can't talk about it openly there. That's why you were all brought in."

Meeker had known this trip to Camp David had to be about more than just giving her and her companions some much-needed rest.

"Your job is to figure out who's behind this and quietly return those documents to Fort Knox. If you can accomplish that, there are several other missions the President would like you to team up on."

"You're asking us to become an intelligence unit," Reese noted.

"A secret one."

"What would that entail for us?" Bobbs asked.

"Alison would be moved into Helen's position at the White House, allegedly serving as an aid to the President. In truth, she would be the conduit for information to get from the team to the President and back. Dr. Mills would remain in his position and serve in a similar capacity."

Meeker glanced from Alison to Mills and back to Barnes. "And the rest of the team?"

"I'm an electronics expert. Henry is skilled in crime solving, explosives, and weapons. Spencer is a trained code breaker. Rebecca is the best crime-scene investigator and laboratory technician in the country." Barnes winked at Meeker. "And we all know what you can do."

"Well, I'm on board," Meeker announced. The rest nodded.

"Great." Barnes released a deep breath. "Now, how do you feel about being dead?"

"What?" Bobbs asked.

"In order to unravel this mystery, we need to be able to do our work in complete secrecy. Except for Alison and Dr. Mills, we all have people looking for us. So we'd need to send an announcement of our deaths to all the papers. The most logical story would be a plane crash. Once the war is over and the need for this unit ends, we can miraculously come back to life."

Meeker glanced around the room and smiled. "Guess this isn't a bad group to join in the tomb."

"Why not?" Bobbs chimed in

"I'm in," Reese added.

Ryan nodded. "Two beautiful women, plenty of action and intrigue, hopefully a good budget. I can live with that. Or should I say, die with that?"

"Before you all sign on, there's one more thing that needs be addressed. FDR had in mind a very specific way this group was to function, and if the members don't all agree to it, then the team will be dissolved before it even begins."

"And what's that important little detail?" Reese asked.

Barnes took a deep breath. "The President insisted that Helen be in charge. We will all have to work under her orders. She has the President's confidence far more than any of us." He looked at Meeker. "I know Helen well, so I'm fine with that. But can the rest of you deal with having a five-foot-four-inch dynamo calling the shots?"

Ryan announced he had no trouble with that rule. Reese looked into Meeker's eyes. She couldn't read what he was thinking. The room was still for one of the longest minutes of Meeker's life. Finally, the FBI agent nodded. The team was set.

CHAPTER 20

Thursday, March 26, 1942

8:10 p.m.

Austin, Texas

Dressed in a white shirt, tan jacket, and blue slacks, Reggie Fister enjoyed a stroll across the campus of the University of Texas. To most of the ten thousand students enrolled here, the war raging in Europe and the Pacific was little more than words in a newspaper.

On this mild spring night under a beautiful full moon, Fister carried two textbooks under his arm. Beneath his jacket he'd hidden a Luger.

He stopped beneath a live oak tree beside the Memorial girls' dorm and casually watched coeds enter and exit the residence hall. Finally, a short, full-chested brunette walked out the front door and stepped onto the main sidewalk. Fister sauntered up beside the nineteen-year-old. "Aren't you Suzy Miller?"

She stopped, her dark eyes studying Fister's face. "Yes."

"I think you're in my history class."

"I don't recognize you."

He grinned, then grabbed her elbow and pulled her against his side. "What you feel pressed into your ribs is a gun. If you so much as raise your voice, I'll pull the trigger. You don't want to die, do you?"

She shook her head.

"Now, at the end of this sidewalk, there's a white car parked at the curb. That's where we're going. When we get there, you'll get in on the passenger side and scoot over behind the wheel. I'll follow you. When I close the door, you'll start the car and pull away from the curb. I'll tell you were to go. Do you understand?"

"Yes," she whispered.

"All right, then. Let's start walking. Not too fast or too slow. Just act like we're on a date."

The girl moved down the sidewalk on trembling legs. When they were about halfway to the objective, three sweater-clad girls met them. "Hey, Suzy," a blue-eyed blonde said. "Who's your fella?"

"Just a friend," came the hushed response.

"Didn't know you had any friends like this." A short redhead smoothed her orange coat. "Aren't you going to introduce him?"

"I'm visiting from back home," Fister said. "We're going to grab a soda and catch up on old times. Aren't we, Suzy?"

The girl nodded.

"Don't do anything I wouldn't do!" The blonde laughed.

As the three marched off, Fister leaned close to Suzy. "You

played that real smart. If you continue to use your head, you'll live through this. And it'll make a great story for your grandkids. Now, keep walking."

Fifty steps later Fister opened the door of the 1938 Oldsmobile and signaled for Suzy to enter. After she was behind the wheel, he slid in and closed the door.

As the Olds coupe pulled away from the curb, the three coeds who had teased Suzy earlier stood in front of the dorm and waved. One of them screamed out, "Have a good time!"

CHAPTER 21

Friday, March 27, 1942

7:30 a.m.

Camp David, Maryland

At the President's suggestion, the new secret team stayed at Camp David while news of their deaths in a private crash was circulated in the media. Since the accident had allegedly taken place in a remote section of the Blue Ridge Mountains and a massive explosion had burned the bodies beyond recognition, the stories soberly announced that a memorial service would be conducted at a later date.

Since neither Bobbs nor Ryan would be readily recognized, they headed out to the rural areas outside Washington to find a suitable location for the group to live and work.

While Reese sorted through the evidence gathered by the various intelligence agencies and military on the two missing men from Fort Knox, Meeker and Barnes met in the retreat's main study, engaged in a heated discussion.

"You're supposed to be dead," Barnes argued, his normally subdued tone nearly shaking the windows. "You can't blow your cover on day one. I'm sure the President will allow you to have him transported here."

"Look, this guy has knowledge that we need. And it won't matter if he knows we're alive. He's in solitary, for heaven's sake."

He pointed a finger at her ace. "We can't take chances. We have to be smart."

Meeker gave him a sly smile. "The President put me in charge for a reason. Women sense things that men miss. Most of you are too proud to even ask for directions!"

"But what you're asking isn't at all logical."

She shook her head. "Look, Barnes, you're a bachelor, so you haven't been around females enough to know this. But there's one rule every man needs to learn, and that's to never doubt a woman's intuition."

The ringing desk phone created a momentary ceasefire. "You going to get that?" Meeker asked.

"Go ahead. You seem to have all the answers."

She picked up. "Camp David."

"Helen, it's Uncle Franklin."

She stood a bit straighter. "What can I do for you, Mr. President?"

"A student from the University of Texas is missing. Her name is Suzy Miller. The kidnapper told the girl's father that if legal authorities were notified, she would be killed."

"Typical."

"Helen, I'd like your team to work this."

She blinked. "But, sir … I thought we were supposed to be finding the missing documents. Isn't that more important than a kidnapping?"

"Normally, it would be. But Suzy Miller's real name is Susan Kranz. Her father escaped Nazi Germany six years ago. He's one of my economic advisers."

Meeker recalled meeting Mr. Kranz.

"Helen, they're not asking for money. They want to exchange the man for his daughter."

So this was somehow tied to the war.

"I want you to shadow Kranz, but don't give yourself away unless it's absolutely necessary."

"We'll do our best to save the child," Meeker assured him.

"A plane will be ready for your crew in four hours. I want every member of the team on this. Barnes can fly, so you won't need a pilot. The meeting point is Brownsville, Texas."

"Yes, sir."

"One more thing, Helen. Three coeds saw the man who took the girl. The description they gave matches that of the man you asked to be sent to Camp David so you could interview him."

Meeker's pulse kicked up a notch.

"I tried to talk Jacob out of going to Texas, telling him there's nothing he can do for his daughter there, and he might actually get in the way. But he flew down today. The kidnappers told him to check in to the Raleigh Hotel and wait for them to contact him."

"I'll join him there as soon as possible."

"Keep me informed, Helen. You can call my private line. Or call Alison at your old apartment."

"I will, sir. Goodbye."

She set the receiver back onto the cradle, then explained the situation to Barnes. "We need to talk to Fister before we leave. Bring him to Camp David immediately."

CHAPTER 22

Friday, March 27, 1942

9:15 a.m.

Camp David, Maryland

Meeker glanced across the hallway at Barnes. “You want to be in on this? Henry’s joining me.”

“Sure.” He shrugged. “If he’s going to see that you’re not dead, he might as well know I’m not either.”

“All right, then. Let’s go see what we’ve got.” The two of them entered the dining room.

Fister looked much better than he had the last time he was face-to-face with Meeker. His eyes were clear and there was a bit of color in his cheeks. Though he was dressed in a nice pair of blue slacks and a white cotton shirt, he lacked the charm that she’d noted in the British Embassy. Fister was no longer capable of owning a room with the power of his charisma.

Taking the chair across from him, Meeker held her tongue until the two men sat down on each side of her.

"Can we get you anything?" she asked, no doubt surprising her partners with her gentle manner. "Would you like something to eat or drink?"

"No, thank you," Fister answered quietly.

"I'm Helen Meeker. Do you remember visiting me the night you were captured after the train wreck?"

"No," came the emotionless reply. "I don't recall much about that evening."

"So this is the first time you've seen me?"

He nodded.

Barnes slammed his fist on the table. "We both saw you at the farm in New York when you tried to kill the President."

"No, we didn't," Meeker said. "We saw his identical twin. And the man who did escape from that train wreck realized I'd figured it out. That's why I was shot."

"There are … two of them?" Reese asked.

"After the parents died, Reggie was raised in Scotland, his father's native country, and the other boy in Germany. The twin who tried to kill the President and the prime minister is Alistair Fister." Meeker turned back to their prisoner. "Did you know you had a twin?"

"No one ever told me that."

"Orphanages often withhold information about siblings." She gazed at him with deep sympathy. "Where were you before you were taken to the train wreck, Reggie?"

"I was held in a laboratory of some sort. I escaped once. All I remember was that the land around it was flat. Lots of corn fields."

"Probably somewhere in the Midwest," Reese noted.

"Before that, I was in someplace dry and hot." Reggie ran his hand through his hair. "I was there for a year or more. The seasons didn't change much. But if the wind was right, I could smell salt air. Kind of reminded me of being on the coast back home."

"And before that?"

"I was held in Germany."

Meeker glanced at a clock on the far side of the room. Rebecca and Spencer would be back any minute, and the plane was on its way. They needed to get out of here within the hour.

"Reggie, would you like to help us catch the folks who were behind kidnapping you and holding you prisoner all these years?"

"Absolutely," he replied, a bit of life appearing in his eyes.

She turned to Reese. "We need to talk." Meeker excused herself from Reggie and walked out into the hall, followed by the agent.

"It sounds to me like Fister was held in south Texas before he was moved to the Midwest."

"Could've been California."

"Texas makes more sense. It's closer to the Midwest. I think we should take him with us and see if something triggers his memory."

"I don't know. Sounds risky."

"Well, we can't leave him here. Besides, we need him more than he needs us."

Reese shrugged. "You're the boss."

"You got that right."

"But first I need to ask Fister one more question."

"Lead the way."

They went back into the room, and Reese leaned forward on the table. "Reggie, did you ever see who held you?"

"Not in enough to light to make out features. Even when they talked to me, they stayed in the shadows."

"Did you ever hear them talk about plans or operations?"

"I overheard things a few times. But I couldn't make much sense of what they were saying."

"Did they ever talk about a plane crash in Nevada?"

Reggie smiled. "Yes. I remember a lady talking about a movie star dying in the crash."

"Carole Lombard."

"That's it! The lady was mourning the loss, but the man in charge told her there was something much more valuable on that flight and that was why it went down."

"Did you hear anything else?" Reese asked.

"Not about the crash. But I did hear them talking about a French explorer in Arkansas. I don't remember any details about that."

Reese grinned. "Reggie, you're going to Texas with us. If you remember anything along the way, be sure to tell one of us, okay?"

"Sure."

Back in the hallway, Meeker peered at Reese. "What was that all about?"

"I'll explain later." He wrapped his arms around Meeker and kissed her cheek. "Let's go to Texas!"

CHAPTER 23

Friday, March 27, 1942

Noon

St. Louis, Missouri

Fredrick Bauer wiped crumbs off the ripped vinyl seat of a back booth in the Downtown Diner before sliding into it. The small, cramped, noisy eatery was immersed in a thick nicotine cloud. With its greasy food and dirty floors, this was the last place anyone who was health conscious would want to visit. Which was precisely why Bauer chose it for his meeting with Ralph Mauch.

A former boxer, Mauch was a health fanatic. He worked out daily and carefully monitored everything he ate. He didn't allow alcohol or cigarettes in his home. He went to bed early and got up with the sun.

Bauer sipped coffee and listened to the tunes playing on the Wurlitzer jukebox for ten minutes before Mauch strolled into the establishment, with a frown so pronounced it made his whole face sag. Bauer stood and waved at his guest.

"I hate travel," Mauch muttered as he sat across the marred tabletop from Bauer.

"I enjoy it," he replied with a smile. "Being alone in a car gives me a chance to reflect on life as I take in the sights of this beautiful world we live in."

Before Mauch could respond, the plump waitress appeared at the table. The stains on her dress indicated she'd spilled nearly as much food as she'd delivered. "You boys want to hear about the special today?"

"No," Mauch grumbled. "Just bring me coffee … black."

"And you, sir?" Her voice revealed a bit of Midwestern charm tempered by a heavy dose of fatigue.

"Ham on rye."

"Chips with that?"

"That'd be fine."

After the woman waddled off, Mauch leaned across the table. "Why'd you pick this place?"

"We won't be noticed in a crowd. None of the patrons here will be able to describe us after we leave. Besides, I like watching Americans rush around. They're always in a hurry. Even when they eat. Look at that guy, for example." He pointed to a table across the aisle, where a man sat alone, wolfing down a sandwich while reading the newspaper and humming along with the jukebox. "As soon as he's finished with his meal, he'll hastily pay his bill and practically sprint back to his office."

"So?"

"You're the same way. Always in a hurry to get things done.

And what good does all that rushing around do? You should relax and enjoy life."

"We're in a war, remember?" the former boxer growled.

"No, we're not. A lot of other folks are. But nobody's shooting at us. We're thousands of miles away from falling bombs and the smell of constant death."

The waitress brought Mauch's coffee and Bauer's order. When she was out of earshot, Mauch whispered, "What have you got to report?"

"We have the girl." Bauer bit into his sandwich. "This is good. You should get one. My treat."

"Where is she?"

"Texas." Bauer savored another bite. "This is the best ham I've had in years. As good as anything you'll find in the Black Forest."

"What about Kranz?"

"He's flying down today. You can tell Hitler he'll have a house guest soon."

"What's going to happen to the girl?"

Bauer shrugged. "How she dies will be decided after we get Kranz on the U-boat."

Mauch appeared to relax. "And the papers?"

"They were on the plane when it went down. My sources tell me no files were recovered, so they're probably still there." Bauer sighed. "Too bad Lombard had the misfortune of being on that flight. I really enjoyed her work. Did you see the movie she made with Jack Benny, the one that made fun of Hitler?"

Mauch's eyes darted around the restaurant.

"Relax, Ralph. No one here is going to shoot you for enjoying Hollywood poking fun at the Führer."

Mauch took a sip of his coffee. "So, the papers are gone?"

"Not at all. They were in a fireproof container. Covered in snow, no doubt. But we can go out there and look for them in the spring." He popped a chip into his mouth. "You sure you don't want a sandwich?"

"I've got to get back home." Mauch slid out of his seat.

Bauer caught the sleeve of his jacket. "Tell your boss I want certain pieces of art in payment this time." Reaching into his inside pocket, he retrieved the list and handed it over.

Mauch scanned the handwritten note, then looked back at Bauer with wide eyes. "These things come from the Amber Room."

Bauer smiled. "You just see that he gets that. And tell him when I come through, the price will seem like a bargain."

CHAPTER 24

Saturday, March 28, 1942

1:10 p.m.

Brownsville, Texas

Dressed in a brown suit, matching pumps, a large-brimmed hat, and sunglasses, Helen Meeker sat in a chair in the lobby of the Raleigh Hotel, pretending to read a movie magazine. Beside her, Henry Reese, the swelling and bruising now almost gone from his face, had his head buried in a newspaper.

"You reading about our deaths?" she asked with a grin.

"No. I already scanned that article. You got way too much ink, and I was only a footnote. So I moved on to the sports page. Joe Louis knocked out Abe Simon in the sixth round to retain the heavyweight crown last night in New York. I'm surprised it took that long. No one can touch the Brown Bomber."

As Reese continued to chatter about the world of sports, Meeker glanced back to the table where Henry Kranz was nibbling on his lunch. She studied the man for a moment. He appeared to be about fifty and athletic. He wore large, thick-rimmed glasses and had a dark, neatly trimmed beard. His shoulders were wide and his back straight. There was a mature charm about him.

"Henry, how tall would you say Kranz is?"

Reese glanced up. "Six foot or so. About my height."

"And your build too."

"He's a bit thicker in the middle." He winked.

Meeker leaned close. "I've got a plan."

Reese set the newspaper to one side. "I'm all ears."

"I'm going to gather the team in our room. You follow Kranz back to his. Even if you have to bind and gag him, you keep him there."

"What's this all about?"

"You just do your part. I'll take care of the rest."

CHAPTER 25

Saturday, March 28, 1942

7:35 p.m.

Brownsville, Texas

Helen Meeker smiled as Rebecca Bobbs put the last bit of makeup on Henry Reese. He slipped on Jacob Kranz's glasses and placed the man's hat on his head.

"Well, what do you think?" Bobbs asked as she stepped back from the frowning man sitting in the hotel room chair.

Meeker glanced from the agent's face to Jacob's. Though they'd never pass as identical twins, they looked similar enough. She hoped. "I think we have a good chance of pulling this off."

Bobbs sighed. "I haven't done any kind of theatrical makeup since college."

Meeker turned to her. "Fortunately, the instructions called for a meeting outdoors, at night. And they've never met Kranz face-to-face." She looked back at Henry. "How's your accent?"

“I can speak American as well as any other German,” he assured her with a guttural twang to his voice.

Barnes, leaning against the far wall with his arms folded, shook his head. “Maybe you’d better not talk too much. Just act distressed a lot.”

“Do you really think it will work?” the real Reggie Fister asked, wringing his hands.

Meeker put a hand on his shoulder. “Your brother has never seen Kranz in person, only in photos.”

“Assuming they believe your agent is Jacob Kranz, what will they do to him?”

“Take him to the girl. If she confirms that he’s her father, they’ll likely try to put him on a plane bound for Mexico.”

Kranz groaned. “And what if they find out the young man isn’t me?”

“In their eyes, Henry is expendable. He’s not an economic guru funding the underground, like you are. But don’t worry. He’s tough. He’ll survive.”

Kranz stiffened. “But if they uncover this charade, they will take my daughter to Germany and put her in a concentration camp.”

Meeker moved to where the man sat on the queen-sized bed. “No, they won’t. Your daughter is a pawn. If they think they’ve got you, they’ll have no more need of her and let her go. If they realize they don’t have you, they’ll continue to use her as bait.”

Kranz did not look relieved.

On the other side of the room, Reese studied Bobbs’s handiwork in a mirror. “You know, I’m beginning to think this plan of yours just might work."

It had to. "When they take you, we'll do our best to follow you. But we'll have to stay pretty far back so they don't spot us. If we lose you, it'll be up to you to save the girl."

"Yeah, and since they'll probably search me, I won't be able to have a gun on me. Guess I'll have to survive on my wits."

"That's a scary thought." Meeker grinned, but as she leaned into his shoulder, she couldn't bear the thought of losing him again.

"Hey," Barnes said, "where's Fister?"

Helen glanced around the small hotel room. The man was nowhere in sight.

CHAPTER 26

Saturday, March 28, 1942

9:00 p.m.

Brownsville, Texas

Henry Reese walked out of the hotel into the moonlit night. He crossed the nearly empty street to a five-and-dime store that had been closed for three hours. Pulling Jacob Kranz's hat low over his forehead, he stopped on the sidewalk, outside the direct light of a street lamp.

A few seconds later, a light-colored sedan parked a half block down the street switched on its lights and slowly rolled toward him. It stopped in front of the store, and a large man, dressed in dark pants and a plaid sports coat, stepped out of the front passenger seat. The top three buttons of his shirt were undone, revealing a hairy chest. His pointed boots looked to be at least a size thirteen.

The stranger quickly covered the three steps separating them, then studied Reese's face in the dim light. After glancing both directions to make sure they were alone, he frisked the agent and then pointed toward the car. As Reese approached, the back door opened. No one had to tell him to get in.

"Welcome, Mr. Kranz," a familiar voice called out from the other side of the backseat. "My name is Fister."

Even though he knew the man, Reese didn't respond.

"I'm glad you decided to do this the smart way." Fister looked to the driver. "Let's go, Hector. We have a plane to catch."

"My daughter?" Reese whispered.

"She's fine," Fister assured him. "You'll see her soon."

"And then you will let her go?"

Fister grinned. "My dear Mr. Kranz, you should know better than to make a deal with the devil. Your daughter will be accompanying you back to the land of your birth."

The Buick sedan headed south. Several miles down the road, Fister ordered the driver to make a U-turn.

CHAPTER 27

Saturday, March 28, 1942

11:00 p.m.

Outside of Brownsville, Texas

After traveling for a dozen miles or so, the sedan pulled up to a small adobe farmhouse. With two men in the front seat and Fister in the back, Reese had remained quiet during the trip. Now it was time to size up the operation and formulate some kind of plan.

After the driver shut off the eight-cylinder engine, Fister stepped out and looked at the large tin building a hundred yards to the south. "Hector, take our guest to the plane. I'm going to step inside, make a phone call and get the girl."

As the big man yanked him from the seat, Reese took in the barren Texas landscape. It was going to be hard for any car to approach without being seen. So even if Meeker and the team had managed to tail them, it was doubtful they could make a surprise entrance. It appeared this plan was going to be up to him to pull off. And with two guns pointed at his back, the odds weren't good.

"You got a cigarette?" Reese asked Hector.

The big man didn't respond.

"How about you?" he asked the other man.

He remained mute too.

Reese didn't smoke. He just hoped a little small talk would loosen up his guards. No such luck.

Hector pointed his revolver toward a small metal building. When Reese didn't move, the man shoved the barrel into his back.

"I get the point," he snapped, then started walking.

The full moon revealed a dirt lane behind the shed. *Must be the runway.* With no wind or clouds, it would be easy to take off tonight.

As they approached the building, three more armed men stepped out. Reese saw no way out of this mess. Once the plane was in the air, he could try to overpower the pilot and take charge. But since he didn't know how to fly, there was a large downside to that idea.

A door opened and Hector pushed him inside the makeshift hangar, revealing a black DC-2. Only a few of these babies had been put into production before they were replaced. "Are you sure this is safe?"

None of the armed men responded.

The trio that met them at the shed opened the building's back door and pushed the plane outside. A lanky man dressed in flight gear stepped through a side door. “You must be Mr. Kranz.”

Reese nodded.

“As soon as Fister gets here, we’ll take off.”

“Where are we going?” Reese asked.

“We have a rendezvous with a sub that will take you to Germany. I hear they’re going to throw a big party for you when you arrive.”

The guy didn’t sound like a Nazi. Reese figured he must be a paid contractor, someone who worked for money, not causes. Life was safer that way. No matter who won, men like this would always have work. And stay alive.

The pilot looked at Hector. “Tie his hands. I don’t want him causing problems on the flight.”

The big man practically yanked Reese’s shoulders from their sockets as he secured his wrists behind his back. He’d just finished tying the knots when Fister walked in.

“Where’s the girl?” the pilot asked.

Fister smiled. “I’m keeping her here for a while. After I take advantage of her charms, I’ll kill her.”

Reese gulped, torn between voicing a complaint, as any distraught father would do, and causing Fister to examine him more closely. Best to remain quiet and appear resigned, at least for the moment.

“Your call,” the pilot muttered. “Let’s get the package on the plane and get out of here.” He headed for the exit.

“Not so fast,” Fister ordered. “I just got word the sub is late. We’re supposed to delay takeoff for forty-five minutes.”

“That wasn’t the deal,” the pilot snarled.

"Would you rather wait on the beach, where the Mexican officials might drive up and start asking questions?"

The man frowned at Fister. "At least put Kranz on the plane."

"Fine." Fister nodded at Hector. "Take him out there and tie him to his seat. I'm going to have a cup of coffee."

CHAPTER 28

Saturday, March 28, 1942

11:45 p.m.

Outside of Brownsville, Texas

"How many do you see?" Helen Meeker asked as she crouched on a small rise overlooking the adobe house, the metal barn, and acres of farmland.

Clay Barnes pulled the binoculars away from his face. "Six hired guns, a pilot, and Fister."

"Do you see Henry or the girl?"

"No. They might already be on the plane, or perhaps in the house."

"You stay here." She turned to Bobbs. "Rebecca, Dr. Ryan, and I will circle around to the left and look in the house. If they're there, we'll bring them back."

"You sure you don't want me to come with you?" Barnes asked.

"Absolutely." She smiled. "You're the best shot, and we might need some cover."

He nodded.

"Okay, gang, let's go."

Within two minutes, the trio had made their way down the hill to the small home. The back door was unlocked. With her Colt ready, Meeker led the way through the kitchen and into the front room. Sitting on a small couch, curled up like a puppy, was Jacob Kranz's daughter.

Meeker signaled for the frightened young woman to remain quiet as Ryan and Bobbs checked the other three rooms.

"There's no one else here," Bobbs called out.

Meeker rushed to Suzy and gently touched her face. "Are you all right?"

"Yes," she whispered. "How's my dad?"

"He's safe."

A loud rumbling noise came from outside.

"They're firing up the engines on the plane," Bobbs announced.

"You two get Miss Kranz back to Barnes," Meeker ordered.

"It won't take both of us to do that," Bobbs argued. "I can go with you."

"No. Our job is to save the girl and her father. You make sure she's safe."

"Where are you going?" Barnes asked.

"To see if I can free Henry."

Not waiting for the argument she was sure would follow, Meeker hurried through the kitchen and back out the rear door.

Though the area between her and the plane was wide open with no cover and the moon was full and bright, she'd caught a break. There was no one outside the building.

She sprinted across the dirt to the shed. Pressing herself flat against the metal wall, she peered around the side.

"We're taking off *now*," a man shouted. "Plane's ready, motors are fired up, and it's been forty-five minutes. Let's get this over with."

"We wait until midnight." Fister's voice sent chills up Meeker's back. "I want to give the sub plenty of time to get to the rendezvous point."

"I'm not sitting around here any longer," the man roared. "My instructions were to take you and that Kranz guy, and I'm leaving now. You can either get on the plane or be left behind."

"Fine," Fister grumbled. "I'll grab my bag."

The pilot bolted out the back door and hurried to the DC-2. A few moments later, Fister emerged from the shed, suitcase in hand. After saying something to the men, he watched them shut the large doors. Then he made his way to the black plane. With a final look around, he entered the aircraft. Surprisingly, he didn't bother shutting the door.

Seizing the opportunity, Meeker raced toward the plane's open entrance with two objectives on her mind. The first was to free Henry Reese. The second was to make sure Alistair Fister did not escape.

The twin engines stirred up clouds of Texas dust as she approached the rear of the plane and crept toward the side door. With gun drawn, she took a deep breath and leaped inside. Two revolvers greeted her, both aimed at her forehead.

"Drop it, Helen," Fister ordered.

Before she had a chance to comply, the pilot kicked the Colt out of her hand. It skidded across the floor, coming to rest under one of the back rows.

Fister ordered Meeker to take the seat next to Kranz. After she complied, he turned to the pilot, who had retrieved her gun. "Get this plane off the ground."

As the man rushed to do as he'd been told, Fister turned back to Meeker and grinned. "You're going to love Berlin in the spring."

Meet Helen Meeker—In the President's Service

In her first three adventures, Helen Meeker finds herself in a race to save the life of a man on death row as well as those of the leaders of the Allied Nations, Roosevelt and Churchill. Working directly for the President, Meeker's life intertwines with the most powerful men of the 1940s in situations that take her from the White House to points all across the country. As she dodges bullets and unravels mysteries, she begins to form a team that will take on an evil presence whose goals and visions extend far beyond World War II. In the President's Service is filled with action, adventure, intrigue, mystery, and romance, along with a cast of colorful characters and a woman whose strength, intelligence, and courage stuns everyone she meets.

The books of the In The President's Service series show Ace's writing at its most versatile—from wartime intrigue to personal crisis to murder mystery to political scheming, and then back again, all in the space of a small number of pages. And the story keeps the reader hooked from beginning to end. If you are a fan of World War II fiction, of great detective stories, or of just plain old excellent writing, get into this series. Ace will not disappoint you!
—**Mike Messner**, Mountain View, CA

Episodes: In the President's Service

Prequel: The Yellow Packard

1. **A Date With Death**
2. **The Dark Pool**
3. **Blood Brother**
4. **Fatal Addiction**
5. **The Devil's Eyes**
6. **The Dead Can Talk**
7. **Bottled Madness**
8. ***Shadows* in the Moonlight**
9. ***Evil*ution**
10. **Uneasy Alliance**
11. **The 13th Floor**
12. **The White Rose**
13. **The Cat's Eye**

Made in the USA
Middletown, DE
09 February 2022